She hel[...]
"I want [...]
but mys[...]

Egill nodded. "Then I will ensure that you do not. We will make your pottery a success, and then you will be my free, willing and wealthy wife. All I will give you is pleasure. If independence will make you happy, then I will make it my goal to help you achieve it."

Mila shrugged and stared down at the half-eaten apple, her appetite gone. She would force herself to eat it. She could never waste food. "The *pleasures* are not worth it."

A wicked glint shone in his eyes. "Oh...I'm sure I can change your mind regarding that at least!"

She glared at him, and then, because she could not seem to help herself, she laughed. "Such arrogance!"

He leaned forward, keeping his voice low so that she would have to lean in to hear him. "I am arrogant, and charming with a serpent tongue." The laughter turned into a swallowed gasp, and he found himself captivated by the little sound that came from her full mouth as he spoke. There was no denying their growing desire. It would consume them both eventually. "But...my promises are as strong as steel, and I *never* disappoint."

Author Note

Egill is an Old Norse name, pronounced "Ay-Gill." Grimr is pronounced like the Brothers "Grimm." Hakon like "Hoe-Con." The Old English pronunciations are as follows: Wynflaed "Win-fled," and Mildritha "Mill-drith-ah." But use whatever works in your head. I am sure the ancestors will forgive us, especially as these are dead languages and we can only make educated guesses about pronunciation. The use of saunas in the Viking age has not been proven, but there is an Old Norse word for a steam bath, *baðstofa*. I like to think they did exist, and for ease, I have used the word *sauna* in this story. Very little Viking-age pottery has been found in Iceland, and there are many theories as to why this is the case. I found *Icelanders in the Viking Age* by William R. Short a useful guide while researching this. However, there are some beautiful ceramics in Iceland today. Finally, Iceland's landscape has changed over time. After all, it has an active volcano! However, I have tried to remain faithful to the intrinsic beauty and dramatic nature of Iceland in my storytelling. I hope you love this magical land as much as I do!

A VIKING TOO WILD TO WED

LUCY MORRIS

Harlequin

HISTORICAL

If you purchased this book without a cover you should be aware that this book is stolen property. It was reported as "unsold and destroyed" to the publisher, and neither the author nor the publisher has received any payment for this "stripped book."

Harlequin® HISTORICAL

ISBN-13: 978-1-335-83152-1

A Viking Too Wild to Wed

Copyright © 2025 by Lucy Morris

All rights reserved. No part of this book may be used or reproduced in any manner whatsoever without written permission.

Without limiting the author's and publisher's exclusive rights, any unauthorized use of this publication to train generative artificial intelligence (AI) technologies is expressly prohibited.

This is a work of fiction. Names, characters, places and incidents are either the product of the author's imagination or are used fictitiously. Any resemblance to actual persons, living or dead, businesses, companies, events or locales is entirely coincidental.

For questions and comments about the quality of this book, please contact us at CustomerService@Harlequin.com.

TM and ® are trademarks of Harlequin Enterprises ULC.

Harlequin Enterprises ULC
22 Adelaide St. West, 41st Floor
Toronto, Ontario M5H 4E3, Canada
www.Harlequin.com

Recycling programs for this product may not exist in your area.

Printed in U.S.A.

Lucy Morris lives in Essex, UK, with her husband, two young children and two cats. She has a massive sweet tooth and loves gin, bubbly and Irn-Bru. She's a member of the UK Romantic Novelists' Association. She was delighted to accept a two-book deal with Harlequin after submitting her story to the Warriors Wanted! submission blitz for Viking, medieval and Highlander romances. Writing for Harlequin Historical is a dream come true for her and she hopes you enjoy her books!

Books by Lucy Morris

Harlequin Historical

A Nun for the Viking Warrior
The Viking She Loves to Hate
Snowed In with the Viking
How the Wallflower Wins a Duke

The Eriksson Brothers

"Her Bought Viking Husband"
in *Convenient Vows with a Viking*
Wedding Night with Her Viking Enemy

A Season to Wed

The Lord's Maddening Miss

Shieldmaiden Sisters

The Viking She Would Have Married
Tempted by Her Outcast Viking
Beguiling Her Enemy Warrior

Visit the Author Profile page at Harlequin.com.

For my newsletter readers, you asked for more from
the Eriksson Brothers, and I hope I have delivered!

Chapter One

Iceland, Yule, 910 AD

Even the gods would think Mildritha beautiful.

Egill was certain he'd never met a more beautiful woman than Mildritha, and doubted even the goddess Freyja could rival her—at least, in Egill's opinion. Nobody could challenge her in his eyes, he was so captivated by her, and he suspected he always would be until the last draw of his breath.

Warm chestnut hair braided in a long rope down her back. Her dark, almost black eyes that appeared sultry in the firelight and added to the sweetness of her features. But it was her mouth that he admired the most, especially when she smiled, as she did now. Her lips lush and full, with a wry lift at one corner. Even when she was happy, she expected disappointment, and who could blame her for her cynicism?

He wanted to take away that inner darkness. To make those hooded eyes sparkle with desire, and those plump lips call out his name with a cry of pleasure. He wanted to banish those shadows and brighten her world. But he would have to tread carefully with her. She used her suspicion like a shield and was as clever as a fox. Getting her to dance with him had been difficult enough.

'Master Egill!' she laughed, tugging him out of his stupor and towards the archway of raised arms, the beat of the music urging them forward. They ran under, raising their own arms up at the end to continue the archway for the following dancers. Her callused hands were warm and silky from her daily task of working the oily wool on his sister-in-law Orla's looms.

Mildritha, or Mila as she was known by her sister Wynflaed, did not enjoy making cloth. He had noticed her scowling at the looms more than once this winter, as if they were her sworn enemy.

Oddly, she preferred the harder labour of working in the kitchens to the intricate work of the looms. But each bondswoman had to repay her debt to Orla with a hundred ells of cloth, and so Mila would grit her teeth and work the looms. Never once complaining that she still struggled with the craft, making her cloth dutifully so that she could slowly repay the cost of her freedom.

As each couple ran beneath their clasped hands, Egill took a moment to enjoy the sight of her, distracted as she was by the festivities. Her lips absently moving along to the song being sung by one of Orla's women. Her sweet voice only rising to join the others as the revellers sang the chorus together. Egill was not familiar with it, as it was a Saxon country song. Most of the weavers were from Northumbria or Ireland, and naturally they had brought their own songs and dances with them to Iceland.

Orla had originally been a thrall from Ireland herself, and did not mind the mix of cultures in her hall. She encouraged it, as the varied choice of music, dance and traditions at this feast had proven.

Mila looked so relaxed and happy singing along to the country songs of her motherland, it made him wonder if she missed her home.

Was that the reason for her sad smiles? Did she miss her land or someone she had left behind?

He hoped she didn't miss a person. There was little he could do if that were the case. Perhaps that made him a selfish man, but he wanted her heart and smiles to himself.

The song ended, but Egill only realised it when Mila let go of his hands and thanked him politely for dancing with her, even though he had insisted she join him. She began to turn away, and he grabbed her elbow lightly with one of his most charming smiles. 'Come and sit with me, Mila. Tell me more about that song. You seemed to know it well.'

With a blush she nodded, and followed him to a bench at the far end of the hall, closest to his chamber. As they approached the bench, he turned towards her. She swallowed nervously, her eyes darting around the room self-consciously, until she noticed Wynflaed on one of the nearby benches. Then she seemed to breathe a sigh of relief as if her sister's presence calmed her.

'It is just a country dance. It makes sense to dance it at Christmas—I mean, Yule...because you need a lot of people to make the tunnel work.'

'I see.' Amusement twitched at the corner of his mouth, and he had to fight not to laugh. Mila was painfully blunt at times, pointing out all the detail, but missing the obvious—the reason he wished to sit with her.

She was about to sit down on the bench when he gestured a little farther down it. 'I think I saw Gunnar spill his ale there. You wouldn't want to stain your dress.'

He winced at the lie, but he had a very good reason for not wanting her to sit in that spot, and it had nothing to do with keeping her drab servant clothing clean. Thankfully, she didn't seem to notice and only nodded, then followed his suggestion to sit farther down the bench. She primly folded her hands neatly in her lap as he took his seat next to her.

'Do you like this time of year?' he asked.

'Yule?' At his nod, Mila merely shrugged. 'It can be a fun time of year, I suppose. Especially when the stores are well stocked.'

Always practical.

He chuckled at her begrudging acceptance. 'The festivities and traditions are a welcome distraction during the darkest days of the season.'

She nodded grimly. 'It is very dark here. I am half-afraid the winter will never end.' She shivered, the thought seeming to dampen her spirits.

Cheerfully, he reassured her, 'Spring will come. The seasons come and go, but the cycle of life is always the same. No matter how dark it becomes, light will always return.'

She smiled at his words, but it was a strangely sad smile—one she often wore. It always made his heart ache for her. He asked gently, 'Do you have anyone back in Northumbria? Family or…anyone else left behind?' It was a question he had longed to ask her since the day he'd arrived at his brother's hall nearly two months ago, but he had been afraid to learn the truth. So had kept silent, until now.

Relief washed over him when she immediately shook her head. 'Wynflaed is my only family,' she said, her dark eyes warming with affection as she looked over at her sister, who was playing dice with Tyr in the corner. She was obviously winning, too, by the shout of outrage from Tyr and the giggle from their friend, fellow bondswoman Nora, who followed the two sisters everywhere they went.

Mila laughed, the sound as merry as the string of bells

hanging from the rafters. 'Wynflaed won't be fetching any water for the rest of the year at this rate!'

'Your sister is lucky.' It was a common compliment that the Norse used often, but it seemed to sour Mila's pleasure.

'Not always,' she said, and then was quiet for a moment, staring blankly ahead, oblivious to the joy around her and swept up in her own dark memories.

'Because you were captured?' he asked gently, and was glad when she snapped out of her gloom and answered honestly.

'Yes, but…before that too.'

That surprised him. He had heard the story of how Mila and Wynflaed had been captured. How they'd been walking along a beach in Northumbria, not seeing the slave trader's camp until it was too late. But he had not heard anything about their time before their capture.

'What happened before?' He asked the question softly, as if he were waiting for a buck to emerge from the trees and was afraid if he spoke too loudly, he might frighten it away.

'We used to live in Jorvik. Our mother was a potter—we all were. We struggled, but we got by. But then there was a fire…' Her eyes clouded with painful memories. She blinked rapidly as if forcing the tears away. 'We went to the coast, hoping for a better future, but then…'

'You were taken,' Egill said grimly.

She sighed. 'Yes… But I suppose things could have been worse. It sounds odd, but I am grateful Orla bought us… Our life improved in some ways, and I realise it could have been much worse for us.'

'What about your mother? Will she not wonder what became of you? I could pay for a message to be delivered to her if you wish?'

She stared at him as if startled. 'You would do that?' But then her eyes narrowed with suspicion. 'Why?'

She was slow to trust.

That was why it had taken him this long merely to be able to speak with her for more than a moment before she made some excuse to hurry away to her sister and Nora.

He shrugged. 'It is a simple enough task. I merely give a few coins to a trusted man on the next ship out. It would be no trouble, and I will have the satisfaction of repaying you for the kindness you showed my brother. He said you helped tend his wounds on the slave ship.'

Mila shook her head dismissively. 'We did very little—it was obvious he was a strong and powerful man despite his chains. He'd already been travelling with the slavers a week before they stopped and captured us, so he was already healing. You should know that before offering us any kind of repayment for our kindness.'

Egill laughed. 'Are you trying to dissuade me from helping you?'

Mila looked away from him and sighed. 'No, I am only telling you the truth. Besides, there is no need to send a messenger. We lost everything in the fire, including our mother.'

He leaned closer, catching her eye to show his sincerity. 'I am sorry to hear that.'

Mila simply shrugged, her shoulders stiff, and he feared he had only made things worse between them. He did not dare ask about her father. He presumed he was dead or absent, considering the fact she had never mentioned him, even when speaking about her mother. He did not imagine that was a cheerful story either.

Odin's teeth! He was making a mess of this!

'But thank you,' she said quietly, 'for the offer. It was very kind of you.'

He decided to change the conversation to a more cheerful subject. 'Forget Northumbria. It is a terribly damp and miserable place. You can build a much better future here. After all, Iceland is the most interesting land I have ever seen.'

'It is? But you have been to so many!'

He had her interest now, and he was determined to keep it. 'Where else can you find hot pools, frozen lakes as high as a mountain, and golden waterfalls? It is a magical land of fire and ice... Do you not agree? You seemed to enjoy the winter lights—I saw you sneaking out to see them whenever you could.'

Mila blushed, but nodded enthusiastically. 'I have never seen the sky look like that before, with swirling colours... It was magical. I hope we see them again before the spring.' She gave a deep sigh of pleasure, as if recalling the beauty of the spectacle that had graced their skies during this winter season.

Egill grinned, leaning a little closer. 'You can see them in my homeland too... But here, you can sit in a hot pool with a horn of mead and enjoy them without getting cold.'

She turned towards him, only a breath of space between them, and chuckled. '*You* may have enjoyed them in a hot pool. *We* only see them while fetching water or feeding the animals.'

The sparkle of amusement in her eyes was like a beacon of hope, and he turned ever so slightly towards her, allowing his thigh to brush against hers. The hands in her lap tightened, but she did not move away. 'I will beat Tyr in every dice game he plays just so that he will be the one to fetch the water and feed the animals. That way you will be free to join me.'

'Join you?'

Her eyes reflected the flame from the surrounding torches, and she bit her bottom lip as she stared back at him. She was on the precipice of falling into his embrace. His heart thudded in his chest so hard he felt it pulsing through his whole body.

'There are no lights tonight...' she whispered, but her gaze had trailed down to his lips, and he knew she wanted to be kissed.

'We do not need lights to enjoy ourselves. Besides... have you not noticed something?'

'What?' she gasped, her chest rising and falling in an alluring way.

He raised his eyes deliberately towards the bundle of mistletoe above their heads. It wasn't *actual* mistletoe—but a woollen model of the plant combined with twigs.

Mila thankfully seemed to realise the significance of the Norse symbol of love, because her eyes widened and then flew back to his with a shocked gasp. 'It isn't real mistletoe,' she said, as if that made a difference.

'True,' he agreed. 'Mistletoe does not grow here. But just like you weavers, I wanted to celebrate yule with some traditions from my homeland. Orla was kind enough to make it for me.'

'I see.' Mila's face darkened, and he wondered what he had done wrong.

'I asked her to make it because I wanted to kiss you. You are beautiful, and I want you, Mila. I want to make love to you and look after you.' The confession escaped him in one rush of heavy breath, surprising him with the nervousness and uncertainty that quickly filled the space left behind. He was never nervous around women, and yet, here he was babbling like a lovesick youth.

'It's not real!' she snapped, and there was genuine anger in her voice, as if she were offended by his words. But then she took a deep breath as if to calm herself, and followed it by speaking in a deliberately cool but polite tone—it might as well have been a slap. 'I think you are a good man, Egill. But I have a future here, a life of security that I want to protect. Being with you…it could put that future at risk. So please do not ask me again.'

Before he could think of anything more to say, she stood up briskly and brushed down her skirts as if she were dusting off his words of admiration like a muddy stain. 'I wish you well,' was her final parting blow before she hurried back to her sister.

Egill ran a hand through his hair, thoroughly shocked. *What had happened?*

A drunken Hakon dropped down on the bench beside him a few moments later, sloshing a little ale on his boots. 'Oh, dear, brother! I have never known you to fail in charming a woman! Not even a kiss on the cheek?' Hakon tutted with a mocking reprimand.

'Shut up!' Egill hissed.

But his brother took no notice of his ill humour, laughing lightly before thumping him in the arm. 'I used to think I was the only brother unlucky in love… Perhaps, now that I have Orla, my bad luck has washed over to you?'

Egill scowled at the suggestion, which was enough to make the drink-addled Hakon blink in surprise. 'Do you…?'

'Shut up!' Egill growled again.

'Oh, I see… You *really* like her.'

'What's this?' asked a cheerful Orla as she handed Egill a horn of ale. 'Are you talking about Mildritha? Egill, you really should—'

Egill stood up quickly, not wanting to discuss his embarrassment any further. 'Hakon, kiss your wife under the mistletoe. Someone should get some use out of it!'

Hakon roared with laughter and grabbed his red-headed wife, pulling her into his lap. 'I think I will!' he declared before dipping his squealing wife low and kissing her soundly.

Egill wandered away, raking through his past behaviour.

What had he done to offend Mila? Why had she rejected him?

He could think of nothing.

Did she not want him?

But surely his instincts were not wrong, he had bedded enough women to know when there was a mutual attraction, and he had seen it with Mila!

A few weeks after his arrival in the late autumn, Egill and Hakon had decided to ease some boredom after the harvest by training the men. Her eyes had watched him with admiration as he fought bare-chested with Hakon's men.

Afterwards, he had sought her out, inviting her to join him in a walk by the stream. Mildritha had stared at him in horror and shaken her head vigorously. 'No, thank you, Master Egill... I, please...don't... Mistress Orla doesn't approve of such things...' She had looked genuinely frightened by his suggestion, and he had felt like a complete wretch for making her uncomfortable.

Taking a step back, he had calmly pointed out to her that she did not need to have anyone's permission, that she was free to choose for herself either way, and that he would rather cut off his own hand than touch a woman without her permission...regardless of status.

He had hoped to reassure her, but she had simply thanked him and hurried away. It had taken until Yule for her to become relaxed in his company.

And now he had ruined it…again.

But if Egill was anything, he was resilient and tenacious.

He took a long sip of his ale, a silent toast to himself, as he remembered the way she had looked at his mouth. She *had* wanted to kiss him, that much was certain.

Like the seasons, she would eventually change her opinion of him… He would make certain of it.

Chapter Two

Iceland, Early Spring, 911 AD

'Mila!' called a cheerful voice from across the bustling feasting hall. The booming voice belonged to the handsome and considerably arrogant Egill. The master's youngest brother and biggest thorn in Mila's side.

Pointedly ignoring him, she carried on with her work—as she had done for weeks. It was infuriating that the man had taken to using the nickname her sister and friends used for her.

When would he finally accept that she was not interested in being seduced by him and leave her alone?

Not today, apparently.

He called again, this time more loudly, from his seat at the high table, drawing more than one curious gaze upon her. 'Mila! Come, sit with me!' He thumped his fist on the bench beside him with a smile that she was certain would melt any other woman's heart.

Thankfully not hers, although…it did beat a little faster at the sight of him, but that was surely due to irritation?

'He won't be happy until you at least answer him,' murmured Wynflaed quietly, an amused smile twisting the corner of her mouth as they both served the last of the rye bread.

At first, Mila had been frightened that Egill might force himself on her, as many men in his position might have done. But weeks had passed since her rejection of him at yule, and yet nothing had happened, except her own patience had finally snapped.

'I want to sit with you,' Mila grumbled. 'I am not here for his entertainment. The Konudagur festival is meant to be enjoyable for *every woman*. Not a jarl's brother who thinks far too highly of himself!' She said the last words with a dark glare towards Egill, who merely laughed good-naturedly at her open rejection and went back to sipping his ale.

No, he hadn't forgotten her. Blue, sinfully seductive eyes followed her every movement above the rim of his cup, doing strange things to the heat of her body and the peace of her mind.

Wynflaed frowned as she took her seat. She gripped Mila's arm, dragging her down onto the bench beside her, whispering, 'Remember our place, Mila! You would never have dared such a thing a few months ago. Perhaps we should not be too comfortable in our position here? Especially when it comes to the master's youngest brother.'

Mila nodded, immediately repenting her behaviour.

Wynflaed was right.

She would never have dared to say such a thing only a few months ago, when they had first been offloaded like cattle on Iceland's shores and sold to Mistress Orla. 'Sorry, you are right to scold me. We do not want to ruin our prospects here. I should not let him rile me so. At least he will be gone soon… He said he would only stay for one year.'

She still could not quite believe their change in fortune,

and she was thankful every day that it had been Orla who had bought them, and not one of her neighbours. Many thralls were not as well cared for as they had been, and certainly very few were given the opportunity to buy their freedom back.

Truly, there was a lot to be thankful for. The pestering of a spoilt and handsome warrior was hardly a hardship.

They had survived the long and dark winter of this new land, and were in the final days of Thorrablót, the month dedicated to the Norse god Thor. It began with a feasting day celebrating men, and ended with a feast dedicated to women. It had taken a while to get used to the many festivals in Iceland, as Mila had been born a Christian, and had lived her entire life in that small patch of Northumbria, until that fateful day when she and Wynflaed had been captured by a slaver.

She was not entirely sure if she should curse that day or not. It had been a hellish time, and yet…their lives had improved drastically ever since.

After all, they had not been happy in the city of Jorvik. They'd struggled every day to make a living there and put bread on the table. It had never been an easy life, and despite having freedom, they'd never been as well-fed as they had been here.

It was a sobering thought.

Some of the men began to gather in the middle of the hall, carrying large sacks and pushing benches and furniture out of the way.

'What is this?' asked Orla curiously. Their red-headed mistress glanced at her husband, Hakon, beside her, who wore an equally confused expression.

Hakon, who looked very much like his golden brother Egill, gave a confused shrug. 'I would imagine it is our evening's entertainment, although I know nothing about it. Egill, what is the meaning of this?'

Egill gasped with mock outrage. 'Why do you immediately think I have anything to do with it?'

'Because if there is mischief, you are usually the cause!' Hakon grumbled with a badly concealed smile.

Egill shrugged. 'It is a saga performance. I may have helped with the poetry...a little.'

Tyr stepped forward from the group. He had once been a bonded servant just like Mila and Wynflaed. As was common with Orla's people, Tyr had worked off his thrall's debt but had decided to stay afterwards, swearing allegiance to Master Hakon and Mistress Orla. Tyr's presence had always reassured Mila that Hakon and Orla were true to their word and would grant them their true freedom once the debt of buying them was repaid.

Mila glanced beside her at Nora and Wynflaed. Nora was a friend to both of them, but Wynflaed and Nora were closer. They spent many hours talking together as they weaved. Mila wished she had someone like that, but she had always struggled to make friends. Most of her friends she had made through Wynflaed.

Tyr gave a respectful bow, and then proclaimed loudly, 'On this day we perform a play. In honour of our mistress Orla, we tell her tale of marriage on *Thorra...blot.*'

The *blot* was muttered quietly, and the crowd laughed at the poor rhyme with *Orla*.

'I can tell you helped, Egill!' joked their neighbour Snorri from one of the benches. Snorri was a bad-tempered and miserly man and yet was the most loyal friend to their master and mistress.

'I am sure you will love it!' Egill gave him a sly smile, and Mila suspected Snorri would also make an appearance in the tale. He'd certainly had a part to play in the saving of their hall.

Tyr was handed a wig out of one of the sacks by one of his fellow players, and he quickly put it on.

It was a short-cropped mop of yellow wool. It even had a yellow beard attached that swung in front of Tyr's face. 'I am the strong and righteous Jarl Hakon Eriksson! Being betrayed and made a slave is no fun!' He then flexed his muscles dramatically.

A loud cheer erupted from the back of the hall, and Mila chuckled at realising the loudest shouts of approval were coming from Tyr's wife, a fellow weaver.

Tyr then held out his hands dramatically, allowing himself to be bound by ridiculously loose chains. Mila was sure they had been used to hang up the rolls of smoked mutton that now sat on the platters of cabbage and turnips in front of them.

Two of the other players put on long brown woollen wigs and stood beside Tyr's rather poor version of Hakon. They spoke in unison with high-pitched voices: 'Two pretty girls from Northumberia's land. Picked up like flotsam on the way to Iceland.'

Mila felt every eye in the hall turn towards her and Wynflaed. Heat burned her cheeks, and she fixed a brittle smile on her lips. It was a comedy show, and nearly everyone was ridiculed in such a performance. But the misery of her capture was still difficult to swallow, and she tried not to let the hurt show.

Wynflaed saved her from embarrassment by shouting in a deliberately high-pitched voice, 'We don't sound like that!' which caused the hall to erupt into more laughter.

Her sister squeezed her leg beneath the table, and some of her shame fell away. Piercing blue eyes, the colour of jewels that she would never own, caught her gaze from across the room, perceptive and filled with sympathy. She stared back at Egill, wondering if *this* was how he saw her, tragic and pitiful. She had thought the same at one time. She hated that this might be how he viewed her.

She didn't want to be pitied. She had suffered enough of that to last her a lifetime already. Independence and freedom were the only things she wanted or needed. Two things that could never be found in the arms of a man.

However, before Mila could think any more about it, she was distracted by the arrival of Gunnar from one of the back chambers. The old right hand of Mistress Orla strode into the centre of the room proudly in a forest-green dress, a red woollen wig slapped on his bald head. Howls of laughter filled the room, including those of Mistress Orla, who took no offence at one of her elderly warriors impersonating her.

Gunnar's voice filled the room, and the fact that he did not even try to hide his deep voice only made his poem funnier. 'I need a husband, and you will do! Help me defeat my wicked uncle—even if you must run him through!'

Tyr flexed his muscles extravagantly, dropping the loose chains and letting them crash to the floor. 'I will marry you, but you must buy them too!' He gestured to the two men impersonating Mila and her sister. 'They have been kind to me and tended my wounds. I have revenge to win, but will stay twelve full moons.'

Mila relaxed a little and began to enjoy the spectacle of the performance. Snorri was introduced, as well as his brave white bear, which was one of the children wrapped up in a snowy fleece. As were Orla's evil uncle and cousin, who had always coveted her land and had plotted against her—until Hakon defeated them.

Snorri wiped away a single tear when his beloved pet was killed by Orla's villainous cousin's hand. But cheered for Hakon when he killed Orla's cousin and saved Wynflaed from his clutches. The final battle between Orla's uncle and Hakon was done surprisingly well, with threads of red wool thrown from clenched fists to show the blood that flowed that day. Mila was humbled to see herself and her sister depicted so bravely protecting the hall with pieces of broken furniture. Even in the face of certain death.

But, of course, their deaths did not follow, because when all appeared lost, a great shout came from the side of the hall, and Egill, the *real* Egill, sailed in on a miniature longship, made with old barrels and rolled out on squeaky wheels.

It must have been hidden by the piles of woven cloth on that side of the room, because Mila had not seen it until now. Egill had gone to great effort to keep this as an entertaining surprise.

Of course he would be the only person to play himself! she thought with amusement.

Egill jumped from his boat and swaggered into the centre of the room with an ale in one hand and his axe in the other, declaring, 'We will save you, brother! Rescue you and your lover!'

Orla rolled her eyes with an indulgent smile, while Hakon grumbled, 'I do not see Grimr. Interesting that you should forget to include his part in your tale!'

'I'm here!' croaked a little voice from the boat, and everyone chuckled to see one of the tiny elderly women sit up from the floor of the boat with an axe in hand, a yellow woollen beard dangling from her chin. She must have been hidden beneath one of the cloths in the boat.

'Come, Grimr! Help me defeat these wicked men!'

shouted Egill, and the elderly woman gave a war cry before awkwardly climbing out of the ship—with a little help from the those around her.

Egill began to charge around the performers, lightly swinging his axe towards them. They dramatically fell to the floor despite the blade not even touching them, making gurgled screams of pain and throwing red woollen thread up into the air in an extra flourish of pretend blood.

Tyr got up onto a stool and proclaimed, 'As my enemy, you fall! But swear allegiance and you will stand tall!'

Even the fallen quickly got to their feet, standing straight and proud. 'We swear!'

Mila gave a loud snort of disdain when she saw the two men playing herself and Wynflaed swoon at Egill's feet and say in breathy voices, 'The Eriksson brothers are mighty and fair!'

The crowd laughed again at Egill's arrogance. He grinned at her until she could not help but laugh as well. She tried to hide it, raising her horn cup to mask her face before drinking from it.

Perhaps she *should* smile about her past... Those days of uncertainty were behind her, and she needed to build a future for herself and Wynflaed...one not reliant on anyone but herself! She had learned her lesson well.

You could not rely on handsome men like Egill, no matter how charming and sweet they might appear, because Mila knew the truth... Men would swoop in as a hero and play to a crowd, but when they were *really* needed, they were nowhere to be seen.

No, Mila would have a future of her own making. Courage and determination swelled within her, and she gripped the fabric of her skirts tightly as she turned towards Wynflaed and Nora and waited for a lull in their conversation.

She would take this opportunity of revelry to speak with Mistress Orla about her plans, but first she would see if Wynflaed approved of her idea. She was sure she would—they agreed on most things.

Excitement sparked in her veins. Her future plans would begin today, and she would never play the victim again.

Chapter Three

Egill sat beside Orla at the high table. She grinned at him and said, 'A wonderful performance, Egill. Although I do question some of your choices.'

'Thank you, sister! But you are right. Gunnar did not do your beauty or courage justice.'

She frowned before answering, 'That is not what I meant. It is fitting to pick Gunnar to play me. He has known me since I was a child. I do not mind his mockery. But the other women...' Orla paused, her eyes deliberately sweeping over to the one woman he could not avoid for long—even if he wanted to!

He could not help himself. It was as if his obsessive eyes had been granted permission. His gaze instantly sought and found Mila, her dark eyes twinkling with firelight as she talked with Wynflaed and Nora excitedly.

So struck by her beauty, he almost did not hear Orla's question: 'Why would you make light of their enslavement?'

Egill was offended by the censure, and he flinched. 'That was not my intention... I wished only to remind them of how far they have come. They are freewomen now and can choose their own fate. Something I wish Mila would accept.

Perhaps then she would not work her fingers raw weaving mountains of cloth every spare hour.'

Orla shook her head sadly as if he were dim-witted. 'You reminded them of their past, which is now lost to them. It is a bitter truth. One that probably pains them greatly.' She fixed him with a stern expression, and he was quickly reminded that Orla would understand first hand what he could not. His sister-in-law had been a slave herself as a child, and knew more about their suffering than he could ever imagine. 'And...they are not truly free—they have at least fifty ells of cloth each to produce before they repay their debt to me. That is the way of things. I buy as many female slaves as I can and use them for my looms until the cost of buying them is repaid. I wish it were different, but our neighbours would revolt against us if we did otherwise... They have their own thralls to manage.'

'I have offered more than once to repay her debt.' Egill snapped bad-temperedly, 'She is too stubborn to accept it.'

To his surprise, Orla nodded. 'I can see why she refuses.'

'I cannot. She is just being proud!'

Hakon leaned around Orla to add his own thoughts on the matter, and Egill really wished he hadn't bothered, especially when he seemed to agree with his wife. 'It is well-known that you like her, have invited her to your bed more than once. But she always refuses you—something which would be considered impossible in any other hall. If you paid off her debt, she would feel as if she owed you—or worse. She might even believe you had bought her solely to grace your bed—and others would presume the same, even if you had no plans to do so. Do not scowl at me, brother. You know I speak the truth. Let her do as she wishes. Unless...you can offer her something more, better even?'

Egill stiffened; he knew his brother was hinting at marriage. He had been debating such a thing himself most of the winter. A year ago, he would have balked at the idea, but after meeting Mila, his opinion had waivered considerably.

In the end, he had realised that it was indeed time for him to settle down. Where he would settle and what he would do were still uncertain, but beginning the next stage of his life with a wife seemed a sensible first step...if Mila wished it. 'I want her to choose me freely. Not because she feels she must.'

Hakon nodded thoughtfully, biting into his blood pudding with relish and then mumbling through a mouthful of food. 'You cannot blame her, then, for wanting the same.'

Orla smiled knowingly. 'Give it time. She will be free to choose by the end of the summer.' At Egill's frown, she added, 'I hope you are not impatient because you plan to leave when Grimr arrives? If you are simply trying to bed her...'

Egill was offended for the second time since he had joined them only a few moments ago. It was true he had never had any intention in the past to settle down, but he'd had his reasons for that. 'Why do you think so poorly of me, sister?'

Orla rolled her eyes. 'Because your brother has told me that you are the most outrageous flirt and charmer of his family.'

Egill clutched at his chest as if she had wounded him with her words. 'Sister, those days are behind me! Honour and family mean everything to me. Now that my brothers are married, I must look to my own future. I merely dallied in the past—while I waited patiently for Hakon and Grimr to find their beloved wives. But I never hurt anyone or spoke falsely. How could I ever take a wife when my dear brothers were so unhappy and lonely?'

Orla gave an amused huff at his defence. 'Then I will not stand in your way. But do not rush her either. She has been through so much, and struggles to trust in—oh!' gasped Orla before quickly raising her horn of mead to cover her face and whispering covertly, 'She is coming over! Pretend we are not talking about her.'

Startled, Egill's eyes immediately searched for Mila, and he realised she was now only a few feet away from them. Hakon loudly asked him something ridiculous about the weather, but he ignored him, his eyes drinking in the sight of Mila like a man dying of thirst.

She had filled out since autumn—which suggested she had been starving before her arrival to Iceland. Her willowy body was still elegant but had softened with delicious curves. Her face was rounder and more lovely than before, and her arms considerably stronger from pulling on the loom and working in the kitchen. She wore a simple linen shift with an ochre apron dress fastened with simple bone pins. Nothing like the elaborate dresses and jewellery Orla wore, but she was still far better dressed then most thralls.

She crossed her hands in front of her and gave a formal bow to her master and mistress, which suggested she wished to talk to them about something of importance.

'Master, may I speak with you about the terms of my bondage?'

Orla sat up a little, and Hakon waved a hand respectfully to his wife. 'You made your deal with my wife. Speak with your mistress.'

'Thank you, Master,' Mila said, the deep swallow of her throat the only indication she was nervous. 'Mistress, I believe I have made forty-two ells of cloth in repayment, and Wynflaed has made fifty-two.'

Orla nodded. 'That sounds about right, although I would

need to check your record to be certain. Would you like me to get it?'

'No need. I do not question the amount,' said Mila, clearing her throat.

If Mila did not wish to question the amount, then why had she mentioned it?

Egill knew Orla kept the records on rectangular panels of wood. One for every bonded woman bought from the slavers' ships. Each ell of cloth carefully scratched into the wood. Once it was filled with a hundred marks, Orla would brand the wood with her seal to proclaim the woman was now free. Many stayed on after their debt was repaid, happy with the small income and safety of Orla's home. Others married local farmers, and some worked a little longer and bought passage home. That was the possibility worrying him the most with Mila...that she would leave, and he would lose her forever. At Yule she'd told him no one was waiting for her...but perhaps she longed for her home in other ways?

Mila took another deep breath, and his foot began to tap impatiently beneath the bench. He was eager to learn more. Why had she decided to speak with Orla about her repayment...did she wish to leave?

'I wish to propose...something. A way to reduce my debt while also benefiting you and Master Hakon.' Mila's hands twisted together, and he could see the calluses and pink marks from the loom and tools she worked with daily.

Mila had worked hard to produce cloth, but many of her marks had been from helping her mistress in other areas rather than in producing cloth, because Mila was not a natural with the loom like Wynflaed. She struggled to find the rhythm of the craft, sometimes having to undo most of her work to correct mistakes. At times it had been painful to watch, but Egill knew Orla was a kind mistress. She regularly added to Mila's count with some excuse or other to ensure the sisters would both be free around the same time.

'Go on,' said Orla.

'Back in Northumbria, I was a potter. I learned the craft from my mother. I have a talent for it, and it would have been my livelihood if…we had not been taken…' Mila grimaced and swallowed nervously as if the thought made her stomach churn. 'Anyway.' She shook her head as if clearing away the bad memories. 'If you would permit me to dig a firepit, I am sure I could make pots, beakers and all manner of pottery to serve your needs as well as to sell at the market.'

Snorri, Orla's neighbour, snorted loudly, drawing everyone's attention. He turned towards Mila with a raised brow. 'Do you see much pottery here, girl? The natural clay of this land is too poor to use. It crumbles as soon as it fires. We Icelanders use carved soapstone, wood, and bone. Not *pottery*!' He said the final word as if it were a curse.

Mila stiffened, but gave an accepting tilt of her head. 'True. But I have seen some clay that holds promise not far from here. If I can produce workable clay, surely that would benefit everyone?'

Orla nodded and then called over to Wynflaed, 'What say you, Wynflaed? Do you think it possible? Is Mildritha a good enough potter to work a miracle?'

Wynflaed nodded enthusiastically. 'She is excellent, Mistress, and if anyone can make the clay of Iceland workable, it would be her. If it pleases you, I will work longer at the looms to make up for her absence.'

Snorri gave a loud, disbelieving grunt before leaning forward with a sly smile. 'If you are eager to pay off your debt, Mildritha, then consider my second son, Bolli.' He gestured towards his big bear of a son beside him, who blinked in surprise at the sudden mention of his name. 'His wife died last winter, and he has not coped well with her loss. Now his farm is filled with children and no wife. He could do with a pretty, hardworking girl like you to *work* him.' Snorri sniggered at his own jest before adding dismissively, 'I will pay off your debt, and that of your sister too—if she agrees to join you. Bolli needs all the help he can get!'

'Father, I am managing perfectly well, and I only have three children!' grumbled Bolli, whose face had reddened with embarrassment during his father's speech, his cheeks now matching the russet colour of his hair and beard. But then he looked shyly up at Mila with a sincere expression. 'Although... I would not object to another marriage...' Bolli was a quiet man, but strong as an ox. He was also reliable and in the prime of his life. Egill had no quarrel with the man and even liked him... Until now.

Mila stared at Bolli, her mouth dropping open a little with shock. Egill had the quick and grim realisation that in Mila's current position, this was a *decent* offer, and she could be taken away from him in a matter of moments.

'Absolutely not!' Egill shouted, his voice filling the room like thunder, and the entire hall turned to stare at him in surprise.

Including Hakon, who raised a golden brow and reminded him gently, 'It is not up to you, brother.'

Scrambling to find a decent reason for his outburst, Egill said, 'We should give Mila the opportunity to prove herself. To do what *she* wants...'

Mila's expression softened, and she gave him a tiny appreciative smile of gratitude. Which only made him feel more guilty, because he had interrupted for purely selfish reasons. They just so happened to align with Mila's own plans.

Hakon and Orla exchanged a thoughtful look before Orla said, 'I have no objection to your trying...at least for a short time—say, two weeks? But I can offer you no help. We need our men to plant the fields and tend the animals. While the weavers will be taking advantage of the better light, now that spring has finally arrived, it will be a busy time, and...' She paused, glancing at Egill before adding, 'Grimr will be visiting us this spring, hopefully with more supplies and news from Norway. If all has gone well with his marriage alliance to Sigrid, he will probably leave again before the end of the summer. Mildritha, are you sure you want to lose potential weaving time on a craft that may never bear fruit?'

Egill knew the implication of her words. Orla was a wise and clever woman—it was how she had retained her power in a land full of brutal men. Orla was reminding them both of two very important things.

Firstly, that Mila could be eating into the time she had left for weaving—time that she could use to repay her debt. Ultimately, the pottery might fail, meaning it would take longer for her to weave her remaining ells, potentially missing the boats returning to Northumbria in the summer—if she did wish to leave.

Secondly, she was reminding Egill that he had originally planned to try life in Iceland for only a few months. *He* might decide to leave with Grimr and return to Norway—without Mila. Nothing was set, and as such, she was trying to protect Mila from making a foolish mistake.

He wished he could argue against her assumptions. Unfortunately, Egill was still undecided and could not be sure of anything himself. He enjoyed helping with the farm, but also found the labour dull and repetitive. He'd never had ambitions to rule or find glory for himself. It had always been for the good of his brothers and family honour. But what if Grimr's marriage hadn't avoided war? He might need to return with him to fight for their family name. It was a small possibility, but one he couldn't dismiss.

Besides, Mila had never given him reason to think she might consider him. In fact, she had done the opposite, refusing to indulge in his flirtations. Even during the winter, he had never spoken that long with her, barely knew anything about her, if he were honest... He had not even known she was a potter in her previous life, and what did that say about him?

He needed to consider his future carefully now that his brothers were settled on opposite sides of the world. He had so much choice compared to Mila, and yet he struggled to decide anything. Paralysed by the sheer breadth of the endless horizon, he almost wished someone would tell him what to do. But he was no longer a child, or a youthful third son without cares or responsibility. He was a grown man, and all men had to find their own path in life eventually.

Iceland was an interesting land, although he had spent most of his months here sheltering in the hall away from the icy claws of winter. There were aspects he enjoyed about Iceland and farming...most of them being the company he had kept.

But was it the life he wanted?

He could no longer continue to follow his brothers everywhere. Grimr was a jarl, with a wife and an alliance to manage. Hakon had given up his jarldom for a simple, happy life with Orla.

But did Egill want the same?

He was unsure. Responsibility and duty had never appealed to him. His only loyalty was to his brothers, but they had moved on with their lives, and now he felt as useful as a blunt axe.

Shouldn't he find a place for himself? A purpose? His eyes were drawn to Mila as she answered her mistress, and he realised with startling clarity that he had been waiting for her...for her debt to be paid, and for his charm to finally bend her stubborn pride like a reed in the wind.

Mila nodded vigorously, drawing him back to the present.

He hoped it was because she was eager for an alternative to Bolli.

'I understand, mistress,' she said, 'and I am happy to do all the work by myself. If you permit it, I would like to take the old pony with me, and some tools and supplies. There is a travellers' shelter close by the bed of clay I wish to use, and I can live there while I experiment. If my work does not bear fruit by the end of my two weeks, I will accept your wisdom and return to weaving.'

After finishing her speech, she lowered her eyes to the floor and seemed to almost hold her breath, waiting for Orla's judgement.

Her words did not comfort Egill. The traveller's shelter was a rickety shack that helped wanderers avoid dying of cold in the thick of winter. There were the hot springs nearby at least, but very little vegetation or shelter. It would not be a comfortable home, and worse, it was close to Bolli's farm. Even though he trusted Bolli to be respectful, he did not like the idea of him being so close.

'Still...' said Orla, who thankfully took the safety of her people very seriously. 'I do not like to think of you alone out there. It is half a day's walk from anyone. Perhaps we could spare someone to go with you—'

'I will go!' Egill declared, not wanting this opportunity to pass for Mila. He also did not want Bolli to offer her shelter instead, as he suspected Bolli was about to do when he started to rise from his seat.

Mila's head snapped up, and she stared at Egill with what looked almost like irritation. He ignored it, adding quickly for Orla's benefit, 'It will be much quicker if I help. She will need a firepit, clay dug, fresh water...and other such things...' He wasn't entirely sure what else he would do, but he was sure there was plenty. 'And, of course, she will be safer in my company.'

Mila glared at him but said nothing. Orla turned to Hakon and asked for his opinion on the matter.

Thankfully, his brother was feeling generous and agreed that Egill could be spared for a short time. 'Besides, I will have to manage without him anyway if he leaves with Grimr and returns to Norway in the summer. Better that I get used to his absence now.'

'I am still undecided on that matter,' said Egill, not wishing to spook Mila with talk of his leaving.

Hakon rolled his eyes. 'Perhaps you should take this time to *finally* decide, brother? Before your lack of planning causes more harm than good.'

Egill squirmed at his brother's valid point, but outwardly grinned and inclined his head in agreement. 'You know I can be very decisive when I want to be.'

Orla fixed Mila with a firm look. 'Well then, Mildritha. You have two weeks to bring me a decent piece of Icelandic pottery.'

Mila's face broke out into a dazzling smile, as she realised she had finally been granted the approval she needed to get on with her plan. 'Thank you, Mistress! I will not let you down!'

The feast continued. Mila returned to her seat, where Wynflaed and Nora gave her a tight hug of congratulations, and others came to wish Mila luck with her endeavour.

Egill sat and watched, wondering when he could make an excuse to speak with her. They would need to make plans, decide on what to take. It was a perfect excuse.

Two weeks! He would have her all to himself for two weeks!

Nervous excitement thrummed in his veins like the night before a great battle. This was his chance to finally win Mila's heart and decide his fate.

Chapter Four

A little shake of her arm woke Mila up. She squinted up at Wynflaed, who was already tying up her bedroll in the dim light of the fading torches. Soon the oil would burn down to nothing. But that was fine, because once dawn had fully arrived, they would open the great doors to let in daylight and fresh air. It was much needed, judging by the smell of stale sweat in the hall that caused Mila's nose to wrinkle. But it was always the way after a feast with their neighbours. Too many people crowded together in one room.

'Come on, the others are already up,' whispered her sister, before she left the little space behind the beer barrels that they used as their sleeping space.

Mila shivered; the damp cold always seemed worse when the warmth of her sister was no longer curled up beside her. She winced at the prick of pain in her head—she should have watered down her ale more last night, as she would suffer for it today.

She wished she could cover her head once more with her blanket and sleep until midday, but there was no point. She could not shirk her duties, especially as today she had been granted the honour of pursuing her pottery and would need to ensure she did nothing to endanger it.

She smiled at the reminder of her triumph, and threw

off the blanket, quickly rolling the straw mat and woollen blankets of her bedroll and tying them with the attached cord. Standing, she glanced around the hall, relieved to see none of the guests were awake yet. Her fellow servants were the only ones up, quietly moving around the kitchen like shadows, each knowing their task and purpose.

As always, they were expected to begin their day well before the family, and at feasts this sometimes meant not sleeping at all.

Last night had been a welcome exception for the female thralls. They had enjoyed the celebration, while the male thralls took over many of their chores in honour of 'women's day.'

Wincing at the dull throb of her head, Mila quickly got herself ready for the day, using the wash-bowl and latrine. On her way back to the kitchen, she crept through the sleeping crowd, being careful not to wake the many guests on benches or slumped in corners—some of them still with a drink in hand.

She noticed Bolli was sleeping in a sitting position. His broad back against the wall, his head tilted back and his arms loose at his sides. She paused a little to consider him. In the excitement of mistress Orla granting her request, she had almost forgotten about the shy farmer who had casually offered marriage to her last night.

He was not a bad man, had never pawed at her like some of the other guests, and had treated his previous wife well—as far as she knew. She had died of a chronic malady, but Mila had never heard Bolli complain about caring for her, as some men might have done. Neither was he ugly or old... His face was plain, but with a strong jaw, and he had all of his teeth. His shoulders were broad and thick, his russet hair full and shiny. Not only that, but he owned land, a prosperous farm, and had family connections across the island.

He would make a good husband.

Why, then, did the sight of him leave her cold? And why was she considering him like the master might consider a stallion or a bull?

Marriage was not what she wanted.

Still, she would never be disappointed in him, like she'd been by Dunstan. Mila frowned. She had not thought of her first love in a long time, had tried her best to forget him and his false promises.

Bolli snored loudly, waking her from her daydream, and she hurried away in case he woke up to find her staring at him. It would be wrong to encourage him, especially when she had other hopes and dreams.

Goals! Not dreams, she reminded herself.

Something not reliant on the fickle heart of a man or the whimsy of fate!

Wynflaed glanced at her from the kitchen area, and then lifted a wooden bucket in question. Mila nodded, and they walked to the hall entrance, Mila picking up two buckets along the way.

The smaller door cut inside the huge hall doors was unbolted, and they stepped out into the crisp spring air. The day had fully begun, milky golden light warming the flat stones around the doorway and causing the frost to sparkle like cobwebs in the sunshine.

Mila shivered against the cold breeze. 'Maybe we should have worn our cloaks?'

Wynflaed smiled into the light, closing her eyes for a moment before briskly stepping forward, her leather boots crunching through the veil of ice. 'No, we'll get sweaty if we do—better to keep them off.'

Mila couldn't argue with that, and so she quickly followed her sister, avoiding the icy patches of snow that had yet to melt completely.

They went to the stream first. 'How many?' asked Mila as she dipped down to fill her buckets in the bubbling brook. She tried to ignore the pain as icy water splashed against her fingers.

'Four will do. Tyr did a couple of trips yesterday, so the water barrel still has plenty in it.'

Mila nodded, grateful that Tyr had been so thoughtful.

As they gathered their now full buckets and plodded back towards the hall, Wynflaed asked, 'When do you think you'll leave? Today?'

'Yes, today. I do not want to give Snorri any time to change the mistress's mind. But I will do all my morning chores first, and help with preparing *dagmal* before I pack.'

'How do you feel about Master Egill joining you?' Wynflaed asked quietly, glancing around them as if afraid the handsome devil might appear from the banks of swept snow.

Mila snorted. 'How do you think I feel?'

Wynflaed chuckled, and then with mock innocence replied, 'I do not know how you feel. That is why I asked.'

Mila gave a grumbling huff and adjusted the grip on her buckets. 'I am praying he does not ruin things... He will probably get bored after a week and come flying back for his home comforts.'

Wynflaed said nothing for a few steps, and then asked slowly as if afraid to anger her, 'Maybe you will *enjoy* spending time with him?'

Mila paused a moment, paralysed by the disturbing thought. She could not risk enjoying *anything* with Egill. He was the master's brother, and although he was kind and amusing to be around, there was not a responsible bone in his body. That meant he was dangerous to someone like Mila. Not physically, but in a far worse way, in the same way that she had been hurt by Dunstan.

Mila's grip tightened, causing her knuckles to ache in the cold breeze. She would never allow such a humiliation to repeat itself. She would rely on herself and no one else.

At least Egill was not the type of man to force himself on her or punish her for rejecting him. He had never seemed offended by her rejection, had never even threatened her as some other men might have done. But she thought it wise to remain cautious anyway. Wounds of the heart were so much harder to heal—she should know.

Wynflaed stopped and turned towards her, probably curious as to why she had stopped walking. 'Mila?' she asked, worry filling her features, as she hurried back to her. 'I only meant… You might enjoy his company… Egill isn't a bad man…'

'We've lived in worse places,' Mila said, gesturing with her chin towards the long turf-covered hall set into the rolling hillside, the barn buildings surrounding it, and the tendrils of smoke coming from the smoke holes.

Wynflaed's eyes widened. Then she turned to join her in admiring their Icelandic home, so different and far from the land of their birth.

'It's certainly better than Jorvik,' she agreed.

Their previous home had been a muddy hut in a crowded and smelly city. But it still hadn't been the worst place they'd slept. Travelling to the coast had been far worse. They'd been forced to curl up in ditches or climb trees to find a safe place to sleep. Too afraid to draw attention to themselves with a fire, and too scared of getting lost to leave the main road.

Mila shivered at the painful memory. In the end it had all been for nothing. The only person waiting for them had been a slaver with an armful of chains.

'I want...' Mila struggled to find the words, ignoring the dragging weight of the buckets in her hands. 'I want to make it work for us...so that we can build a life here. One that doesn't rely on anyone but ourselves.'

'People always need each other. That is life, unfortunately. We just have to hope it will work out.' Wynflaed smiled, but there was a bittersweetness to her expression that made Mila's heart ache in response. It was not the first time they had been disappointed, and she knew how hard it was to put your hopes into a future that could be snatched away from you at any moment.

'If the pottery works out, we can have our own home.'

Wynflaed nodded, but added thoughtfully, 'But if this is all there is for us, then I am content. I have friends and a sister I love. Food, honourable work, and warm shelter. So...' She fixed Mila with a firm look. 'Don't be disappointed if it doesn't work out—the pottery.'

Mila's bristled at her sister's words.

I want more for us than this! I don't want to have to rely on anyone!

But she gave her sister a reassuring smile and nodded cheerfully before walking forward. 'Come on. If we hurry with our chores, we might even be able to bathe in the hot pool before I go.'

After fetching the water, milking the cows, and starting on the porridge, they fed the hens and filled the troughs for the animals they kept close to the hall. Gunnar and the other men looked after the animals in the fields, so it was only the barn animals to care for. But it was still a rush to get their chores completed and the first meal prepared in time.

The guests were slowly beginning to wake, and Mila focused on ladling out the now cooked porridge. She had eaten leftover crusts of rye while they fed the animals, so at least her stomach had something in it. It would have been embarrassing to have a grumbling stomach while she served the food. After the guests and family had eaten, she and Wynflaed could take their bowls with the rest of the thralls and sit in the sunshine for a while before beginning the next set of chores.

Her eyes were drawn to the back of the hall as the doors opened to reveal Mistress Orla, Master Hakon and Egill emerging from their private chambers.

Their mistress greeted her guests and settled at the high table. Usually she was not so formal, but appearances needed to be kept up in front of their neighbours. Orla sometimes found the mornings difficult with her recent pregnancy. It was not common knowledge yet, so Mila imagined she would want her meal quickly before the nausea set in.

Mila ladled three bowls of porridge, spooned on some honey and dried fruit, and then carried them over to the high table on a wooden tray.

'Thank you, Mildritha,' said Hakon, passing the bowl she gave him to his wife before taking his own with a grateful smile.

Orla took a bite of the porridge and said, 'Perfect!'

Egill gave Mila a bright smile as he took his seat and the porridge she offered. 'Good morning, Mila! Are you excited about our trip? You will want to eat well. We've a long day ahead of us.'

Mila nodded politely but did not meet his eyes in case he saw the disrespect burning within them.

Why did he irritate her so?

Perhaps it was because he seemed to think her day had only just begun when she had already been up for hours.

A long day!

He knew nothing.

How could a jarl's son know anything about hard labour? That was not to say he had not seen suffering. Of course he had. She knew he had fought under King Harald's banner and for his brothers, but the glory and horror of battle were different to the daily, hopeless grind of the common folk. In her world, people fought for survival, not for treasure or honour.

However, she kept her words polite and her eyes low. 'I am. When do you wish to leave?'

'Hmm...' he said thoughtfully, and she was sure he was teasing her by taking his time to answer.

How was she going to bear two weeks with this man?

It would be like looking after a child while she worked. Not impossible, but irritating. Perhaps she could ask him to go hunt, or fetch supplies? Anything to keep him out of her way.

He will grow bored, she reminded herself firmly. *He will indulge in flirting with me, and then, when nothing comes of it, he will leave...as men always do.*

Egill seemed to still be pondering her question, but when she lifted her eyes a little, he finally answered with an easy smile. 'Whenever you wish... You are the one in charge. Order me about. I am all yours.'

Mila's stomach flipped, and she replied curtly, trying to ignore the sudden blush that heated her cheeks. 'Just after midday, then. I will come and find you.'

'I look forward to it!'

Mila wished she could say the same.

Chapter Five

Egill was almost done packing. The cart was filled to the brim, and he had a large pack of supplies waiting on the ground to be strapped to his back. It was common courtesy to always leave the traveller huts well stocked with firewood and flint. No one knew when they might be stuck in a blizzard and forced to rely on a shelter to save their lives. But Egill would rather be over-prepared and comfortable.

He had a feeling the cabin would need a lot of work to make it a pleasant home for the next two weeks. Travellers' huts were basic and draughty at the best of times, and he didn't want Mila to catch a chill. She had been bad tempered about him joining her, but he imagined that was just because she was nervous about being left alone with him, and anxious about the challenge ahead of her.

Some nerves were understandable, and after a short time, he was sure she would relax in his company. Especially when she realised how helpful he could be. He knew how he could appear, quick to laugh and slow to anger. Not bad characteristics, but ones that might lead her to question his commitment to her cause. She'd definitely not seemed pleased by his enthusiasm that morning, refusing to meet his eyes and being dismissive of his words.

Egill had always relied on his wit and charm to get his

way. With two very large and stubborn older brothers, he'd had to growing up. But perhaps Orla would require action rather than words? She was slow to trust. That much was abundantly clear.

'Are you taking *all* of that?' asked Mila from behind him, and he spun round to grin at her. She had a bedroll under one arm and two medium sacks in her hands.

He nodded enthusiastically, 'Better to be prepared.' Glancing up at the sky, he noticed the sun was not yet at its highest point, but it was close enough. 'Should we set off now? It will give us time to get settled in before nightfall.'

Mila turned away from him, placing her bedroll and sacks into the cart carefully, and patting them down to ensure they wouldn't topple out. Her gaze then shifted to the rest of the cart, assessing everything within it with a thoughtful expression. When she finally gave a curt nod of approval, he felt ridiculously proud of himself, as if he had passed some silent test of hers.

'As you wish. May I say goodbye to Wynflaed first?' she asked, her tone humble, but her dark eyes bright with rebellion.

Guilt struck him as heavy as a hammer, and he realised that Mila had probably not been away from her sister for any length of time—certainly not since her initial capture. 'Of course! Take all the time you need… I can delay leaving if you wish?'

'No,' she said firmly, 'you are ready to go, and I will not be long.'

As she turned to leave, he called out to her, 'You might want to mention we're leaving to Hakon and Orla. I am sure they will want to wish us farewell and good fortune.'

'I will let them know,' she said swiftly as she strode back into the hall. He liked how she moved, with firm, long strides. There was never any doubt in her movements. She always knew where she was going in life and what she wanted. He envied her that simplicity.

True to her word, she was gone and back again in only a short amount of time. Hakon and Orla followed closely behind as well as a few of the other servants, including Wynflaed and Nora.

'We heard you were leaving,' said Hakon cheerfully. 'We came out to wish you luck.'

'Thank you, brother! I will miss your hospitality, Orla, but I am excited to help Mila with her challenge.' He gave Hakon a grateful thump to the shoulder and kissed Orla's cheek.

Mila was talking very quietly with Wynflaed, but he distinctly heard her say, 'Do not worry. All will be well.'

'Yes, do not worry Wynflaed!' he declared cheerfully. 'Mila will be perfectly safe with me, and I will help her with her goal in every way that I can.'

Wynflaed gave a polite bow. 'Thank you. I feel happier knowing you will be there to protect her.'

Mila turned to him expectantly, her voice crisp as the spring air. 'Shall we get going, Master Egill?'

He frowned at the politeness of the title. In the past few months, he had come to see everyone at Hakon's settlement as one big family. The reminder of their difference in status was strange after so many months of informality. 'Yes... Mila. I am sure you are eager to begin our work.'

Had she rolled her eyes as she turned away?

Oddly, he was pleased by the thought. Hopefully she would be comfortable enough to curse and laugh with him by the end of their time together...or more, and he could not deny that he hoped for more.

It wasn't entirely honourable, but Egill had vowed to

himself that even if—at the very end of their time together—she still rejected him, he would ensure that she was still glad of the help he had given her. He would ensure she wouldn't regret him joining her.

She had captured his attention from the very first moment he had seen her. Standing with a broken chair leg in hand, ready to fight for her mistress and protect her home—despite her only arriving a few weeks before. It appeared that when she did give her loyalty, it was as unshakeable as a mountain, and he liked that about her. It was one of the few things they had in common.

Thankfully, he and Grimr had arrived before Orla's attackers could harm them, and he had never been more grateful for Grimr's dogged determination in rescuing Hakon. Even when his own injury had made him miserable throughout that time, it had all seemed worthwhile in the end because of that moment.

Mila had been shy of him at first, was still wary of him even now, despite the fact he had given her no reason to fear him.

Odin's teeth, she was pretty!

With her long, shiny chestnut hair and dark brown eyes, she had a rounded face, with thick lashes and a wide mouth—which was often pursed, as if she were constantly trying to hold her tongue. He wished she would speak those words she kept so closely contained. Perhaps she would not frown so much if she let them out occasionally, if she allowed herself to speak freely and without reservation?

As they began to leave the settlement, she took to walking on the other side of the pony, using a slower speed that he was sure she wouldn't have used normally. It meant he couldn't see or speak to her easily because he was leading the pony. Which was frustrating, as it suggested she wanted to keep a distance between them even now.

He was hoping he would get to know her better on the journey. As he'd begun to do at Yule, before she had built an invisible stone wall between them.

Those first few weeks of getting to know her after his arrival had been pleasant. She had even smiled and spoken to him warmly after her initial wariness of him as a stranger had disappeared. But after yule, the blushing smiles and friendly chatter had quickly disappeared and never returned. He only received polite words now, and very rarely a genuine smile, only false ones without heart or meaning. Sometimes she would even suffocate her own laughter when he made a jest, simply to stop herself from appearing friendly towards him.

It was beginning to frustrate him.

He glanced over at her ochre skirt, the only visible part of her, as the heaped cart kept her head and shoulders blocked from view.

Did she refuse to consider him because he'd not offered her marriage first?

If he were honest, his reluctance to proclaim himself was due to his fear of failure—of not winning her heart fully. He wanted her to want him. But was he wasting precious time?

Might she accept someone like Bolli instead? Purely because he was more open about his intentions?

It seemed bizarre, but perhaps a woman in Mila's position would prefer a more stable offer of protection over desire?

Egill had mulled it over after his conversation with his brother last night. He had never liked the idea of marriage before now. Had always thought of it as another kind of bondage. One of duty and responsibility, two things he had never been very good at maintaining, which was why he was reluctant to offer it without knowing Mila's feelings.

However, to a bonded woman like Mila, marriage offered freedom, protection, and a happy future for both herself and her sister...*if* she made the right choice.

Egill knew from his own parents' unhappy marriage that not everyone did make the right choice.

His mother had been clever and compassionate, his father disciplined and honourable. But there was no love between them. They had lived separate lives under the same roof.

Egill had not been like his brothers, who had taken after their stoic and serious father. He had been more like his mother, quick to laugh and easy in temperament, but always led and guided by his own heart. Sometimes he wished he had the focused ambition of his brothers and father. At least then he would know what he wanted in life.

Until recently he'd never felt strongly about anything, other than family loyalty.

But when Bolli had been propositioned as a potential suitor for Mila, Egill had not been able to allow it, had fought against it. Now he wondered if he should listen to his instincts. If he was going to lose Mila to someone as unworthy as Bolli, he wanted a fighting chance at wooing her first...if she would allow it.

He needed a plan of seduction.

A way to draw her out of her shell.

A light drizzle began to fall, and he quickly realised there would be no chance of talking with her on this journey. She was determined to place him well out of arm's reach.

Thankfully, separation and distance would become impossible once they reached the tiny traveller's hut. He was determined to take advantage of their closeness and prove himself the better suitor in every way. She would succeed in her pottery and choose him freely because of his help. He would learn all about her past and her hopes for the future. Her plans would become his own, and he would do everything in his power to fulfil them. She would no longer fear her desire for him, but would relax and rejoice in his embrace. She would know that despite his light-hearted temperament, loyalty ruled him, and he would always keep a promise.

He would make it impossible for her to resist him.

Chapter Six

The banks of snow were beginning to thin and shrink in the spring sunlight, but they had not fully disappeared, and Mila's feet were like blocks of ice by the time they arrived at the little hut that would be their home for the next two weeks.

Egill had not spoken much on the journey, which had been a blessing, but she suspected that had more to do with the grim drizzle than his choice. Her carefully placed position on the other said of the cart rather than beside Egill had been a deliberate avoidance of conversation, but at least it meant they arrived in good time and reached the cabin well before nightfall.

The sight of the cabin, however, did not reassure her about the upcoming two weeks with Egill. The last time she had seen the cabin had been in the autumn, when every servant in the hall had helped gather in the sheep from the furthest fields. They had eaten a meal here and slept one night. But it had looked distinctly better then, filled with people and chatter, and she had been excited by the sight of the potentially good clay close by to care too much about the condition of the hut.

She shrugged off her disappointment and vowed that she would make such a success of her pottery, that she and

Wynflaed could one day build a proper home for themselves here—when their bond to Orla was repaid.

Any place can be made a home...eventually.

As long as they were together.

She paused to examine the building, and Egill joined her, both of them staring at the cabin thoughtfully. It was a squat, square building, with a large wooden door and a peaked roof. Thick stone walls were covered in turf to keep out the chill. But it had not been used in months, and the snow and ice thickly covered it entirely. If it were not for the sheltered door, someone might think it an oddly triangular hill in the landscape, or perhaps even mistake it for a burial mound.

'Go in and light the fire—hopefully the last person to use it restocked the fuel before they left. I will unpack and see to the pony,' said Egill, already turning back to the cart.

'I can deal with the supplies. You should go inside, Master Egill.'

'Egill!' snapped Egill in an uncharacteristically irritated voice, and he turned back to fix her with a hard look before saying, 'You will call me Egill from now on. I am not your master. I am here to help you. Go inside. Your lips are turning blue from the cold!'

Startled by his harsh tone and odd words of concern, she nodded obediently before hurrying inside. The fact that he had ordered her to do so was not lost on her, and she tried to bite back her resentment. For all his bluster and promises of help, she was still compelled to do as he asked.

She lifted the latch and walked into the cabin's central room. The firestone was in the centre of the room a little farther towards the back. Wooden panelling had been used to insulate the hut on the inside. It also created a triangular loft space at the back that could be used as a sleeping space and was reached by a ladder. A bench and table filled up the remaining space, with plenty of empty baskets and pegs hammered into the walls to store their belongings.

There was a tiny window above the front door that let in some light, and it was enough for her to see the basket of fuel and tinder left beside the flat firestone.

She rubbed her hands vigorously to get the blood moving before reaching into the basket to gather up some wooden shavings and a few sticks of kindling. After lighting them with the provided flint, she spent some time carefully feeding and nurturing the flames until the fire was blazing steadily.

Egill began to bring in the supplies he had packed, including her bedroll and his. She tried not to flinch when she saw him throw both up into the loft above.

He had once said he would never force himself upon her, but she still wondered if she was safe in his company, or rather, if *she* was safe from temptation. There had been plenty of times when she had admired him or daydreamed about how it might be to share his bed.

Even if it would be an inevitable disappointment, she longed to feel those initial kisses of pleasure again, that close intimacy with another person who held you tightly as if they couldn't bear to let you go...except, of course, they would.

The Norse were not as prudish or as restrained as Saxons. They thought nothing of hopping into bed with one another for warmth or pleasure, oftentimes both. At feasts, she and Wynflaed had been propositioned by several men. Thralls, bondsmen, warriors and farmers—all manner of men. Thankfully, Orla kept firm rules in her home, and nothing bad had ever happened to either of them. But they had certainly been asked.

Egill must have noticed her staring because he rolled his eyes. 'You have nothing to fear from me, Mila. I would never harm you. But I will not shiver in this draughty building, especially when there is a decent bed loft and another person to share heat with.'

Mila blushed and turned away, busying herself with looking through the supplies to find some ingredients for their evening meal.

'I will go and get some water,' said Egill. 'I'll leave the pony outside until it gets dark, and then I'll bring him in.'

'Thank you,' replied Mila, not sure what else to say. She lifted out the cauldron and set it on the hook above the fire. She had put a skin of water in her sack of supplies and had only sipped from it once, knowing she might need it to start their evening meal, although her head ached and she suspected thirst was the cause. She took a little sip from her skin before adding the rest of the contents to the pot.

There was also a parcel of cut vegetables, some grains, and some mutton from last night that was still attached to the bone. She popped all of it into the cauldron and then covered it to let it stew. It would make a filling soup for later. She had a loaf of bread they could share too, although she suspected that would not last as long as she would have liked. She doubted Egill was used to rationing his meals.

She then went to work organising the space, sweeping out the old dirt and debris blown in beneath the door, making a space for the pony, and putting a net of hay up for him to eat later. She folded their clothes carefully away in the baskets in the loft bed, which she was pleased to see was more spacious than she'd remembered. Then she unpacked all the tools and supplies from the cart. There were…a lot, but all of them were practical, and she was glad to see them.

Especially the hunting weapons and net, as they meant Egill did intend on feeding them with game and fish.

She paused a moment to survey her work, and wrinkled her nose in disgust when she realised she was beginning to smell. She wished she had been able to bathe with Wynflaed before leaving. It was Egill's fault! Proclaiming they should leave early, and she couldn't refuse the suggestion of her master's brother!

Unfortunately, she would have to wait until Egill returned with water before she could wash herself. By then their meal would be ready. Mila gave a disgruntled huff. She might as well change into a fresh shift before bed and wash these clothes tomorrow.

'Mila, can you hold the door?' called Egill from outside, and she hurried to open it. He was carrying six large buckets of water on a beam of wood across his shoulders. 'Can you take them off? I am worried about spilling them.'

Mila nodded and helped him remove them from the pole one by one, more than a little impressed that he had managed so much on his own. There was a huge water barrel just inside the doorway that was raised up on a tripod. Water could be let out from the stopper at the bottom. There was still some water inside, and she poured it out into a small trough for the pony before filling the barrel with the fresh water Egill had taken from the nearby spring.

'Shall we leave one bucket for our meal?' asked Egill as he pushed the trough into position beside the hay net.

'No need. I had some water in a skin, and I have already started cooking our meal. Mutton soup.'

Egill frowned as he straightened up from the trough. 'You should drink some water. I didn't see you stop once on our journey to take a drink.'

'I will in a moment.' She poured the last bucket into the

water barrel and sealed the lid. She didn't point out that Egill hadn't stopped either.

'You have done enough. Sit down and relax. You do not want to overwork yourself on the first day. You look... tired.'

Startled by the suggestion, she found herself snapping back without thinking. 'Perhaps because I spent all of last night working, and have been up since before dawn doing my chores, followed by a long walk that you insisted upon doing early!'

'I didn't insist, you said it was fine to leave early,' he grumbled, but then tilted his head and asked, 'Were you really up before dawn today?'

It was too much!

Egill's oblivious, carefree attitude caused her irritation to burst out of her in one explosive geyser.

'Yes!' she snapped, making her way over to the cauldron to check on their meal, avoiding his piercing eyes. 'Every day, in fact! I have already fetched water, fed the animals and cleaned out their stalls, collected eggs and milk, and made porridge, all before you have even wiped the sleep from your eyes!'

'Sit down,' Egill said firmly. She glanced back at him, a little shocked by the severity of his tone. Was he about to reprimand her for being insolent? 'You have done enough. Let me do the rest.'

'The cooking?' she asked incredulously, and he chuckled as he made his way past her to the cauldron. Conscious of her bad odour, she hurried a few steps away from him.

Egill frowned at her behaviour but began to stir and check on their meal. 'I have cooked for myself many times. Do you think fighting for King Harald was done by stopping at a jarl's longhouse every day?'

Mila sat down on the bench and folded her hands in her lap, careful to keep her arms tight against her chest. 'I thought you had thralls to do such things. Besides, men in my experience would rather starve than look after themselves.'

'They sound like stupid men. When I went hunting with my brothers, we always used to take turns with the chores.'

'Did you go hunting often?' she asked, hoping he would say yes—he'd brought the weapons and nets, she just hoped he was skilled enough to use them. Not that Iceland offered much in the ways of wildlife, but an occasional rabbit would help fill the pot.

'I have hunted everything from rabbit to bear,' he said proudly, and she breathed a sigh of relief.

'A rabbit or two would be nice.'

He raised an eyebrow and poured two horns of mead from the small barrel she had placed in the storage area. 'Are you concerned about our supplies? Do you not trust my planning or ability to provide for you?' he asked, and despite the lightness of his tone, she could tell he was offended.

I do not trust any man.

She wanted to explain, but she bit her tongue and decided to remain silent.

Especially when he had just poured two generous cups of mead. Rather than remind him that they would need to make the mead last the entire two weeks, she said nothing. She did not want to irritate him further, and frankly, she would welcome a horn of mead tonight. She felt as if she were dead on her feet.

'Take it,' he said, and so she did.

The first sip was magical, and she sighed as the honeyed liquid filled her mouth with tart sweetness.

'I am here to help,' said Egill firmly as he sat beside her on the bench.

Perhaps, it was her tiredness, but she could not seem to stop herself from asking him, 'Is that all you want?'

She expected him to deny it, to become defensive or laugh at her fears. To her surprise, he turned towards her and said in a serious tone, 'I have decided I wish to marry, to settle down and start a family. I would like to do that with you, Mila. I admire your strength, beauty and loyalty. I think we are well-suited to one another. But I do not expect you to give me an answer now. In fact, I suggest you do not.'

Her mouth had dropped open at his shocking words of marriage. Surely he did not mean them? He was so far above her in status it was almost laughable. Quickly she snapped her mouth shut when she saw him staring expectantly at it, as if he expected her to say something. She would not. She could barely accept the ridiculous things he was saying were even true.

He took a deep breath, followed by a large drink from his horn, before adding, 'I will help you with your pottery. Perhaps the time spent together will give you the confidence to accept me.'

'To accept you?' she echoed, wondering if she had somehow fallen asleep and was now dreaming. 'Mas...' She paused to correct herself. '*Egill*, I am not in a position to refuse you.'

God in heaven! Why on earth had she admitted to that?

She might as well have lifted her skirts and offered herself to him. But to her relief, Egill did not like her words, seemed to even become uncomfortable because of them, and it gave her the confidence to explain, 'You are a *jarl's* brother. I am...' She could not finish it. She had been about to say *no one*, but she could not stomach such a description, even if it were true.

'You are a free woman. Free to choose me or refuse me.'

'It is not like that in Northumbria,' she said firmly.

No, in Northumbria, a man could offer you sweet promises while he kissed and caressed you, and then pretend not to know you the next time he saw you.

'We are not in Northumbria,' Egill said with a light shrug.

Mila was certain it was not that different in any part of the world. Yes, Norse women had more respect and power than Saxon women...but the difference was minimal in her experience. She frowned and looked away. 'I want to focus on my pottery.'

On something she could rely on.

Words did not feed or shelter you.

Egill nodded cheerfully. 'I know. But I can still hope, can I not? That one day you might change your mind about me.'

'If you wish...but I think you will only be disappointed.' She huffed but sipped her mead thoughtfully. She was not sure what to say. Part of her was horrified by the prospect of Egill courting her, scared even—of the possible consequences. But another, far smaller and vulnerable part of her was...flattered... Hopeful, even.

A terrifying prospect.

It never did any good to be hopeful... You were always disappointed in the end, and yet even her pottery was an act of hope. A wish for a better future, but somehow relying on herself seemed far more reasonable than relying on a man she barely knew.

As they ate their soup and discussed her plans for the upcoming days, she had to admit that Egill did seem to be focused on helping her succeed. He might not have the most honourable reason for assisting her, but at least he was honest about his intentions. Although she wouldn't trust his word completely. What a man said in private to a woman he desired was completely different to what he would confess in public.

Still, she had plenty of work to do, and it eased her mind to know that she didn't have to fear any repercussions from rejecting him.

That night they slept side by side in the cosy bed loft. Mila's meagre sack of possessions deliberately placed between their two bedrolls. A silent but obvious shield against any other intentions he might have.

After all, she couldn't deny his help during the day, but she was determined to not encourage anything more at night.

Chapter Seven

Mila woke just after dawn the following morning, the weak light from the hut's tiny window proclaiming the start of a hopefully dry spring day. Egill was still sleeping, judging by the sound of his steady even breaths. But as she rose from her bedroll, she heard a rustle behind her, and when she looked back, a rumpled golden head emerged from the blankets. A hundred butterflies filled her stomach. A man should not look so disarmingly handsome first thing—*it was unnerving!*

'Wait! I will make you something to eat!' declared Egill, throwing aside the covers, revealing far too much for Mila's comfort. With a fierce blush and a horrified gasp, she turned away sharply.

'Why are you *naked*?' she screamed. She blinked rapidly, trying her best to wash the sight from her eyes, and knowing that it was already impossible. She'd seen *everything*, and would probably still remember the sight of him until she was old and grey with cloudy eyes.

Egill's large body was no longer a mystery to her. He was all golden skin and rippling muscle, just as she'd imagined. Lithe, strong, and…incredibly masculine. There was a lot of…*maleness* on display that had caused her throat to tighten considerably. She'd never thought a man could be that…large.

Egill's husky voice floated into her addled mind. 'I find it more comfortable to sleep like this. Did you not notice when I came to bed?'

'No!' she declared indignantly. 'I… I was not *looking*!'

Had he seen her looking at his…*manhood*? Seen the shock on her face? Mila said a silent prayer, hoping that some angel or saint or Norse god would take pity on her and strike her with lightning.

He won't think I'm interested, will he?

Mila had been very careful to go to bed first, saying that she needed to change out of her dirty clothes. Then, when Egill had come to bed a short time later, she had firmly closed her eyes and turned away from him as he prepared for bed. Even going so far as throwing the blankets over her head to avoid seeing or communicating with him. To her relief, he had not bothered her. The lack of movement beside her had suggested he had fallen asleep immediately. So, with a lot of relief and a tiny amount of confusing disappointment, she had settled down to sleep herself.

'I went to bed first, remember?' she added, hating the way her body squirmed in anticipation of every rustle and creak behind her.

'That's a pity…you might have decided to join me. You wouldn't be the first to do so after seeing me naked.' Mila gave a loud snort of disgust at his arrogance, which then ended in a strangled cough when she realised how truthful that statement probably was. Egill continued as if untroubled, 'Maybe next time you should take a longer look?'

Realising she should probably be doing something other than sitting there waiting for him, Mila hurriedly gathered her spare apron dress from her sack and pinned it into position, being careful not to look at him as she dressed. There was no point going down the ladder, as she would have to turn and face him to do so.

'No, thank you! The sooner that possibility is gone from your mind the better!' she snapped, losing her temper at his constant teasing.

She knelt and ran a comb through her hair before braiding it securely, pinning the plait around her head, and then putting a linen cloth over it to protect it from the wind.

'Your hair is beautiful…it is a pity to cover it,' rumbled a husky voice behind her, and she stiffened, wondering if he'd moved to sit behind her as she'd braided it.

Was he admiring her?

She shook off the thought like an insect.

'It's more practical this way. I've a lot of work to do… Are you dressed yet?' she asked tartly, running out of patience with his foolishness.

'Yes,' he answered, and while avoiding his eyes, she turned to hurry backwards down the ladder. She was vaguely aware that he was indeed sitting behind her, but was now at least dressed and currently pulling on his boots, the ties of his tunic undone at the neck and showing a liberal amount of golden chest and dark blonde hair.

He really was handsome—she wished she didn't think so.

Mila swallowed, her throat suddenly dry, and had to concentrate on the placement of her feet as she fumbled with one of the slim steps.

At the bottom, she rubbed her arms to fight off the chill before heading over to the fire to rake the ashes and throw on some more tinder and logs. They would need the fire for their morning meal and to warm up the hut.

A few moments later, Egill was downstairs, and they

were awkwardly taking it in turns to use the wash basin and latrine and prepare for the day. Moving around each other like the sun and moon.

When she started to ladle oats into the pot for their porridge, Egill firmly wrestled the cauldron from her hands and said, 'I meant it. I am your helper. You do not need to cook.'

She sighed as she released the handle, then grabbed a sack and started to sort through her tools. 'Fine, I should pack anyway. I am going to dig for clay today and might be gone most of the day.'

'After *dagmal*, I will help you dig.'

'It would be better if I did it.'

'Then show me where you will be so that I can bring you food and drink. Presumably you will need help carrying the clay back too.'

'As you wish,' she said, feeling more than little put out by his interference, but she couldn't really argue against it. He was *trying* to help her, and if she was honest, she didn't like the idea of lugging all that clay back on her own.

Once her sack was filled, she placed it by the door with her empty baskets and returned to sit on the bench by the fire. Watching Egill as he cheerfully moved around the fire, busying himself with serving their meal of porridge, berries and honey.

'How is it?' he asked, his eyes bright with anticipation.

Swallowing her first mouthful, she nodded with approval. 'Good.'

He turned away, a beaming smile upon his face.

How long would it be before he grew bored with her company and the tedious labour of helping her? And which would he tire of first?

Her or the chores?

***

It was messy work, digging for clay, and even though Mila had put down a few branches of heather to cushion her knees and avoid too much mess, that still hadn't stopped her from getting stains on her dress or getting mud up to her elbows.

At least Egill was not here to witness it. She had shooed him away after showing him her location. To her surprise, he had left without argument—probably realising how dull watching her dig was going to be, and how little he could help with the task.

The bed she had found was close by the shallow stream that ran through this valley—which was lucky, as Mila suspected she would need to wash her clothes later. The bed of clay was a dug-out area that looked as if it had been a cow's or sheep's shelter from the wind. It thankfully didn't involve much heavy digging to reach the clay she needed.

Mila had noticed it in the summer and had been intrigued enough to mould a little in her hands. The texture had shown promise. But now, as she stared at the strange threads of yellow and silver that ran through the bed, she was reminded of Snorri's gloomy words.

'The natural clay of this land is too poor to use...it crumbles as soon as it fires.'

How could she stop such a thing?

Perhaps these strange colours running through the clay were the cause of the issue? She tried her best to avoid them, but it was difficult as they ran all through the soil and meant digging deeper into the bed.

'Greetings, Mila!' came a loud masculine shout from some distance away, and Mila popped her head above the bed to stare at the horizon, more than a little confused. It was not the familiar voice of Egill but someone else.

She squinted into the low spring light and quickly realised that it was Bolli striding towards her from the opposite side of the stream. Leaping over stones and splashing in the shallower curves of the water to reach her.

What was he doing here?

She waved hesitantly at him before ducking back down to her work...hoping that she had neither insulted nor encouraged him with her brief greeting.

Perhaps he was just passing through?

She glanced around her, feeling suddenly exposed out here in the open, surrounded by baskets of clay and only one wooden spade. She picked it up and pretended to dig at the earth with it, while glancing to check if Bolli had left.

He had not, and was now striding towards her. Stopping what she was doing, she waited patiently for him to arrive, casually leaning her back against the overarching bank. She gripped her spade with both hands tightly, trying her best not to show her fear.

Her mother's words came to mind.

'No good ever comes from a man who seeks to speak with a woman alone.'

One of the few things her mother had been right about. It was a shame she had never followed her own advice when it came to men.

It was reasonably flat in the valley, so she could watch him approach, the grassy rocky landscape rising and falling like low-cresting emerald waves compared to the soaring mountains surrounding them.

In the distance, she could see wisps of steam and spray from the hot springs. This area was known for its hot pools, and a hot river a short distance away that never iced over regardless of the time of year.

The pools to the north had to be avoided, as they were

dangerous. Some of the boiling mud pools were even roped off or surrounded by low fences to stop livestock and drunkards from falling in. They could—and had—killed people in only a few grisly moments.

Mila had been frightened of the landscape at first, of the strange smells and eruptions of water and steam. But over time she had become accustomed to the sulphurous scent and no longer even noticed it any more, and the *heat*! The glorious natural heat was like nothing she had ever experienced before. It even made the cold winters here worthwhile.

Mila could bathe like royalty in hot clean water with little effort, and in winter the hot pool behind the hall was a heavenly treat that everyone was allowed to enjoy occasionally. Always warm and comforting, even when there was snow on the ground. There were *some* good things about being brought to this land, she reminded herself, hoping that she was worrying over nothing.

Bolli reached her and stopped a few feet away with a pleasant smile upon his face.

He didn't seem like a threat, but just like the hot pools, she decided to tread carefully and keep her wits about her.

'Mildritha! It is good to see you!' he said, and then he seemed to struggle to think of anything else to say, judging by the sudden frown on his brow.

'Greetings, Bolli,' she said politely, her grip relaxing a little on the spade, but she still kept it in front of her anyway. 'What are you doing here?'

'I came to find you… Egill not with you?' He glanced around them at the empty flatlands.

'He's nearby,' she lied. It was not that she suspected Bolli of wrongdoing. It was more that she did not trust anyone… at least, not until they had proven themselves trustworthy, and in her experience, most had only proven themselves to be the opposite.

Bolli nodded and smiled kindly. 'Good. If you...um... need anything, my farm is just the other side of...there.' He gestured to the slope of the eastern mountain.

She nodded. 'Thank you.'

'I brought you some eggs. I left them outside your door in a basket.'

'Oh! That was kind of you.' She smiled nervously. 'Thank you.'

They started at each other for a moment, until Bolli gave a shy, smiling nod and ran a meaty hand through his red hair. 'Farewell, then.'

Blinking back her surprise, Mila nodded, and opened her mouth to thank him again, but was interrupted by the sharp voice of Egill from the side of them. Neither of them had seen him before. He was still some distance away but was rapidly approaching.

'Bolli? Is that you?' shouted Egill cheerfully as he strode towards them, leaping from mound to mound, as nimble as a goat.

Bolli cleared his throat and smiled. 'Greetings Egill, are you well? I was just telling Mildritha that if you need anything, come by my farm. It is not far from here.' Again, Bolli pointed in the direction of his home.

'Ah, yes!' declared Egill, hopping down from the curved bank she'd been digging to squelch into the mud beside her. 'But I doubt there is anything we need. We brought plenty with us...didn't we?' He draped an arm around her shoulders and gave her arm a friendly pat.

Bolli followed the movement with wide eyes before giving them another awkward smile. 'That's good.'

Mila frowned. How many times could Egill say *we* in

a sentence? She shrugged off his touch and took a step away from him.

Was he trying to declare ownership over her?

Regardless of her feelings towards Bolli, she didn't appreciate a man claiming her when he had no right to do so. 'Thank you for the eggs, Bolli. That is very kind of you. I will be sure to give you one of my first pieces—if they are successful.'

Egill stiffened beside her, but said nothing.

Bolli glanced at Egill and then back at her with a serious expression. 'My father is right about the clay here—it is difficult to work with. Perhaps you should consider other...er...opportunities?'

Egill moved over to her baskets filled with clay. He slapped the mud with the palm of his hand. 'It looks good to me, and I have confidence in Mila's skills. I am sure she will be able to make something with it.'

Bolli nodded. 'I meant no disrespect of her skills...only that I have lived here all my life, and I know that this land is not malleable. It is wild and unpredictable... We must accept that some things can *never be tamed*.' He looked meaningfully at Egill before smiling gently at Mila with a polite bow. 'Working with what we have available is always wisest here. It is nothing like your homeland...but it can still become a home. Farewell, Mildritha. Remember, I am only a short walk away. If you need anything, my door will always open for you.'

Mila watched him stroll away across the rolling landscape of mossy rock and woody heathers interspersed with patches of snow. The steam of the occasional spring and distant geysers filled the air with a warm fog despite the biting cold of early spring. Bolli walked calmly across the meadow, confidently striding through the steam and easily skirting around areas of danger.

She was uncomfortably aware that Bolli was probably right...about everything.

Some things could never be tamed, and she suspected Egill was one of them. His desire for a settled life and his proposal to Mila were nothing more than a foolish idea brought on by his brothers' recent marriages.

Mila was once again nothing more than a distraction, an object of passing amusement. But she suspected what Bolli was offering was far more reliable than the clay or Egill.

She stiffened, realising that she shouldn't even be *considering* Egill in that way! She had rejected him, and that should be the end of it...for both of them.

'Why were you so rude? He was only trying to help,' she snapped.

She turned away from both men and walked over to the baskets. The piles of clay looked almost red in the afternoon light. The mud still glistened with worrying threads of yellow and silver.

Some things didn't change no matter how much you wished they might.

It was just...their nature.

No! She glared down at the clay as if it were her enemy. She was not moulding men—she was making pottery. She'd not sat beside her mother all those years and learned nothing.

She *would* make this work... She had to.

Chapter Eight

'I wasn't rude,' Egill lied with an indifferent shrug. But his words couldn't have been further from the truth. He hated how Bolli had looked at and spoken to Mila—with a completely inappropriate warmth. The man was practically drooling with desire! The sheer arrogance of the man to warn Mila against *him*.

As if Bolli didn't have plans of his own to court her!

What disturbed Egill the most, however, was that Mila appeared to listen to him, and even value his opinion.

As if he were goddess Skadi's wise owl!

She'd watched him depart with a grim look upon her face, as if she were battling with some great indecision, and he doubted it was solely about Icelandic clay.

Egill had a rival, and for the first time in his life, he was actually worried. A disturbing enough thought at the best of times. Was he really going to have to compete against a *cattle farmer*?

'You weren't friendly!' Mila tossed aside her spade. The sight of it reassured him a little. She was not nervous in his company, not like she had been with Bolli. He had seen how tightly she had held it in front of her when Bolli first arrived. It was why he had nearly winded himself trying to get to her quickly.

Grumbling, he said, 'I think that is the most I have ever heard Bolli speak. Shame everything he said was so *dull*. He sounds like a miserable old troll!'

'He has a point,' Mila said quietly, kneeling beside her baskets. She pinched off a small piece of clay and rubbed it thoughtfully between her fingers and thumb. 'This isn't quite right.'

Egill positioned the wooden beam across his shoulders. 'Bolli doesn't know what he's talking about! He grew up slinging manure and feeding cattle! What would he know about your craft?'

Her head snapped up, and she glared at him. 'More than you, I imagine! Considering he has lived his entire life here and you are just passing through!'

Egill flinched at her tone but held his ground. 'You will make it work, and I am not *passing through*. Now, help me by putting the baskets on.'

Mila huffed but did as he asked, grunting as she lifted the baskets onto the pole one at a time. 'Put all of them on,' he said when she looked as if she were going to carry the remaining two herself.

'Are you sure? We could do two trips.'

'I can manage,' he said firmly, and she lifted the remaining ones onto the pole, then turned to pick up her tools.

He took a deep breath and said, 'Bolli doesn't *want* you to do well. It would not serve him.'

She gave a snort of disdain as they began to walk home. 'And it would serve *you*, would it?'

'I want you to do well because it would please you.' He grunted, taking care with his steps so as not to unbalance his load. His shoulders would ache tomorrow, but it would be worth it to spend more time in her company tonight beside the fire.

Mila's voice drew him back to their current unpleasant talk of Bolli. 'He seemed...genuine. I do not think he is saying it to be unkind.'

'He wants to court you. Surely you can see that?' Egill grunted again as he had to take a large step over a dip in the land.

Mila steadied the baskets with her hands and seemed convinced that he was managing well, judging by the little nod of approval she gave him. 'He wants a wife and a mother to his children. He does not want *me*. I could just as easily be Wynflaed, Nora or any of the other unmarried women.'

Relief washed through him. 'Good, so you see through his words and will not consider him.'

She paused before answering. 'I didn't say that.'

His whole body went rigid, and he stopped walking to turn and face her. She stared back at him, her face emotionless in a way that he found utterly devastating. 'Why? Why would you *ever* consider *him*?'

She did not flinch at his words, simply tilted her head a little and spoke slowly as if she were explaining it to a child. 'I am not making any decisions yet. Just as you have not! You have not decided whether to stay or leave, have you?' she snapped accusingly.

He turned back and began to walk again, throwing over his shoulder dryly, 'Why would I leave when I am treated so well here?'

Mila strode forward, matching his pace. 'I want independence for myself and Wynflaed. That is why I want to do my pottery, not because it will *please* me. It is the only livelihood I know...' She sighed miserably. 'What choice do I have otherwise? Wynflaed doesn't want to leave, and there is nothing else that I am good at...but I could manage a household, and I do not mind hard work. Perhaps marriage is my only option.'

Indignation burned through him, and he struggled to temper it. 'So, you would accept *Bolli*? A man completely unworthy of you... But you will never even *consider* me?'

She stopped, her back stiff as she turned back to face him. A rush of colour painting her cheeks that finally allowed him to see the emotion beneath her cold mask. 'I am a *distraction* to you! A *dalliance*! Do not pretend to have feelings for me! That would make you worse than Bolli. At least he is honest about his intentions!'

'When have I not been honest?' he asked, appalled by her accusation, especially as he was currently carrying his intentions across his shoulders.

'You are *never* honest, Egill!' Mila shouted. 'You are all laughter, games and silly flirtation. Teasing promises with no substance! Even your own brother has said as much! Do you know how people see you? How they talk about the Eriksson brothers? Hakon is wise, Grimr is fierce, and *you*—*you* are the serpent tongue of the family! I know what *that* means! You leave women behind with nothing more than a handful of tears! Well, I will not be your fool!'

Egill flinched at her words—there was some truth to them. 'No, you are no one's fool, Mila. People talk about you as well. They say you are beautiful, but *cold*—as distant as the moon. I have never thought of you that way. I know you must have your reasons, that you are slow to give your trust but are passionately loyal to those that have earned it. I judge you on what I have seen and heard with my own eyes and ears, not on the opinions of others. *Perhaps you should do the same?*'

He saw the moment of doubt in her eyes, and he pushed forward, grunting loudly with the effort, his arms wrapped around the pole so that he was unable to do anything more than stare into her eyes. 'And listen well to what I have to say. I want you, *Mila*. I want you whether your pottery is a success or not. I want you in my bed and by my side. I want you like I have never wanted a woman before, or will again. I want to care for you, if you would let me. I do not know why I feel this way, but I do. I am undecided about everything else in my life, but that much is certain. If you want me to stay, I will. That is *my* truth.'

Her mouth was slightly agape as she stared up at him. But he could tell that she was still uncertain by the way her grip tightened on the handle of her spade.

Did she wish to strike him with it?

Deny his feelings once more, as if she could silence his heart with another cruel blow? Her words had hurt him deeply in ways that he couldn't fully understand. Was he really nothing more than a charming serpent?

'Think on it,' he said finally, and walked ahead, allowing her time to consider his words.

As they arrived back at the cabin, Mila began to realise how truly ungrateful she'd been towards Egill. Not only had he carried back all of her baskets without complaint, but he'd obviously been very busy in her absence.

A new lean-to shelter had been built beside the cabin. It consisted of a single drystone wall and a wooden canopy covered in bracken. It was not large, could only fit a couple of people inside it. But it allowed east and west light in from both sides, which meant it would benefit from natural daylight throughout the day, and more importantly would keep her clay dry from any downpours.

'You built this?' she asked quietly, staring at the little storage area with wonder.

'I am not completely useless,' grumbled Egill, and guilt gnawed at her stomach. She'd not expected him to be so thoughtful.

It seemed churlish not to be grateful. His arms were still wrapped around the pole. She reached out and patted his chest, the plate of muscle just above his heart. Blushing and removing her hand immediately when she felt the hitch of his breath beneath her palm. 'I never said you were useless,' she told him sheepishly, but the tightness in her throat reminded her that she'd said far worse. Questioning his reasons and honour, as well as calling him little more than a charming fool.

On the way back, they'd walked in silence, and she'd thought about what he'd said.

Was she being unkind—ignorant, even—for judging him without truly knowing him? How could she consider one man and deny the other when they were both sincere in their claims?

Egill cleared his throat and gestured to the shelter with his head. 'I found the rocks by the stream. It didn't take long to build it. Now, help me take these baskets off.'

'Sorry!' She gasped, horrified that she'd kept him waiting. She hastily helped him take off the baskets, not missing the way he tried to hide his wince when he finally set the pole down and rolled his muscles.

'It will help your work—to have a shelter with ample light that is also dry and out of the wind and rain.' He reached for her hand, the same one that had betrayed her moments earlier by reaching for him.

Damn it! She needed to stop encouraging him!

He began to vigorously rub her muddy hands in his. 'You are cold!'

Mila's insides squirmed like a worm, and she snatched

her hands away with a half-hearted laugh. She didn't like him touching them. They were peasant hands, rough and dirty. 'You've already said that once,' she joked with a half smile, and he tutted.

'*I* never called you cold, and the men who did were only bitter because you would not accept them.' He flinched at his own words, and she smiled, knowing that he was wondering the same thing about himself. After a moment he shook his head as if dismissing the thought. 'Come, let us go inside and warm you up.'

She followed him in, and Egill quickly revived the fire. He put some mead into a pan to warm while she took off her cloak and hung it up.

'We're going to run out of mead quickly,' she warned. 'No need to pour any for me in future. I can drink the water.'

'Nonsense, I can always go back for more.' Egill continued to swirl the golden liquid in the pan until it began to steam, and then he transferred it into two bone cups and handed one to Mila.

It was then that she noticed her shift and dress hanging up on a peg beside the fire.

'You washed my clothes?'

He glanced over at them and nodded. 'They looked as if they needed it, and you don't have anything else to wear, do you?'

She shook her head. 'No... That was really thoughtful of you. Thank you.'

'Why don't you ask Orla for some cloth? There is plenty in her hall, and I'm sure she won't mind you using some of it for clothes.'

Mila shook her head. 'I can't. It would be taken off my total number of ells...and I am not as good a weaver as Wynflaed. I need every scrap of cloth I make to pay off my debt. Even that dress was made by Wynflaed. She and Nora made it for me as a yule gift.'

'But why the rush to pay off your debt? Orla is not a bad mistress; and it would only add a short time to your labour.'

She sipped from her cup, her hands laced around it for warmth. Remembering a far less pleasant time when her hands had ached with cold. 'I don't like to be in debt.'

'But if it means greater comfort in the present—'

She interrupted him sharply, not liking the path this was heading down. 'Your life is your own. Mine is not. As soon as I am truly free, I can choose how to use my coin. Until then, I am the same as any other thrall. Mistress Orla is a good woman, and I am thankful every day that she bought me. But she still *bought* me.' Her eyes met his blue ones, which softened with sympathy as he finally seemed to understand her.

Egill nodded. 'I see.'

Her stomach grumbled with hunger, and she smothered it with her arms, saying conversationally, 'Bolli said he left us some eggs?'

'Always practical,' he laughed, and she found herself returning his smile. 'Yes, he did. I was washing the clothes at the time, so missed him. I have put them in the store.'

He waved dismissively over to the baskets and pots beside them. Mila wondered if that's why he'd come to find her when he did. It had been a little earlier than she'd expected, although she was grateful for it now. She'd managed to do a lot in a short time...they both had, she acknowledged, looking over at her clean clothes.

Egill followed her gaze and frowned at the puddle of water beneath them. 'I don't think I wrung them out very well. They may take a while to dry.'

Mila smiled. She imagined this was probably the first time he'd attempted to wash a woman's clothing...or any clothing, for that matter. He *really* was trying to be helpful. 'They will dry eventually. The shift will not take long, and that is all I need for tonight.' She took another sip of her mead and then said quietly, 'I would like to apologise, Egill. You are right, I should judge you on your actions, not on the opinions of others...and your actions have been very good to me. Thank you, Egill, and I am sorry for what I said earlier.'

He blinked, as if surprised by her change of heart, but the truth was she had never truly thought bad of him. She just knew that he was everything she should fear.

'Will you consider me then?' he asked quietly, swirling the amber nectar in his cup. 'The same as Bolli?'

A hot blush crept up her neck, and she choked a little on her mead, wiping at her mouth with a trembling hand and avoiding his gaze. 'I suppose so...in that... I would prefer to have my pottery become a success before I am forced to choose *any* husband... Does that offend you?'

'That you would prefer a pile of mud to me as a husband?' he asked, then shrugged playfully and sipped his drink. 'As long as you don't prefer Bolli, I am content.'

She laughed. 'I am sorry.'

He grinned, then reached into a basket and offered her an apple, which she took gladly and began to eat. Egill got one for himself as well, and crunched into it with one decisive bite before asking through a mouthful of food, 'Why do you think so lowly of us men? Who has disappointed you in the past to tarnish your view of us so thoroughly? I wish to know so that I can reassure you about my own character.'

Mila stiffened, her mind screaming to deny him an answer, to laugh off her fears and pretend they did not exist. But Egill had been truthful, considerate and brave. How could she repay him with lies?

Chapter Nine

Egill was worried he had pushed her too soon, because she stared into the fire a moment as if trying to decide whether or not to speak. The apple was forgotten in her hand—despite the fact she must be hungry after all her digging.

To his relief, she eventually answered him. 'There is no great villain in my past—I am as much to blame for my disappointment as any other. I have been foolish and naive more than once.' She took a bite out of her apple as if that were answer enough.

'Who has disappointed you?' he asked softly, his fingernails biting into his own fruit so hard they pierced the flesh. He was trying to keep a rein on the outrage that had quickly followed her confession.

Who would dare betray Mila?

She was a wise and kind-hearted woman—as her recent apology to him had shown. She wasn't the type to hold grudges without justification.

She shrugged dismissively. 'Men.'

'Who?' If he was going to hate a man for all time, he should at least know his name.

'Well...my father.'

An old pain ached in his chest, and he nodded. 'You are not alone in that.'

Mila gave a bitter laugh. 'I suppose it is a common truth—nothing special.'

Egill flinched. Firstly, because as a man, it felt wrong to judge his own sex so harshly. Secondly, because he had his own complicated feelings towards his own father—so he could not even deny her words with an alternative view. He could tell Mila did not wish to speak any more about it. She ate her apple absently, staring into the fire, avoiding his gaze.

But if she were to trust him, she would need to open herself up to him. Perhaps she would do so if he revealed his own uncomfortable secrets first. His mother once told him that the quickest way to make an ally was by sharing common ground. And if she thought him lacking in substance and truth, then perhaps he should confess something more personal...let her see the darker sides of himself that he usually preferred to keep hidden.

In a few short bites, he finished his apple and tossed the remains on the fire. Her eyes flickered towards him at the movement.

Resolved to show her another side of himself, he took a deep breath. 'My father never loved my mother, but he was always honourable towards her. In his mind, that was enough, because everybody had a place and a purpose. Do you know what my purpose was?'

He smiled when she shook her head.

'He said that as the youngest son, my sole duty was to support and honour my family. My life would have no meaning unless one of my brothers died or they failed in their own responsibilities. He warned me not to seek anything more, that chaos and suffering was the only result of a third son's ambition. I decided early on that I loved my brothers dearly and would do everything in my power to ensure they never failed in their duties. I wanted more than anything to make my father proud of me, even if all I could do was protect and support them. However, I do think my father failed in one regard... He should have loved his sons and the mother of his children more. All we ever did was try to please him. My mother even died giving birth to yet another child for him, when she had already done her part! Three children in a loveless marriage and he wanted more? He shouldn't have asked it of her...' Egill paused, but only saw sympathy in Mila's eyes. It gave him the strength to confess. 'Hakon and Grimr are born leaders. I knew they would eventually find their place in the world. But I have not. I want a purpose, and a home of my own... And yet I am still plagued by indecision.'

He paused, and she stared at him, wide-eyed. 'Why?'

'Because how can I choose between my brothers when they live so far apart? Who should I help? Who should I abandon?' He tried to laugh, to shrug off the fears that had recently plagued him. 'I got badly hurt—the night Hakon was betrayed and sold into slavery.'

He had never confessed how badly he'd been hurt by the incident, both physically and emotionally. It had always felt like a weakness to admit it. But he found himself confessing the truth to Mila now. 'Hakon was due to marry Sigrid, Ingvar's sister—it was meant to form an alliance between our two feuding families. But the night before the wedding, Ingvar attacked us in our beds. Sigrid tried to warn us, but there was little she could do. We managed to fight our way out into the main hall. We were surrounded and outnumbered, and I had drunk heavily the night before... I was not as quick with my reactions. Something hit me on the side of my head, so hard that the world went black, and when I came back to my senses, something else hit me... I think I heard something crack, and I became sick with dizziness. I thought my fate was set, that I was going to die there and then. But Grimr grabbed me and never let go. It wasn't until I saw the doors closing that I realised Hakon was no longer with us.' His chest tightened at the memory, and his voice became raw with emotion. 'I will never forget the look of acceptance in Hakon's eyes—when he realised that he was surrounded by the enemy, with no way out.'

Mila leaned close, reaching for his hand, which lay against his thigh. She took it and squeezed it lightly. 'But it all worked out well in the end. I am sure he is even glad of it now, as it brought him to Orla...'

Hakon covered her hand with his remaining one, unwilling to let her go, and turning in his seat to face her better and look into her lovely dark eyes. 'You misunderstand me. Hakon was not upset... He *smiled*. That is what haunts me...because in the face of death...he was *grateful*. Glad, even, that his brothers had escaped. My *only* duty was to protect and support them, and I failed them both... because I am a fool. Who never cared about consequences until it was too late.'

'It wasn't your fault,' Mila insisted, and he finally let her go. Realising belatedly with disgust that he did not deserve her comfort.

'It was my fault. We were in the home of our enemy, and I should have kept my wits—like Grimr urged me to do. If I had, then maybe we could have escaped together. I should have suspected betrayal, but instead I trusted in the rules of hospitality. In the bread and salt we had eaten. I should have known that Ingvar was not worth his salt.'

Mila sighed deeply, gently nodding with understanding. 'But...he was the one at fault, not you. Hakon does not blame you. I am sure of it.'

'No, he would not. Hakon is the best of us...but I am still plagued by my failings that day. We might have all escaped if it were not for my thoughtlessness. In the days and nights that followed, I was consumed by guilt—but I was useless. The blow to my head had addled my mind. Grimr said I slurred as if I were drunk. I struggled to concentrate or even stand. My mind did not feel my own. Even now, I do not remember much of those days after the attack. When Grimr was rallying our men to rescue Hakon, I was unable to help. My body was not my own. I have prepared for injury, or death in battle...but not that...that complete loss of control, of your mind constantly drifting away. I only remember one night...' He stopped, uncertain if he should confess his darkest secret of all.

'Go on,' Mila urged, and her brown eyes were so soft and warm that he found himself admitting what he had never dared tell his brothers.

'I... I was weak...' He had cried, wept like a babe in a faceless woman's arms. *Pathetic*. Even now he tried to laugh about it. 'Sobbed like a babe... I vaguely remember a woman comforting me. Pressing cool cloths to my head and reassuring me that all would be well. I was so grateful to her... And when I did regain my senses, Grimr had already gathered a force to attack Ingvar. I did not say thank you to her. I am not entirely sure she was real... Did not even recall who she was except for fragments of her touch and her kind words. But...that experience made me realise something...'

Mila's head tilted. There was no judgement in her expression, only curiosity. 'What?'

'I realised that I do not want to be alone for the rest of my life. That even though I do not know what I want to do, I am certain that I want to spend my life with a family of my own. Not to build a legacy like my father. But to build an honourable life, a home...to fall in love...like Hakon... And... *Mila*, the only thing that I am certain of... is that... I want it to be with *you*.'

His heart plummeted when her initial shock drifted into a sad smile. 'That is a worthy ambition, Egill. I am sure you will find the perfect woman to love... But—'

Her inevitable rejection was like a rusty blade dragged across his heart, and he deflected it quickly, forcing himself to smile brightly even though it hurt to do so. 'No answer yet, Mila! I am happy to wait. But...now that I have told you of my father and my darkest moments of shame, tell me how yours failed you... I wish only to know you better.'

Mila looked away from Egill's kind expression. She could feel herself already falling under his spell. Listening to his deep, husky voice and the struggles of his past had softened her heart to him, and she was afraid she might be tempted to do more than comfort him in return.

To do so would only cause her greater pain later on, and she could not stomach another disappointment. There were only so many times she could remould herself without crumbling.

Perhaps confessing the miserable truth about her past might put him off courting her? After all, he'd been dismissive of Bolli because he was a farmer. How might he feel about her when he learned the grim truth about her humble background? He might lose all interest in her. She wasn't just a stolen woman sold into slavery. She was much more pitiful than that.

Mila swallowed and stared into the fire. She shivered as memories of flames and humiliation blinded her. Absently Egill put another log on the fire, misreading her behaviour.

'My father was my greatest disappointment.'

'How?'

'It is a long story... But in Jorvik, our pottery didn't earn us much. However, it was just enough to survive. My mother had a little workshop on the edge of the city. We made pots, crucibles and lamp bowls. Nothing too elaborate. My father worked on his uncle's farm farther North. He'd met my mother one day at the market and had instantly fallen in love with her. Unfortunately, he could not live with her—because there was no room on his uncle's farm, and no other way for him to make an income. So they lived apart, my father visiting whenever he came to market. We loved him, cherished the short time we spent together. He was saving coin to buy a larger workshop for my mother. So that one day, we could all live together and my mother could create larger, more decorative pots to sell. We had difficult years—times when the pots he took to other markets did not sell or were broken along the way. But my father was determined to see our family dream come true. Then the fire happened, nobody's fault. Such things happen regularly in the towns. But this fire was particularly bad and swept through the workshops quickly, leaving only devastation behind. Wynflaed and I had been out selling our pots at the market. We did not know about it until we saw the smoke rising in the distance. Our neighbours had managed to get our mother out, but she still died from the smoke. With her dying breaths, she begged us to go to our father.'

Egill's brow was furrowed. 'What happened then?'

Mila took a sip of her mead and then replied bitterly, 'It took us a while to find him—we only had the clothes on our backs and a loaf of bread from a friend...' She paused, remembering the second devastating loss she'd suffered that day. But she couldn't face confessing it yet. So she continued on, 'The farm he had spoken of was farther north, and nearer to the coast than we had been told. We slept out in the open and walked all day to reach him. We were starving and frozen to the bone by the time we reached it. However, our father did not welcome us. You see, he was already married, had several sons and daughters with another woman—his true wife. You see, it was *his* farm, not his uncle's. *Years* of constantly lying had finally caught up with him. The man I saw that day was unrecognisable to the father I thought I'd known. He told us not to seek him out again, that he could not help us, because we were not his *real* family. Our mother was a whore he'd taken pity on—according to him, at least. I did not know what to do. We walked to the beach, hoping to find enough firewood to keep us warm and some seaweed to eat... That is how the slaver found us. *Remember?* We were easy pickings, like driftwood on the beach. Too weak to fight or run.' She held Egill's gaze firmly as she explained, 'I want to be independent. To rely on no one but myself.'

Egill nodded. 'Then I will ensure that you do not. We will make your pottery a success, and then you will be my free, willing and wealthy wife. All I will give you is pleasure. If independence will make you happy, then I will make it my goal to help you achieve it.'

Mila shrugged and stared down at the half-eaten apple in her hand, her appetite gone. But she would force herself to eat it. She could never waste food. 'The *pleasures* are not worth it.'

A wicked glint shone in his eyes. 'Oh... I am sure I can change your mind regarding that, at least!'

She glared at him, and then, because she could not seem to help herself, she laughed. 'Such arrogance!'

He leaned forward, keeping his voice low so that she

would have to lean in to hear him. 'I am arrogant, and charming with a serpent tongue.' The laughter turned into a swallowed gasp, and he found himself captivated by the little sound that came from her full mouth as he spoke. There was no denying their growing desire. It would consume them both eventually. 'But...my promises are as strong as steel, and I *never* disappoint.'

Mila blushed furiously and leapt from her seat. 'We should prepare our evening meal.'

Egill knew he had rattled her composure, and he couldn't help the sly smile that spread across his face as she busied herself with the stores. 'Come sit,' he said gently, and her back stiffened. 'Come sit,' he repeated, rising from his seat. 'I will cook.'

'No.' She shook her head. 'Not tonight, I insist! I owe you for all the work you have done today.'

Egill sighed and returned to rolling his aching shoulders absently. 'If you insist. But you owe me nothing, Mila. Always remember that.'

Mila didn't turn to look at him, but she paused and nodded silently.

Chapter Ten

The next day, Mila asked Egill to dig the firepits while she worked on the clay.

The meal she'd cooked last night had been an exception, because Egill seemed more than happy to continue with his chores the following day. Preparing *dagmal*, fetching water, tidying up the kitchen and all the other tasks she would have normally performed as a bondswoman. All of this before obediently starting on the firepits she'd requested.

At first, it had felt odd working alongside someone so far above her in station, but after their talk last night, she found herself forgetting the chasm of difference between them. She was beginning to see him less as the master's charismatic brother and more as...well, just... Egill—a man with his own struggles and doubts.

He was an easy man to spend time with, cheerful, talkative and helpful. Always putting her at ease with a teasing comment or looking ahead to see what she might need next. Like the shelter she currently worked in, or the clean shift she now wore.

Today she'd decided to keep her dirty apron dress on from the day before, as the preparing of the clay was dirty work. She'd emptied out the clay from her baskets into a wide half barrel and mixed it with plenty of water. Beating it with an old milk-churning oar and removing the larger pebbles and rocks from it as she went until it was a smooth consistency.

But despite working on it for most of the day, it still wasn't the exact texture she needed, so she took a break to think about it.

The sun was at its highest point, and her upper body ached from pounding the clay. Glancing over at Egill, she noticed he'd removed his tunic and was digging out the firepit several feet away from her. She walked over to check on his progress, and *not* to admire the fine lines of his bare chest.

I need to check he is doing it properly! she told herself, although she couldn't help the flutter in her stomach as she watched his broad back flex.

Egill straightened up as she approached and turned to face her. Grinning proudly and gesturing at his hard work. 'Two shallow pits with a connecting tunnel. Are they large enough?'

She nodded, trying to avoid staring at the mountains of bronze flesh on display, or the rivers of perspiration running down his hot skin. Instead, she tried to focus on the firepits. 'Perfect, thank you.'

'I will start building the kiln tomorrow. How is the clay?' he asked, leaning casually against his spade and gesturing with his chin towards her workshop.

She sighed. 'Not ideal. It looks right but does not *feel* right. Does that make sense?'

Egill nodded enthusiastically. 'Like a badly balanced sword... It looks fine but is awkward to wield.'

She laughed. 'Yes, that is a very good comparison.'

'Let us take a break and talk about it some more,' Egill

said, thrusting the spade into the pit and leaping out with one step.

Mila wasn't entirely sure taking a break was a good idea, especially with Egill standing so close and half-naked. But she could not deny that she needed to consider all her options when it came to strengthening the quality of her clay. So she walked towards the cabin, Egill following close behind.

As she entered the dim hut, Egill said, 'The weather is pleasant. Let us stay outside. I will put out the stools if you bring some food and drink.'

'Agreed,' Mila said, moving to the back of the room. 'But we will need more water soon. I used a lot of it to work the clay.'

Egill's reply was untroubled, as she heard him picking up two stools. 'I can get that this afternoon. I think we have done enough for now.'

Mila used a pan of water to wash her hands, then gathered some bread, cheese, and a flagon of water. She did not want to waste any more mead—no matter how often Egill insisted it was fine.

When she came out once again into the crisp spring sunshine. Egill had put out two stools and held a blanket in his hands. 'Sit,' he instructed, and she put down the basket of supplies and let him place the blanket over her knees as she took her seat.

He then went inside, presumably to wash his own hands and face, as well as splash his chest with water—at least, she presumed so because of the way little rivers of water were running down his spine and stomach when he returned. He pulled on his tunic and sat beside her.

In the meantime, she had made him a platter of bread and cheese with some cut-up apple on the side, and offered it to him. He took the platter with a cheerful and satisfied sigh as he eased down beside her.

'We did well today,' he said. 'Hopefully it will stay dry for a few more days.'

Mila looked up at the sky. It was bright, with only a few wispy clouds. 'We have been lucky with the weather. It is unseasonably warm.'

'The gods are on our side.'

Mila smiled and bit into her bread. She was undecided on what to believe. She had been brought up Christian, but most people in Iceland were pagan. She had concluded that regardless of religion, people were basically the same. They had ambitions, fears and hopes for the future—regardless of who they worshipped.

There was a time when she had not been so hopeful. When all had seemed broken and lost. That day on the beach seemed like a hundred years ago, but it also burned brightly in her mind—never to be forgotten. A strange contradiction of memory.

She did not like to dwell on the past, so she thought instead about the next task ahead. 'We should burn some wood in the pits to create a solid base. Then cover it with a tent to keep it dry.'

Egill mumbled an agreement while he ploughed into the bread and cheese.

Mila chewed on her own food thoughtfully until Egill interrupted her by asking, 'What do you need to do to strengthen your clay?'

'Back home, I would add sand, crushed shells, grass...' She paused. 'Perhaps I should add dung ash... We have a pony, so there's plenty of dung.'

Egill blinked and swallowed. 'You want to burn the pony's dung?'

She chuckled at his horrified look. 'It sounds strange, but it might add the dry consistency I need, and it's one material we have plenty of.'

Egill nodded with a grimace. 'Fine, I'll rake it all out, let it dry, and then we can burn it...downwind of the hut, though.'

She smiled cheerfully. 'Thank you. But I can do it.'

'I am here to help, remember.'

She rolled her eyes at him and was met by the same cheerful expression as always. 'You can help by fetching the water and putting a tent over the pit—that will keep you busy. I will rake out the dung, and if it is dry enough, I'll burn it today.'

'After such messy work, perhaps you'd like to bathe in the hot river?'

She thought for a moment and then nodded. 'That sounds like a fine plan.'

After eating, they set to work, doing their tasks quickly, occasionally passing one another, and saying a warm greeting or commenting on their work. It led to a pleasant afternoon, even though Mila was doing a foul-smelling chore.

She raked out the dung, and found that most of it was dry, so she put it in the firepit and dotted it with some charcoal and wood they'd brought with them, and then lit it. She was careful to hurry away from the smoke when it caught.

'The wind is working in our favour, at least,' said Egill grimly with a wrinkled nose as he stared down at the contents of the firepit. He'd set up tent poles around the pits but hadn't covered them yet with bracken. 'I'll cover it once your fire is dead... Shall we go and bathe now?'

'We?' asked Mila, startled at the suggestion. She'd presumed they would go separately.

'I will not miss out on bathing, and the sun will set soon.'

She squinted up at the sky. The sun was low. She had

bathed with the bonded men and women of her hall—after all, privacy was a luxury no one of her status could afford. But it still felt strange to do so with Egill. She nodded hesitantly and resolved to find a place to bathe a little away from him when they did reach the river. 'Let me gather some soap and a comb, then.'

A short time later, they were on their way with small packs on their backs. The terrain was difficult at times, with steep, rocky inclines and narrow ridges. But the landscape was truly stunning, and different from one path to the next. Changing from lush green meadows to rocky landscapes, to hot pockets of water and mud.

The great steaming mountain was only a short distance away, and the valley was filled with yet more steaming springs and bubbling mud pools. But these were too hot to bathe in, so they had to keep on walking. They passed a cascading waterfall, but the area around it was full of gravel and very slippery underfoot. They followed the gentler path down towards the hot river, the steam around it like a misty fog glittering in the twilight.

The brown, muddy pools bubbled and squelched as they walked past, and there was one large, rippling pool with water the same shade of blue as a spring sky. The air around it was steaming furiously.

'Stay on the path,' warned Egill, pulling her closer towards him. 'The mud pools are difficult to spot—especially after the snows. If you step through, you could lose your foot.'

She nodded and continued along the well-travelled path, keeping close to Egill's back. 'Have you ever been to the Gullfoss waterfall or the mushroom geyser?' she asked, trying to keep her mind away from the horrible image of her falling into a boiling pool.

Egill nodded enthusiastically. 'Yes, I have explored a lot of Iceland.'

Mila knew that. She had seen him go off travelling throughout the late summer and autumn, sometimes with his brother, but often alone. It was a privilege of the free and wealthy to go and do as you wished—not fearing a lack of food come winter.

'Do the big waterfalls look like the water in that pool?' She turned to gesture back towards the bright blue pool. Egill gripped her elbow as if afraid she might slip off the path and pulled her close before glancing over her shoulder at what she'd gestured at.

'Yes, just like that—but it is as big as a lake, and it's cool enough to bathe in.' He looked down at her, and she eased herself away from his grip, colour high on her cheeks.

'It sounds wonderful.'

'I will take you to see it.' He paused, noticing her frown. 'Once your pottery has paid off your debt, of course.'

She shrugged. 'I could go alone then, if I wished.'

Egill smiled. 'But why go alone when you can have a friend come with you?' Without waiting for a reply, he continued on down the path.

The river, which looked more like a deep stream, twisted and cut through the lush green valley. The heat of the land had melted away most of the winter snow, but there were still patches here and there, the steam rising in clouds above the water.

They put down their packs near a deeper section of the river. It was terribly exposed, without even a bush or tree to hide behind. Mila was beginning to wonder if she'd made a terrible mistake in coming here.

Egill took out a length of linen from his pack, as well as two combs, a shaving blade, and some soaps that he liked to use when bathing, and put them on the riverbank. When he straightened, he noticed Mila was inspecting the river thoughtfully, no doubt trying to work out the best place to hide from him.

'Are you shy, Mila?' he asked mildly. 'Will this be the second time you see a man naked?' he teased, reminding her of the first time she'd seen him.

She stiffened as if it were an accusation. 'No! It is common to bathe with the men and women of the hall. But it is also common courtesy not to stare...'

'Good. Come along, then!' he declared, trying to hide his delight at the horrified look on her face when she realised he'd goaded her into joining him. He unbuckled his belt and let it drop to the floor. 'Although, Mila... I must insist you stare at me. You might grow to like me if you do.'

Her eyes widened, but to his immense satisfaction, she didn't look away, and he stripped off his tunic and undertunic. He bent to take off his boots and woollen socks, and then stripped off his wide trousers and loin-cloth. At which point she was suddenly very busy dealing with her own pack of supplies and emptying them out, a flush of pink on her cheeks.

It pleased him to see it, and with a chuckle, he waded into the river, sitting down to immerse himself in the slow-running water. It was warm, deliciously so, and he gave a guttural sigh of contentment as the heat seeped into his bones and muscles. 'I do love this land!' he declared, and heard an answering giggle from the riverbank.

Mila was sat with a comb and a tablet of soap. She was still blushing, but her eyes seemed to devour him, eagerly eating up the sight of his naked body. She bit her bottom lip and then went back to busying herself with what appeared to be doing nothing but reorganising her few possessions.

'You should join me! Before the sun sets and we have to head home.'

Mila glanced worriedly at the purple sky. 'Will it be safe to return in the dark?'

'I brought torches.'

She nodded and began to fumble with the bone brooches on her dress.

Egill took pity on her and turned away, vigorously soaping up his hair before plunging beneath the water. When he rose, Mila was already in the water, crouched low so that most of her was a pale, shimmering shadow beneath the water.

Her hair was still braided and wrapped around her head, although she'd removed the cloth that usually covered it. She was trying to hold her soap while fiddling with the ties in her hair and seemed to be struggling.

He dropped his own soap and combs on the riverbank and moved towards her. 'Let me do it. Turn around.'

Mila dipped even lower in the water, but did as he suggested.

He unpinned the braid from her crown, and it fell down into his waiting palms like a rope of silk. The scrap of leather at the bottom of her braid was tightly knotted, and it took a little bit of gentle working to release it. He tried to keep his attention focused on the braid rather than the soft curve of her milky shoulders, or the scatter of freckles along her collarbone.

He offered her the leather tie as he released her, and she took it silently, her arms folded across her chest tightly, only peeling away slightly to grab it like a fish biting on a line—if only he could reel her in.

He unwound the braid slowly, enjoying the feel of her lusciously thick hair beneath his fingers. It reached almost to her waist, and she dipped low into the water, tilting back her head to let the water reach her scalp. Her eyes widened as she looked up at him, and he cupped some water to pour it over the top of her head.

When she rose up again, he reached around and took the soap from her limp fingers. She didn't argue, but he could sense her growing panic in the quickness of her breath and the stiffness of her spine.

Lifting the soap to his nose, he breathed in the scent...or the lack of one. 'This will not do. Use mine.' He tossed the plain tablet of fat, ash and lye onto the bank and grabbed his own soap before returning.

With deliberate slowness and care, he began to massage the soap into her hair. 'I buy this whenever I travel through Jorvik or Birka... It is a luxury, I know, but I challenge you to smell anything finer.' The scent of woody herbs and rich aromatic oils filled the air, and even Mila couldn't resist the intoxicating scent, sighing blissfully as she breathed it in, her shoulders finally relaxing as he rubbed the lather into her scalp with circular motions.

'I have decided I will not bed you, Mila,' he said with mock seriousness, and her gasp of outrage made him chuckle. 'Instead, I wish to show you all the pleasures I can give you...*without* fully bedding you.'

There was silence for a long moment, and that's when he knew her curiosity had won the battle. 'What do you mean?'

'This,' he said, massaging her scalp. 'And this...' He dipped his head, bringing his mouth beside her ear, and brushed his lips against her lobe.

She stepped away from him, the water splashing against his chest at the sudden movement. But there was no fear in her face, only innocent shock and a flicker of temptation. It was all he needed to finally catch her.

He stepped closer, but did not reach for her, and instead

gave her the space to decide for herself. 'Marriage to me would give you the security you desire. You know that, and if you wish to make pottery, then I will support you in that also. You are afraid of trusting me. I can understand that. I have done nothing to prove myself to you, and as you say, I have done nothing in my past to reassure you either. So, why not trial being my wife? While we are alone together. You can enjoy all of the pleasures and none of the risk. No one will know what we do.'

Mila stared at him and then said slowly, 'There is always a risk.'

'Not if I do not enter your body with mine. There are other things we can do, kisses and touches...'

She blinked, startled. 'What?'

'You know how children are made...yes?'

Her head tilted, and she glared at him. 'I *know* how children are made.' She turned away from him and dipped fully beneath the water, rinsing the soap from her head. When she rose again, she was facing away from him. 'The sun is almost set. We should return home,' she said firmly.

He glanced up at the sky. It was painted with salmon pinks, purples and reds. Amongst the steaming pools and patches of snow, it looked like the land of the gods, filled with ice and flame. If magic existed in this world, it must have been born here.

'Would you like me to kiss you?' he asked softly, gently stroking her arms, desperately hoping she would turn around.

She said nothing, and his hope slowly melted away until it was almost gone. His arms dropped back to his sides. But when he thought she was about to leave, she surprised him by remaining, and answering softly, 'Yes.'

Chapter Eleven

Mila could barely believe what she'd done. He'd asked if he could seduce her, and she'd said yes! The proof of her idiocy was given only moments later, when he took her arm in his and turned her to face him.

Surely she had lost her wits? Why was she encouraging him?

Had the soft touch of his hands in her hair and the exotic perfume addled her mind? Allowing him any kind of intimacy was a path to despair, and yet she couldn't seem to help herself. She felt removed from all sense and normalcy in this wild landscape. So much so that she was beginning to believe anything was possible.

The sun was setting. They were alone, far from her sister and home. She was losing touch of everything that mattered, and yet she could not seem to help herself.

She trusted him, even though she knew she shouldn't.

That was strange in itself.

In the past she had been pawed, grabbed, and forced to endure rough kisses and touches—at least until she could wrestle herself away. Thankfully it had never been more terrible than that. But she had been disappointed enough by most men's behaviour to never seek more from them. Dunstan was the first and only man she had allowed any closer, and he had given her nothing but false promises in return.

However, with Egill she felt strangely safe. For all his charm and bluster, she had never seen him utter a lie. He had the same strict moral code of his brother, and she knew from experience that Hakon was a good man... One of the few.

When she'd lost her temper and said that Egill only left behind women with '*nothing but a handful of tears*,' she'd been thinking of herself and Dunstan...not Egill, and that was unfair.

But regardless, she was surprised she was still allowing this...or even *wanted* this.

Which she did.

Heaven help her...she wanted him!

One of his hands cupped her face, and then his head dipped, illuminated by the rosy pink sky behind. She closed her eyes, giving in to the promise of pleasure. She had had so little in her life, and she desperately wished to experience it. Egill's words had filled her with reckless hope.

Perhaps she could trust him enough to show her what life *could* be like with him, and if he *really* meant what he'd said, then...maybe...she *would* marry him. Would such a life be so terrible?

Her instinct was to rebel against the prospect, to remind herself of all the reasons it would never be possible.

She was better off alone with only herself to rely on.

Men would always let her down. How many times had she witnessed it with her own eyes?

Very few marriages were ever happy, and it was just another type of bondage. Slavery, with no hope of release.

She'd once asked one of the bondswomen why they had

done it, put their future in the hands of another. She had answered simply, *'For the kisses.'*

Could something so simple cause you to lose your wits?

His lips were close now. She could feel the warmth of his breath against her mouth. She inhaled sharply, expecting the touch, and preparing herself for a rough disappointment.

The brush of his mouth against hers was gentle and coaxing, and the tension she hadn't realised was building inside of her now eased a little at the simple touch. Causing fear to transform into a thousand tingles of excitement that shivered across her lips.

The warmth of his body and the lapping water around them eased her muscles and nerves. It was only a kiss, nothing wild or dangerous as she'd always feared. His lips brushed against hers again, and this time she ached for more.

She leaned forward, unsure if there was more, and Egill obliged, pressing forward to open her mouth with his in an intoxicating tasting of each other. His tongue slid against hers sensually, only to retreat again after a few moments of shared breath.

Egill stepped back, an arrogant smile on his face. 'Come, let's go home, brave Mila. One step at a time until you are comfortable.'

She was sure he was teasing her, but she did feel brave. This was the most dangerous thing she had ever done, and she was still afraid it was going to be a terrible mistake.

They dressed quickly, and Egill lit two torches with his flint. The moon was full and low, so they could see their way reasonably well. Although Egill insisted that he walk behind her so that there was no danger of either of them stepping away from the path.

Returning back to the cabin, Egill added more fuel to the fire before setting to work on their evening meal. Mila worked alongside him, cutting up vegetables and adding them to the pot. There was only a little bit of cured meat left in their supplies, and she tried to hide her dismay when Egill put all of it in the cauldron.

Despite her trying to hide her expression, he must have guessed her thoughts, because he said, 'I will get more supplies tomorrow. Will you be all right alone, or would you like to come with me?'

'I will be fine. But are you sure we need more supplies? It's only been a few days, and I imagine I will be done before the two week deadline. I am sure we can make do with the vegetables we have. I brought a snare with me. Perhaps we could try and catch a rabbit? There are also the eggs. There are enough to have two a day of those. And I really don't need to drink the mead. Water from the stream is fine by me.'

'I think I should go back. We will need plenty of fuel to burn in your firepit.' Egill placed the lid on top of the cauldron, then took a seat on a nearby stool. She did the same.

'What do you plan to do tomorrow?' he asked.

'I will work in the ash. Try to get it to the consistency I need. I might even need to go and fetch another basket of raw clay.'

'So you won't be making anything yet?'

'No, sadly not,' she said with a frown. Icelandic clay was certainly hard work to get right.

Was this already an omen, warning her that her plan would fail?

Egill nodded thoughtfully. 'Then I have time to build your kiln with you.'

'Thank you.' Mila nodded eagerly, glad he intended to

return to help her with that task. She was beginning to wonder if he would return. Staying away wouldn't have made sense after their kiss, but Mila was always prepared for the worst.

As they waited for their meal to cook, Egill asked her questions about the pottery-making process and seemed genuinely interested by her answers.

'So, you like making pottery?' At her confused expression, he added, 'You *enjoy* it?'

Mila hesitated, unsure of how best to explain herself. 'It is...all that I know. I tried weaving, but I do not have the talent for it like Wynflaed. At least with pottery, I know what I am doing.'

Egill nodded. 'I only ask because I do not know what I want to do with my life. I am curious if I am the same or different to everyone else. My brothers always seem to know.'

'You don't? But you have so much choice...' she asked, confused. He'd said as much before, but he seemed so confident otherwise, she just couldn't imagine it. A man with so much opportunity, plagued by doubt.

He shrugged. 'For years I followed my brothers. But now they have built separate lives on opposite sides of the great sea. Hakon has always been our guiding voice, more of a father to me than my own. But...he has a wool farm now and a wife. Should I join him? When I have spent many years fighting battles and leading men into war? Or should I live in Norway with my second brother, Grimr? He is now jarl in Hakon's place. Should I become his second, now that the dust has settled, help him negotiate treaties and run his lands...?'

'I always wondered why you didn't leave with him in the summer... Were you waiting for him to grow used to his position? Or were you worried your people would not accept Grimr as jarl?' Mila quickly shut her mouth, cursing her runaway tongue. It was not her place to question the decisions of men like Egill and Grimr, men who dined with kings.

Thankfully, Egill didn't even blink at her curiosity.

'Grimr is an ideal jarl. As loyal as a dog and as fierce as a bear. But he lacks confidence in himself, and is slow to trust...' Egill paused, giving her a knowing look that made her bristle and his smile widen. 'Because of Hakon's decision to remain in Iceland, Grimr all at once had a reluctant wife, a new role, and an angry king to appease. Normally I would help my brothers with anything, but I knew in this case it might be better for Grimr to handle things alone. At least at first. Give him time to claim his position and be confident in his right to rule without my interference or aid. Our people, too, would feel more confident in Grimr if they saw him manage them alone.'

Mila was left stunned by his explanation. 'So you stayed in Iceland to give your brother independence?'

Egill nodded, and then chuckled with an embarrassed inclination of his head. 'Yes...but I realise that is arrogant of me, and not the only reason. Hakon's enslavement and my injury made me realise...how uncertain and fragile our lives can be. I think I should finally find a place for myself in this world...' He scratched his freshly shaved jaw thoughtfully. 'I have always enjoyed travelling. Perhaps I should become a merchant trader? I could sell your pots.' She didn't return his smile because a part of her never wanted him to leave, and he shrugged. 'But I have also grown to love this land. Maybe I should farm? Orla has plenty of land after her uncle's demise. I might buy some from her...or I could go back home and fight under Grimr or King Harald. Perhaps he will send me to Constantinople... I hear they need warriors there.'

'You have lots of choice,' she said, more than a little envious. She had lived in only two lands, and neither had been by choice.

He nodded. 'I do....and so would my wife. She could do whatever she wished, whether it be pottery, weaving, farming, or simply bathing with Arabian soaps and wearing only Byzantine silk.'

Mila scoffed at that. 'You would need to be a very good merchant indeed to afford that!'

A twinkle sparkled in his blue eyes as he answered, 'When I want something, I usually get it.'

For some reason, his statement caused a shiver of excitement to run down her spine.

After they ate their meal, Mila excused herself to go to the latrine outside before getting ready for bed. She took a torch with her and made quick work of her visit as the night air was clear but chilly.

When she re-entered the cabin, she noticed Egill had finished cleaning up, and must already be up in the loft as there was a glow from an oil lamp in the triangular space above. She extinguished her torch and slowly made her way up the ladder, feeling with her hands and feet for the bars.

At the top, Egill sat up in his bedroll, his hands resting loosely in his lap. The breadth of his naked torso was visible above the blanket and showing him off in his golden glory. Mila swallowed and concentrated on climbing up into the space, not realising until it was too late that Egill had rearranged the packs so that they were lined up against the beams, and the bedrolls were now placed close together in the centre.

'Nothing will happen without your say-so,' he told her

firmly at her panicked expression, and then smiled cheerfully before continuing, 'But I thought we could enjoy the greatest pleasure of the marriage bed...one I have never experienced myself, but feel inclined to try with you.'

Mila stared at him, feeling as if this were some kind of strange and weird dream. 'What...haven't you tried before?' Surely this confident traveller of the world had experienced every pleasure known to man.

Mila swallowed again, this time more deeply as if she were trying to digest a boulder.

Heavens! What debauchery could he possibly want to perform on her?

Egill grinned, his face almost glowing with gleeful excitement, and he slapped her bedroll beside him. 'I have never slept with a woman in my arms.'

Mila stared at him, trying to work out if he were trying to mock her. 'What?'

His face fell. 'Have you slept with a man before...like husband and wife?'

'Not *slept*,' she whispered, embarrassed.

Egill breathed a sigh of relief. 'Good. I had hoped as much. I wanted it to be something we experienced for the first time together.'

Unsure of whether to laugh or cry at his odd statement, she decided to turn away instead, and took the opportunity to regain her composure and take off her apron dress and boots.

When she turned back a short time later, he was still waiting patiently, so she eased herself into the bedroll beside him. They were divided by their bedding rolls, which were open-ended quilted tubes of cloth—much like a sock. She tucked her head beneath her hands as she turned onto her side, facing away from Egill.

'Can I hold you?' he asked.

She gave a little nod of agreement. 'Extinguish the lamp first. We need to save our oil.'

A moment later, the light disappeared, and they were covered in a blanket of darkness. Her spine was rigid, but she forced her breathing to remain calm and steady. There was loud shuffling as Egill shoved himself deeper into his bedroll and turned towards her.

A large, heavy arm draped over her waist, warm and solid. It curved around her a little but did not touch or grope her in any way.

She waited, and when nothing happened, she breathed a sigh of relief.

Then Egill's arm pulled her towards him, her whole body and bedroll sliding across the loft to be fully wrapped in his embrace. He nuzzled her hair and sucked in a deep breath, releasing it with a loud groan of pleasure.

'You smell of spice and snow,' he mumbled, and then his body seemed to slump into hers.

She blinked into the darkness as Egill's steady and even breath filled the air.

Was he asleep already?

She waited again, and realised that he had been true to his word. He had just wanted to hold her while he slept. She smiled into the darkness, oddly pleased that he would choose her for this unusual *first* experience.

The warmth of his body reminded her of Wynflaed sleeping at her back, and she found herself drifting off into a peaceful and easy sleep.

Glad she wasn't alone.

Chapter Twelve

Egill was up at dawn. It seemed living alongside Mila meant he now naturally rose early. He ate porridge with her and then hitched the pony to the empty cart. Mila watched him from the doorway, a cloak wrapped around her shoulders.

Perhaps it was her imagination, but she felt as if the weather had turned for the worse. There was a cold and biting wind that seemed to rattle through her bones.

Egill paused in what he was doing and glanced over at her. 'I will be back before nightfall.'

Mila gave an absent nod but didn't reply. She couldn't think of anything more to say.

Egill walked over and gripped her shoulders with both hands. When she looked up at him, startled, he smiled down at her warmly and said, *'I swear.* I will be back before nightfall.'

She wanted to reply, *I know*, but she couldn't bring herself to do that, because she *didn't* know. She couldn't control the actions of others any more than she could control her own foolish heart. Instead, she forced a carefree smile and shrugged out of his embrace, stepping back into the shadow of the hut. 'Farewell, then. Say hello to my sister and Nora for me.'

'I will.' He nodded, seeming to accept her sudden indifference, despite the fact they'd woken up in each other's arms. After walking back to the pony and cart, he moved off with a cheerful wave.

Mila didn't watch him leave. Instead, she shut the door of the hut firmly and went back to sit by the fire. There was no point fretting over it. He would return or he wouldn't. There was nothing she could do about it either way. She glanced over at the supplies, taking stock of what was left. It was only for another week. She'd survived on far less, and she still had Bolli's basket of eggs.

A strange, cold emptiness swept through her, as if there were a draught in the hut that she'd never noticed before. The room was suddenly a lot larger than she remembered, the earthen floor dirty and scuffed from their boots.

No good will come of this! she reprimanded herself harshly as she stood up and brushed off her skirts, then strode around the room, gathering what tools she would need for the day's work.

In a short time, she was outside under the shelter, pounding the dung ash into her clay and concentrating on creating the perfect texture for moulding. The cold, empty feeling was thankfully replaced by the strenuous efforts of her labours.

Several hours later, she was done working on her clay. The ash seemed to have helped bring together the consistency she needed. At noon she dug into the bank and filled one more basket from the clay bed. This one was meant for sealing the kiln and would require less working through with ash, although she found herself doing that too, until all the ash was gone and all the clay was prepared, ready for moulding.

Exhausted, she finally stopped working when she noticed the sun dipping towards the horizon. Walking to the nearby stream, she took the opportunity to wash herself and her filthy clothes. She knew she must look terrible after all her messy work, and she was sure she could smell the dung ash on her fingers despite rinsing her hands in water several times.

The nearby stream was much shallower than the hot river, and although it had some residual heat from the hot springs, it was nothing compared to those steaming waters. Which meant it wouldn't boil the wool, at least, and was ideal for clothes. She scrubbed them with her ash and lye soap, then used Egill's soap for her body. It was pure vanity to use it, but if he did return, she didn't want to smell of clay and dung ash. She shivered as she remembered the way he had breathed in her scent last night.

Spice and snow.

She liked that description. It made her feel interesting and exotic. Neither of which was true, but she appreciated it all the same. Dunstan had called her '*the prettiest girl in Jorvik,*' but it was false flattery. There was always someone prettier, wealthier, better... Somehow, being compared to *spice and snow* felt more...honest, in a strange sort of way. Timeless. A force of nature within its own right, and not comparison or competition.

She trudged back from the river, shivering, wearing only her damp shift and boots, and carrying all of her sodden clothes in a basket. Once inside the hut, she hung up the clothes on sticks and wall pegs around the fire. Hoping that at some point she would warm up.

Washing clothes was hard, and they'd had to do it far more regularly than normal because of the messy nature of her work. Perhaps, if her pottery did fire well, she could finally use some ells of cloth to make a new dress and shift? She could use one of her old dresses purely for pottery making. That way she wouldn't have to wash her clothes so often.

She was about to throw another log on the fire when she stopped herself.

What if she needed to ration her fuel?

She hadn't thought of that!

She stripped off her damp shift, as it was only making her shiver, and then climbed up into the bed loft. Curling up in her bedroll and blankets, she finally let her heavy eyes close. She would worry about the fuel tomorrow.

'Mila!'

Egill's voice startled her awake, and she jumped up into a sitting position, the blankets pooling around her lap. Cold air puckered her naked nipples, and with a panicked squeal she tugged the covers around her closely. Thankfully she wasn't visible from ground level, so she scooted forward to take a better look at the doorway.

Egill was seeing to the pony, giving it hay and water. It was raining outside, and she could see the water streaming heavily in front of the doorway, wetting the entrance. Egill's hair and cloak were soaking wet, but when he looked up at her, his face shone with warmth and affection. 'There you are!'

A wave of relief washed through her, followed by bubbles of excitement. She felt like that bright blue steaming pool, alive with colour and heat.

'I will come down!' she shouted, followed by a nervous realisation that she was still naked. 'Could you pass my clothes up?'

Egill glanced at the pegged clothing by the fire, and

a slow, wicked smile spread across his face. 'I will bring them up in a minute. Stay there! It's wet down here, and I still need to bring in the supplies from the cart.'

'But... I should help you.'

'No!' he insisted. 'No need for both of us to get cold and wet.' He gave her a firm look. 'I mean it. Stay there.'

Helplessly, Mila watched as Egill trudged back and forth with supplies, chatting cheerfully the whole time. Telling her that the firepits and her barrel of clay were still reasonably dry despite the rain, but that he'd added more canvas and bracken to shelter them.

'Heavens above! Did you bring the entirety of your brother's stores?' she asked with a chuckle as he carried in something bulky that was covered in a blanket.

He grinned up at her before carefully placing it on the ground. 'No, this is a gift for you.'

'A gift?'

She had never had a gift from a man before.

Mila wasn't even sure what to say. Belatedly she realised what she should say and snapped in a rush, 'Thank you!'

'You haven't seen it yet. I am not even sure if you need it. I asked around before we left about what tools you may need for your trade.' He pulled the blanket away, shaking off the rain with a snap of his wrist.

Mila gasped, leaning forward to get a better look. 'Is that...a potter's wheel?'

'One of Hakon's carpenters used to live in Wessex. He said he'd made a couple of these in his time, and I asked him to make one for you. It was going to take him a few days, so I arranged to collect it today.'

Mila stared down at the beautiful polished wheel, her eyes pricking with unexpected tears. She swallowed deeply, trying her best to control her emotions. 'It is...wonderful. Thank you.'

She had been prepared to hand-coil the pottery in the old fashion, knowing that she didn't have the tools to make bowls and cups like she used to. It wasn't just the fact that he'd given her a wheel—it was the care he'd taken to find out about her craft, and then to have commissioned something for her well in advance. There was even a cutting wire, and an assortment of spatulas included, attached by a string to the wheel.

She leaned a little more forward. 'I should come down.'

'No, don't,' Egill repeated as he untied the tools from the wheel and then demonstrated the movement with a light kick of his boot. 'The floor is cold and damp. I can show you whatever you need to see. This is how it works, yes?'

She sat back on her heels, gathering her blanket closer around her. The warm affection rushing through her body made her feel naked and vulnerable in more ways than one. 'It's...perfect.'

It wasn't enough to show her gratitude, but she doubted she could have said anything better. Judging by Egill's bright expression, it pleased him deeply, even though it was a weak response.

He moved it carefully to the side of the room. 'Have you eaten?'

Mila shook her head. 'If you pass me my clothes...'

'No need. Orla gave me some cuts of meat and roasted vegetables from *nattmal*. Plus some bread and cheese.' He raised up a covered basket. 'Take it.'

'You wish to eat in bed?' she asked, horrified at the suggestion.

'Why not?' He shrugged. 'I am cold, it is late, and I'd rather be curled up beside you.' He passed up the basket before she could argue, and she took it, slightly bewildered as to how easily he always managed to get his way.

She scooted back to the centre of the loft and began to rearrange the bedrolls so that there would be room for both of them to sit and eat in comfort. But as she arranged them, fleeces were thrown up beside her, as well as a couple of feather-filled pillows. She smiled at the indulgence.

'Miss your comfortable bed?' she teased.

'No harm in making us more comfortable.'

Egill stomped up the ladder a short time later. After hopping up onto the platform, he turned to sit on the edge, his legs dangling over. He gave her a boyish grin and then began to remove his boots, placing them at the very edge of the platform so as not to get mud on their bedding.

It was then she noticed another bundle beside him, which he handed to her quickly. 'I didn't have time to get a new dress made for you. So I brought some of my old clothes instead. They will be too big on you. But you can roll up the legs and arms, and they will be good enough to work in.'

Stunned, she merely nodded and accepted the bundle. 'Are you sure?'

'They are old—keep them.' He shrugged. 'It will save me washing your clothes, and you can use them whenever you work your clay.'

She'd been thinking much the same thing, but he had saved her from using her ells to make a new dress! 'Thank you.'

He moved to sit opposite her on the fleeces, bedroll and blankets she'd laid out. He'd already hung up his cloak and over-tunic below, presumably to dry off. So he was only in a light tunic and woollen narrow trousers that were tight over his thighs.

Carefully unwrapping the contents of the basket, she was surprised by the delicious and luxurious contents within.

Their meal consisted of a flagon of Frankish wine that was a rich and extravagant luxury she'd never tasted before. Skewers of pork and lamb ribs were wrapped in flatbreads slathered in a herby butter. A little cauldron held roasted turnips, parsnips and carrots drizzled with precious honey and spiced with salt and pepper. To finish, there were two bowls of wheat and hazelnut pudding with scattered dried berries that were as bright as jewels.

A meal fit for a powerful man...and he was sharing it with her.

'How is Wynflaed?' she asked, unsure of what she should take from the array of extravagant dishes. Egill was eagerly filling a wooden trencher with large portions of everything, and she decided to wait until he was done before taking her own portion. She ignored the way her stomach grumbled and her mouth watered at the delicious smells.

'She is working hard at her weaving, so much so that she has already covered your absence,' Egill said, handing her the trencher he had filled.

Startled by his kindness, she took it. 'I hope she is not overworking herself.'

'No...' Egill shook his head. 'I think she is enjoying the challenge, and Orla would not let her carry on if she were hurting herself.'

The food was delicious, and they both ate mostly in silence, occasionally remarking on the flavour of each dish or offering each other more.

At the end of the meal, there was little to clear up as they'd eaten so much. They placed the dishes back in the basket, and Egill set it beside his boots for cleaning up in the morning.

Mila finished her wine, savouring the last plummy sip before handing him the bone cup. 'Thank you. It was delicious.'

Egill smiled, pleased with himself. 'Made better because of your company.'

She blushed, and then yawned, covering her mouth quickly with her hand.

'You are tired?' he asked with concern.

She nodded, but then shrugged. 'I managed a lot today. The clay is fully prepared, and I have enough to build the kiln too. Thank you again for the wheel.'

Egill didn't appear to be listening. He was already adjusting his bedding so that it lay next to hers and settling himself down for the night. It took her a moment to realise he was giving her some privacy, deliberately facing away from her. She examined the bundle of his old clothing, took out the under-tunic within, and put it on quickly. It looked more like a short shift on her, and she draped a blanket around her shoulders as she climbed down the ladder in her hastily shoved-on boots.

'Where are you going?' asked a sleepy voice.

'I need to use the latrine,' she said with a sigh, hating having to admit it to him. 'The wine…'

'I brought a pot for you. It's beneath the ladder to the right. I thought it would save you stumbling out in the dark.'

'Oh…er…thank you.'

'Up to you to empty it, though. There are some things even I won't do for you.'

She chuckled at that, and went down to take care of her needs and prepare for bed. With a cup of water and a strip of linen, she rubbed her teeth clean. She wasn't surprised that Egill was fast asleep when she returned to bed.

He'd also done a lot today.

In fact, he'd worked hard for her all week, and more importantly, kept his promise.

She extinguished the oil lamp and clambered into her bedroll beside him. Snuggling close to his side, glad of the warmth from his big body...and for his return.

Until now, she'd not realised how anxious she'd been about it. Fearing that he would not keep his word and leave her to struggle alone. She would have managed. She knew that. It was why she had worked so hard today, to prove to herself that she could.

But...to have him back felt...good.

Chapter Thirteen

The rain continued the next day, falling in a non-stop miserable drizzle. They decided to stay inside the cabin as the wind was blowing too hard to work in the lean-to.

'At least we'll gather plenty of drinking water today,' groaned Egill, coming in from outside carrying the huge half barrel of workable clay.

Mila hurried to shut the door behind him, frowning a little at the heavy rain and dull skies overhead. They'd moved the water barrel out first, and already it was half full. 'It seems our weather has turned for the worse... Although at least it isn't snow.'

'True, and the rain will melt the remaining patches of ice. Do not worry, though. This will pass, and we'll soon have plenty of bright sunshine again, ready for your firing,' Egill said optimistically, putting down the huge half barrel carefully as if it were a sleeping babe.

The oil lamps were lit, and the fire was burning steadily to give them extra light. Mila had worried it was an excessive use of their fuel, but Egill didn't seem to care, insisting she would need the light to work, and reassuring her that he'd brought plenty of wood back with him for all their needs.

'Hopefully... Otherwise, I might not have anything

ready in time,' Mila said with a frown, more than a little worried about the uncertainty.

'All will be well,' said Egill firmly. 'Do not worry.'

Mila sighed, but nodded. 'No point worrying about it, I suppose...' She didn't like to rely on *hope*, but some things were beyond her control...or anyone's, for that matter. They could not argue with the weather.

Better to focus on what she *could* control.

'How can I help?' asked Egill eagerly, and she smiled at his enthusiasm.

'You have helped me enough, and there is nothing more to do anyway other than make the pottery. After I've done that, it will need to dry out slowly before decoration and firing. Storing it in here should be fine, though, as long as it's not too close to the fire.'

'I will make some shelves for the finished pieces, then... It will be easier to store them that way, and for them to dry more evenly.'

Touched by his offer, she nodded eagerly, and after a long pause confessed, 'Thank you for everything. You have made this challenge...well, *better* than I expected.' It felt weak as a compliment, and so she added, 'I am grateful you are here...truly.'

Egill flushed at her praise, and inclined his head solemnly. 'That means a great deal to me, *Mila*.' He said her name with a husky, raw edge of emotion, like a sharp blade running through silk. Smooth, and yet devastatingly effective.

It was her turn to blush, and she hurried to sit on her stool in front of her new pottery wheel. She briskly kicked the flat wheel below to move the throwing board above, determined to focus on her task rather than the flush of heat rushing through her body.

They worked together, Mila taking time to practice and become accustomed to her new wheel. Egill putting up shelves with some planks of wood and nails he'd brought with him.

Was there anything he hadn't thought of?

When she jokingly asked him that question, he explained that he'd been going to use the wood to reinforce her workshop, but had thought better of it now that he'd seen the poor weather. It would be far simpler and warmer for her to work inside, so by mid-morning he had finished the shelves and was now carefully helping her to load the first completed piece on the bottom shelf.

It was a simple bowl with little decoration. She was going to make two, one for herself and one for Wynflaed. That way, they would be able to eat from them every day, and know that her pottery had given them the freedom and independence they craved. Inside at the base, she'd pressed her thumb into the clay, a simple and discreet mark.

When she started on the next bowl, Egill sat on a nearby stool and began to chop vegetables and smoked sausage for their evening meal. 'What sort of things are you going to make?'

Mila wet her hands in the nearby bucket she used for this purpose, then scooped out a chunk of clay from the half barrel. She warmed it with the kneading of her hands until it was pliable enough to be thrown. 'I will make two of everything that we used to make. Bowls, pots, mugs, spouted jars, flat-bottomed bottles, oil lamps, and loom weights... The last two will be particularly useful to Mistress Orla, who has to trade for them normally. I will start with the larger items, like the pots and bottles, and move down into the smaller pieces. If I have enough clay, I will make more of those.'

'Why start with two small bowls, then?' asked Egill curiously, nodding to the second bowl that was already beginning to take shape beneath her fingers.

'These are for myself and Wynflaed... If they fire well, I won't sell them. They are the first, and I want to keep them... I am being foolishly sentimental,' she admitted, avoiding his eyes, as she finished and pressed her thumb into the bottom of the bowl. She then used the cutting wire to remove it from the throwing table and placed it carefully on the shelf beside its twin.

'Nothing wrong with keeping a trophy. Many warriors do the same,' Egill said, smiling at her with affection as she returned to her seat. She returned it shyly, feeling a little more confident in her plan, and set to work.

They laboured side by side, listening to the steady rain against the roof. Talking about everything and nothing.

When dinner was almost complete, and a good portion of her clay had been used, she decided it was almost time to finish her work. With a satisfied sigh, she poked a hole into her last loom weight and placed it with the half dozen others on the shelf to dry.

'My hands are beginning to ache... I think maybe one more cup and then I am done. Tomorrow they should be dry enough for light decoration, spouts, and handles,' she said.

Egill glanced up from where he'd been splitting firewood. He'd done every chore possible inside the cabin, only going out to fetch more tasks to do. Their evening meal was cheerfully simmering in the cauldron, and there was a huge stack of wood and kindling beside the fire. The water barrel was full and had already been brought inside. The cabin was tidy, the floor swept, the pony well-fed and watered. Egill had even repaired furniture in the cabin and started to carve toys for Orla's babe. Mila had never seen such a busy man. She knew some who would drink ale and sleep all day if they could get away with it.

'May I make one?' he asked. 'If you are willing to show me...'

'Of course. It is the least I can do!' she declared, exhilarated that he would even want to learn. Especially when most people considered pottery a low-status skill. 'Come sit!' she said, jumping off her stool and then wincing a little from her stiff muscles.

Egill noticed and gave her a sympathetic look. 'Are you sure? You are tired.'

'You'll be doing all the work. Now, sit.'

Egill sat down in front of the wheel, and she began to show him how to turn it, pulling up a stool so that she could show him more easily. Not realising how close they were until their hands brushed against one another.

'What do you want to make?' she asked, trying dismiss how the warmth of his touch had made her heart flutter wildly. She forced herself to concentrate on the task at hand, reaching into the half barrel of clay.

'A bowl,' he said firmly, 'to join the ones you made for you and your sister. I also want a keepsake.'

'So be it.' She chuckled, scooping out the right amount and slapping it onto the throwing table. 'Warm the clay with your hands, and add water to soften it,' she instructed, showing him the technique with her own hands, then placing his on top of the clay to guide him.

'Begin to kick the wheel at the bottom, until it is moving at a good speed. Good. Now, guide the clay up, smoothing it as you go.'

She glanced at Egill and had to smother a giggle when she saw the sheer concentration on his face as he struggled to move his feet and hands in different ways.

'It's working!' he shouted, gleeful as the bowl began to form under their combined hands.

'Slow down!' she warned.

'Oh,' sighed Egill as the bowl collapsed.

Egill had thought he was doing so well up until now. He turned a little to look at her and felt his whole body still, as if caught in a spider's web. Transfixed by the warmth of her eyes and the flush of pink high on her cheeks as she laughed in delight. His heart twisted and then thudded back to life, and he tried to smile, to act as if the sight of her didn't devastate him with longing.

'Try again,' she urged, taking his hands and gathering the clay back together. 'You're doing so well—especially for a first attempt.'

Egill used to pride himself on his patience. He could negotiate with rivals for hours, wearing them down with his dogged determination, or wait happily for battle while other men chewed off their nails with apprehension. But sitting beside Mila was pure agony, made worse by her change in manner towards him.

When he'd left the other day, she'd been cold, refusing to even watch him leave. But after his return, he could tell something significant had thawed within her. Not simply because of the gifts he'd brought her, but because he'd returned. Had she really thought he would not stay? After everything he'd confessed?

He turned back to the clay. 'Show me again?' he asked softly, taking her wet hands in his and idly stroking down her fingers with his own. Her chest rose and fell with a gasped sigh. His loins stiffened at the soft brush of her chest against his arm.

Egill sighed, letting her hands fall away from him as

she patted the clay lightly, and demonstrated the technique obediently. 'Now you.'

He began to pedal the wheel, copying the movements she'd shown him. He *could* be patient, especially when she looked as beautiful as she did when she was working.

After a few more attempts, he managed to create a decent-looking bowl, and Mila declared it was good enough for cutting.

'It's lopsided,' he said with a frown, scrutinising the bowl from all angles as he slowly rotated the wheel. He wanted it to be perfect, just like Mila's bowls. But then, he wasn't as skilled as Mila, and he didn't want to tire her after such a long day of crafting.

'It's fine,' Mila reassured him, quickly reaching around him, ready to make the cut that would remove it from the table.

'Wait!' Egill cried, and Mila stopped dead.

'What? Did I knock it?' she gasped, her body frozen.

Quickly he tried to reassure her and explain, 'No, but we haven't marked it with our thumbs!'

'Oh, that.' Mila blushed. 'Go ahead, then.'

Egill took her hand in his and guided it into the bowl. 'I want both our marks, as I couldn't have done it without your help.'

I want you too, he thought, but knew there was still something keeping her from him.

He had no idea what it was, but he could tell she was on the brink of falling into his arms, and he wanted to be ready to catch her when she did. Reassure her that all would be well.

Mila's throat bobbed as he tugged her forward and pressed her thumb into the wet clay. 'I...' She struggled to find her words for a moment, and he squeezed her hand lightly, offering her reassurance. He wasn't entirely sure why she feared love, but he could understand it. He'd felt as if he'd opened up his ribs more than once. Eventually she replied quietly, 'I hope one day we can enjoy eating from them...together.'

She might as well have leapt into his lap, so elated was he by her words. It gave him hope that she was beginning to consider a future with him.

Looking away from him, she busied herself with cutting away the bowl and carefully placing it on the shelf. He focused on cleaning up her tools and wheel. Then they washed their hands and began to serve and eat their evening meal, stealing heated glances at each other occasionally. It seemed the short time apart had only encouraged their mutual desire.

'Thank you for the clothes—they were useful,' said Mila, brushing the worst of the clay from her trousers in a nervous gesture he recognised as embarrassment.

'I have never seen my clothes look better,' he replied, and grinned when she blushed and laughed in response. Easing back into her seat with a relaxed smile, she had truly never looked more beautiful.

'Mila?' he asked mildly.

'Yes?'

'I think we should go to bed early tonight. What do you think?'

Her wide eyes brightened in the firelight, and he was secretly delighted when she answered softly, 'Well... I am a little tired.'

Chapter Fourteen

'Then let us prepare for bed,' he replied, taking her empty dish from her numb hands, their fingers sliding against one another and causing a flood of heat to rise up her cheeks. Nodding, she hurriedly rose and quickly helped him tidy up.

Egill's eyes followed her every movement with the intensity of a predator choosing its prey, missing nothing, and seeing through her feigned tiredness with a smug smile.

Anticipation consumed her, as if she were one of those hot, trembling pools—ready to burst at any moment.

Would he kiss her again?

Bubbles of excitement popped inside her at the thought, and she bit her lip, wondering if she had lost all sense and reason.

Egill was the last man she should kiss! What had happened to relying only on herself? To avoiding all dangerous relationships? Especially ones involving arrogant and carefree men such as Egill!

Needing some fresh air, she went to the door and tentatively looked outside. 'It's stopped raining, at least... The sky looks clear. I won't be long,' she said, taking the opportunity to clear her head and visit the latrine.

The sun was just dipping below the horizon, casting a golden glow across the mountains. The rolling landscape of their valley was free of snow and looked as if it had been newly made. Lush green grass and bushes covered the rolling hills, and she could smell a dewy sweetness in the air.

She stepped out, being careful not to slip on the mud surrounding the hut, and saw to her needs. On the way back, she stopped beside the shelter Egill had built for her and took some deep breaths of fresh clean air.

Perhaps she should stop letting the past rule her future?

Just because it had not worked out for her mother or with Dunstan did not mean that happiness was impossible. Orla was happy, as was Tyr with his wife, and there were others too.

He came back! she reminded herself.

He had promised to help her, and he *had*. In fact, he'd been so thoughtful and considerate that she was now beginning to wonder what she would do without him.

Walking back into the cabin, she washed her hands and face, rubbed her teeth with a strip of linen, and then clambered up to the loft bed as quickly as she could without wanting to look too eager. Her feet stumbled on one of the ladder's steps, and she blushed furiously when Egill asked if she were well.

'Yes, I forgot to bring up a lamp, that's all,' she squeaked, realising belatedly there was still daylight, admittedly dim, pouring in from the window above.

Egill's voice was light with amusement. 'Well, be careful, and I'll bring one up shortly.'

She hurried to change into a clean shift as Egill prepared for bed below. Then she folded her 'new' work clothes for the next day and combed out her hair.

Cuddling up into her bedroll, she covered herself with a blanket just as the light from Egill's oil lamp illuminated the increasing darkness of the loft.

'Are you already asleep?' he asked incredulously, and she rose up to a sitting position.

'No...not yet.' She shouldn't seem too eager! 'I am a little weary, though.'

He nodded, placing the lamp carefully down on the edge of the platform away from the bedding. 'I have something to soothe your aches.'

'You do?' she asked, waiting for some crude remark that thankfully never came.

'Hemp oil. It relaxes and eases muscles.' He knelt beside her and poured a little from a small leather flask into his hands. After a moment of rubbing the oil between his fingers, he lifted her arm from her lap and began to rub the palm of her hand with smooth circular motions.

She closed her eyes and bit her lip, desperately trying to stop herself from moaning with pleasure. After working with her hands all day, they felt sore and tight. Egill's motions were wonderfully sensual on her dry skin and stretched tendons.

'Is that good?' he murmured, and her chest hitched when she thought she felt the whisper of his breath against her neck.

'Yes,' she nodded, turning a little to face him more fully.

'Undo the ties of your shift. I can massage your arms and shoulders then.'

Mila opened her eyes with a start, but obediently unknotted the ties at the wrists of her shift, as if unable to deny him—or herself. She hesitated a little on the tie at her chest, but ultimately did as he had asked and loosened it.

Closing her eyes again, she offered both hands, palms up, and held her breath. She was not disappointed when his hands returned to hers. They were warm and comforting, soothing with gentle circular strokes all the tension from her muscles. He worked on each hand, each finger and thumb. Rolled her wrists gently and stroked up and down beneath the crisp linen shift to smooth away the tension in her forearms and elbows.

Once he was finished with each arm, she heard him kneel behind her. She was afraid to open her eyes in case she broke the spell he'd cast over her. He gently moving aside her loose hair before oiling his hands once again, and working this time on her shoulders and neck.

She couldn't help herself. She groaned loudly this time, and he chuckled, 'Good?'

'Yes.' She sighed. '*So* good!'

The touch of his hands down her neck and shoulder blades was exquisite, and she moaned helplessly when he cracked a tender spot on her neck that sent a wave of relief down her spine.

The heat of his chest enveloped her as he leaned close. 'May I kiss you again, Mila?'

Drifting on a wave of bliss, Mila couldn't find the strength or desire to deny him.

She was a fool for him, as she knew she would be.

'Yes,' she murmured softly, moaning when he unexpectedly pressed a kiss to the side of her neck. A cool breeze puckered her nipples, and she realised he'd pushed the shift down to her elbows. His hands cupped her breasts from behind, massaging them softly as he brushed kisses down from her ear to the nape of her neck.

She turned a little, nervousness finally winning over pleasure, and she gazed up at him scared to confess her fears.

'I have lain with a man before... I did not enjoy it,' she said, hoping that it might warn him against their disappointment later.

'Did someone hurt you?' he asked, his voice gentle and kind.

She shook her head. 'Not like that...'

Egill nodded, no judgement in his expression, only compassion. 'Go on.'

Mila's throat tightened, but she knew that he would never understand unless she confessed her shameful truth. 'His name was Dunstan. I thought he loved me... He promised to marry me. He said he needed time to convince his parents regarding our match. They were wealthy merchants... far above us in station. After the fire, I went to his parents' home, asking for his help in finding my father...' Her voice caught on the painful memory of what followed. 'He pretended as if he didn't even know me. Pushed me away as if I were a leper...and threw us out in the street. The entire market was watching. They all knew the truth, but they looked at me with disgust, just as he had done. Out of pity and to not seem so terrible in their eyes, he offered me a loaf of bread for our journey.' She laughed bitterly. 'I should thank him, really. We would have died without that bread.'

Egill's jaw tightened into stone, but he spoke gently. 'I am sorry, Mila. He did not deserve you.'

She smiled, releasing a breath of relief. He did not blame her for her stupidity. 'For the first time ever... I think I agree with you... He was a lying coward.'

Egill cupped her jaw softly, leaning down until they were eye to eye. 'I meant what I said. You will experience only pleasure with me...and I will not treat you as my true wife... Not until I have bound myself to you in front of everyone—including my brothers and the gods.'

For some reason, she believed him. Even when every past experience screamed otherwise. She closed the gap between them, pressing her lips against his in surrender and hope.

He pulled her to him, the kiss deepening into a passionate embrace. Then he lowered her gently back onto the bedroll, her legs slipping free from the bedding.

His mouth trailed kisses and licks down her breasts as his hand stroked up her legs to gather the soft linen at her waist.

'Open your legs for me,' he whispered against her neck, and she obeyed him, her hips lifting a little with an eagerness she had never imagined possible. It had never been like this with Dunstan. Their ruttings had been quick and painful, leaving her sore for days after. Dunstan had said she was too cold, her body not responding as it should. She had thought there was something wrong with her.

Blocking out the memories of before, she waited, praying that *this time* would be different...in every way.

He rose up above her and pressed gentle kisses against her lips until she softened beneath his embrace. Her hands snaked up his arms to grip the cloth of his tunic as his fingers sought the ache between her legs and eased it with the same soft circular motions he'd used earlier on her hands.

She groaned under his touch, and it was enough encouragement for him to move his attention back to her breasts. He licked and tasted them with soft caresses that had her hips grinding against his hand, seeking release.

Would it be like the release in her neck? A tightening pain, followed by bliss? She hoped so. She had only felt pain before, and she longed to feel more.

'Egill,' she whimpered as his hand drifted away from her aching centre and moved to spread her legs a little wider. She thought he would remove his clothes now and enter her. She braced herself.

But she was shocked when he seemed to settle his upper body between her legs. 'May I kiss you here?' he asked softly, the heat of his breath so close to that intimate part of her that she moaned beneath the whispering caress.

'Yes,' she whimpered, arching as he began to lick and suck at the entrance between her legs and the bud of tension that seemed to throb with anticipation as soon as he latched on to it.

Her heels dug into the bedding. She was unsure of what to do. He calmly draped each of her thighs over his shoulders while not moving away from her or stopping the kisses he rained down upon her body. His tongue began to stroke and lick every inch of her flesh. When he sucked on the bundle of nerves again, it was too much for her, and the tension within her shattered.

There was no pain, only wonderful pleasure, and her eyes flew open to stare in shock at the ceiling above as wave after blissful wave rushed through her like an unstoppable tide.

Egill's handsome face rose from between her thighs. A wickedly sinful smile spread across it. 'See, Mila... I never disappoint.'

The next few days passed in idyllic happiness. They worked together, adding the handles and spouts to her pottery as well as a simple glaze. Then they built up the kiln in the spring sunshine, around the carefully arranged pottery and straw.

In the second firepit, they stacked the wood, ready for lighting. A tunnel between the two pits would ensure the smoke and heat poured into the kiln to bake the pottery. Mila stood with the flint in her hand with hesitant excitement.

Everything now rested on this firing time.

'Wait a moment,' said Egill, and he hurried inside the cabin.

Mila gave a huff of impatience, and checked the seal of the kiln for a third time to be sure there weren't any gaps in the rock, clay and turf that covered it. By the time she'd completed a full circular walk around the beehive-shaped kiln, Egill had returned.

Two stools were held in one mighty fist, and he had a basket in the other.

Mila rolled her eyes. 'Why have you brought those out? It won't take a moment to light it.'

Egill placed the stools down and gestured for her to take a seat. 'And will you walk away and leave it burning, or will you sit and watch?'

Mila tried to hide her smile. 'I may watch it for a while… to check all is well.'

Egill grinned. 'That's why I planned accordingly!' He sat down and placed the basket on his lap, drawing out the flagon of Frankish wine and two bone cups.

'I thought we'd drunk all of it!' She laughed, surprised when the burgundy liquid splashed into the first cup.

'I kept one flask hidden. I saved it for today.'

Mila frowned. 'We should probably wait until the pottery has fired before we celebrate.'

'Absolutely not!' Egill blustered, pouring a large amount of the Frankish wine into both cups and thrusting one into her hands. 'You have worked hard and produced the best pottery this land can offer. If it fails, it will be because of the clay, and not because of you.'

Mila wasn't entirely sure of that, but she smiled at his confidence and nodded. 'Fine, let us celebrate the completion of our hard work.'

Egill nodded, then handed her his own cup to hold while

he bent down to light the fire. The dry tinder flickered with smoke and flame quickly. Soon they were sitting beside a roaring fire, and they had to nudge their stools farther back from the heat.

'Skol!' Egill declared, raising his cup. 'To Mildritha the potter. May she always be as wild and as resilient as this land.'

Mila sucked in a deep breath, which felt as if she were breathing in both smoke and sunshine. She raised her own cup. 'To Egill. I couldn't have done this without you!'

Egill beamed with pride, and he stole a quick kiss from her cheek before he sipped his own wine with a happy sigh.

They ate bread and cheese, even cooking some of the eggs and cured sausage in a skillet on the fire, and had a simple day of talking and laughing beside the flames, ensuring the constant blaze heated the kiln steadily. Egill even left their bed several times during the night to ensure a constant supply of fuel to heat the kiln.

Mila couldn't help the swirling hope building within her. If the pottery burned well, she wouldn't have to worry about her future—especially if Egill remained by her side.

Which she was beginning to believe he would.

Chapter Fifteen

The next day, after a leisurely *dagmal*, they went out to check on the now cooled kiln. Nervous excitement was bubbling furiously in Mila's stomach. So much so that she hadn't been able to eat much of the porridge Egill had heaped into her bowl that morning.

Egill took off his outer tunic and began to work at opening the kiln, first raking out the ash from the firepit and then gently opening up the tunnel to the pottery chamber. He stood up, holding some of the first pieces triumphantly. 'The loom weights worked!'

Mila nodded absently, her eyes searching into the darkness to try and see the back of the kiln. She had expected the weights to fire well as they were so small. But if she were going to make a successful livelihood out of her pottery, she needed the bigger pieces to be intact. She didn't wish for Egill to worry, though, so she took the weights and placed them in one of the baskets with a cheerful smile.

While admiring his handsome profile and the eager way he opened up the kiln, she noticed something moving in the distance behind him. With a frown she leaned forward, squinting at the rapidly approaching horse and rider galloping across the meadow towards them.

'Is that Master Hakon?' she asked, recognising the man

as having a similar build and blond colouring as her master, but not quite seeing his face clearly enough to be sure.

Egill turned and squinted at the rider. 'No...that's my brother Grimr. He must have arrived from Norway.'

Her heart began to race.

Why would Grimr come charging out to meet with them? Especially when they were only days away from returning.

'Do you think something happened—back at the hall?'

Egill shook his head, although he didn't have the same easy smile he usually wore, and he walked a few steps forward to meet Grimr as he approached.

Grimr was an intimidating man, handsome like Egill, but stockier and always with a sour look upon his face—which he wore now as he dropped down from his horse.

'Greetings, brother! How was your voyage?' called Egill, walking forward to embrace his brother with his usual cheerfulness. 'And how have you been? I presume—by your safe return—that Sigrid hasn't murdered you in your sleep. Have you managed to tame the vixen yet? And has King Harald been appeased by your marriage—is the feud between our families over?'

Grimr scowled as he hugged him with a half-hearted slap to his back. 'Yes, King Harald was appeased, and take care when speaking of my noble wife.'

'Noble?' Egill laughed, and then teased with mock severity, 'Ah, so you have made peace with her too. I am glad. I knew you were well-suited, even when you were ordering me to tie her up.'

Mila blinked at their odd conversation, but the Norse had odd ways. Most of the time they preferred to use jesting and boasting to communicate with one another.

Although, she was glad the marriage alliance between

Sigrid and Grimr had worked well in securing peace. Egill wouldn't be compelled to return to Norway if all was well.

Grimr gave a bad-tempered huff, and then his eyes shifted to Mila. He had the same piercing blue gaze as Egill, and just like his brother, he seemed to see something within the heart of her. His gaze softened slightly... with what looked like...*pity*. Her stomach lurched, and she clutched her skirts in a tight fist at her side.

Please let Wynflaed be safe and well!

'Is all well at the hall?' she asked, praying that no one had become ill or injured in her absence. She particularly worried about Wynflaed, who she knew would be working hard to cover Mila's weaving.

Perhaps she caught a sickness from overworking herself?

Grimr nodded. 'Everyone is well. But I have brought a guest with me from Norway.' His piercing gaze slid to his brother with a heavy look. 'A woman called Freydis.'

Egill's brow furrowed. 'Freydis?' he said thoughtfully. 'She lives up in the mountains, does she not?'

Grimr nodded slowly as if waiting for Egill to understand something. When he did not, Grimr said gruffly, 'She demanded I bring her here. She claims you made a promise to her...a promise to marry her.'

Mila's stomach dropped to her feet, and an icy chill swept through her.

Not again!

Her mind screamed with anguish, but she couldn't move or speak, her whole body freezing solid with a familiar dread.

Egill laughed as if it were a fine joke, but Grimr did not return his humour, and Egill's face fell. 'I barely know the woman!' He glanced back at Mila with an imploring look, as if he were caught in a snare.

Mila stared back at him in horror, even now believing the innocent look on his face, when she knew from past experience she shouldn't.

Men lie.

Grimr cocked a brow. 'Well, she says she knows you very well. That she helped you heal after your injury.' Grimr then tapped his head for emphasis. 'You weren't well then, brother. Do you recall anything from that time? Her caring for you, perhaps?'

Mila's world crumbled at that moment, because she saw the sudden realisation on Egill's face—as if a door had opened in his mind. Slow horror dawned across his handsome features, and Mila knew that he was realising who Freydis was.

'I vaguely remember a woman comforting me. Pressing cool cloths to my head and reassuring me that all would be well. I was so grateful to her...'

Egill's words came flooding back to her, swallowing all of the hope and joy she'd managed to build in the last few days. Her heart cracked like stone in her chest, falling apart in a blinding rush of grief. She swallowed hard, the shock stealing all of her reason and tears pricking the back of her eyes as she fought hard to keep her dignity intact.

Egill's head turned sharply towards Mila, as if he'd heard her heart split in two. 'I... I don't remember...' he said helplessly.

'Don't remember *her*, or the promise?' asked Grimr. Then, before Egill could answer, he added solemnly, 'To be honest, that is of little consequence. She is pregnant and claims it is your child. So it is up to you whether you decide to marry her or not.' Grimr placed a hand on his shoulder, drawing Egill's stunned gaze back to him. 'Is it your child?'

Egill looked as if he had been hit by hammer. 'I...do not know.'

* * *

Mila had heard enough. Slowly she crouched down, the weight of his confession dragging her to the earth. Despite the numbing coldness of her fingers, she began to dig out the entrance of the kiln. She couldn't bear to look at Egill a moment longer. If she did, she feared she would burst into tears and clutch at him like she had Dunstan.

Let me keep my dignity this time.

She had caged her emotions before, locked them away to deal with at another time, like the days after they'd been captured by a slaver. When she'd still been reeling from the grief of her mother's loss and the betrayal of the two men she'd relied on.

I will not weep now! she told herself angrily as she concentrated on lifting more of the loom weights out, carefully polishing them with a cloth and then placing them in the basket.

She could not stop. It was as if her body had to keep going, otherwise her shattered heart would stop beating entirely. Her hands did not feel as if they were her own, dirty from the soot and soil. She noticed every callus and scar as if it were her first time seeing them.

'Mila.'

Egill said her name softly, but she couldn't look at his face. She stared at his boots instead, widely planted in front of the firepit. They were fine boots, well made, with expensive fur trim.

They looked odd next to her, with her peasant hands scrabbling around in the mud... She had no right to claim him.

'It seems as if you are needed back at the hall, Master Egill,' she said slowly, careful to show no hurt or anger in her voice. 'Do not worry. I can manage without you. I only need to empty the kiln and pack the cart. The pony will do the hard work of carrying it all back to the hall.'

'Mila,' Egill urged again, dropping down into a squat so that he could see her face.

She stared back, hoping she had the strength to hide her crippling pain. Her vision blurred, and for a moment, she thought he looked a little like Dunstan. He'd had the same piteous look on his face when he'd handed her the loaf of bread.

'I do not remember her... Not in the way I should. Let me go speak with her...' he pleaded, as if he needed her permission to leave her. 'Perhaps there has been a misunderstanding?'

No, women do not forget promises...it is always the men that do.

Mila took a deep breath before forcing a tight smile. She had to remember to be grateful. It was a lucky escape, after all. She should feel...*free*...like a hare slipping out of its snare. 'If you are worried you have disappointed me, then please be reassured, Master Egill. I did not expect anything to come of our time together...' She paused, glancing at Grimr, who stood some distance away. He was deliberately looking away from them as if fascinated at the sight of the cabin. 'I wish you well with Freydis... You wanted a family, and she can provide that for you.'

'I want *you*, Mila.' He groaned, his hands reaching for her, but she shuffled away.

Glaring at him, she allowed her anger to whip out with one cold-hearted statement, hoping to silence him and set them both free. 'You are disappointed. I know that feeling well, and it *will* pass.'

Chapter Sixteen

Egill rode away from the cabin on Grimr's horse, determined to discover the truth about Freydis, but it felt as if he were leaving a part of his soul behind—the better part.

His heart and mind were torn into a hundred pieces and scattered on the wind. Grimr would stay behind and help Mila bring her pottery and supplies back home. He had insisted on that, and Mila had agreed obediently. Gone was the teasing, passionate woman Egill had come to know. In her place was a docile servant that kept her eyes low.

He'd done that to her.

With his careless words and broken memory.

How was it possible to father a child and not remember it?

But it was true. He barely remembered Freydis's face, and yet...some of what she had said to Grimr rang true.

I did seek comfort in a woman's touch...

But he'd thought he'd merely wept in her kind embrace, not bedded her! How could he? He'd barely been conscious...and yet there were huge gaps in his memory. He couldn't even recall leaving Ingvar's hall and making their way down to their boat, or their journey home. Days and nights had passed while Grimr organised an army to retaliate, but Egill did not remember them, only snatches of memories, foggy and incomplete.

Could he truly have slept with a woman and not remember it?

That seemed far-fetched, but not impossible. He grimaced against the wind and urged his horse forward.

Could there be a misunderstanding... Could she be lying?

He had never hoped to be deceived, but he wished it now, with all his heart. Perhaps her words would crumble under his questioning...and he could return to Mila before nightfall?

His heart leapt at the possibility, and he urged his horse forward. But a heavy lump formed in the back of his throat, because he knew without a doubt he had already hurt Mila. She had finally started to trust in him, and his stupid, weak mind had let her down.

If only he could remember the truth.

The sun was beginning to fade as he entered the hall. Everyone was feasting, celebrating the arrival of Grimr's ship. Sigrid sat beside her sister Alvilda, with Orla and Hakon at their high table. The benches were full of Grimr's crew, men he had known his entire life, but he barely nodded at their greetings as he strode to the back of the room.

Wynflaed moved into his line of vision. She was placing dishes down on the high table. Their eyes met, and his step faltered at the accusing look in her eyes. It could have burned a man down to nothing more than ash. But she glanced away from him and disappeared into the crowd.

He walked to the high table. 'Where is she?' he asked, his voice sharper than he'd expected it to be.

Hakon gestured to their chambers behind the hall. 'Resting in your guest chamber.'

Sigrid rose from her seat, a concerned look upon her face. 'The journey was hard on her... Be kind, Egill.'

Egill nodded, his jaw clenched tight. He did not want to be *kind*! He wanted to demand answers and free himself from this curse.

He walked past them, towards the private chamber behind the back of the hall. His guest room was more of an antechamber to the main bedchamber of his brother and wife. They had a large bed box in the centre of the room, while his bed and chests were sectioned off by the timber and tapestry screen.

On the bed lay Freydis, lying on her side, her hands tucked under her golden head, her knees drawn up to her large, protruding belly. She was definitely pregnant. Judging by the size of her belly, she could have easily fallen around the same time as their war with Ingvar…when he suffered his injury.

She was pretty, small and curvaceous, with long, glorious hair and full, pouting lips. Before he'd met Mila, he could well have imagined himself being attracted to her. But when he looked down at her, all he felt was panic and a suffocating sense of duty.

You wanted this! he reminded himself bitterly. *A family…a wife! A life of meaning…*

But this woman left him cold. He wanted Mila.

Freydis's eyes flickered, as if sensing his presence, and then opened wide to stare back at him. 'Egill!' she breathed, relief and happiness washing over her face at the sight of him, and he was sickened by his own lack of response.

A cold marriage beckoned…just like his parents' miserable life together.

Freydis struggled to sit upright, and he rushed to help her. She clutched at his arms with a limp and weary smile.

Groaning, she rubbed at her head. 'Odin's teeth! I still feel as if the world is swaying.'

Guilt rushed through him.

Poor Freydis. She'd crossed the ocean to see him, and he was staring down at her like a burden.

He sat down beside her on the bed and turned to face her. 'Freydis, I am sorry...but my head injury has affected my memory. I do not remember much from those days after Ingvar's attack...'

Her eyes widened and then narrowed with anger. 'You made a promise, *Egill Eriksson*! You swore before the gods that I would be married before this babe came!'

He opened his mouth to speak, but Freydis grabbed his hand and leaned in close, cupping his face with her hands, the anger shifting quickly into desperation. 'Please Egill! I cannot go back! I cannot! My father...he is so ashamed of me! You promised! Even if the worst was to happen—You promised!' Her bottom lip began to tremble, and her eyes filled with tears. 'I came all this way...'

Seeing her cry caused a memory to flicker like fragile candlelight in his mind.

Gentle hands stroking his cheek, a woman sobbing, and him whispering back, 'I swear by all the gods you will have a husband. I will not fail you.'

Dread and horror washed through him in a relentless downpour, capsizing all of his hopes and dreams.

'The child is mine?' He asked, stunned at the possibility he had fathered a child without even remembering it, and his eyes strayed down to the swell of her belly.

'You...don't remember?' Freydis asked, her voice fragile and quiet.

He didn't want to hurt her, but he couldn't start his life with her as a liar. 'I am sorry, Freydis, as I have said... I do not remember much of that time, and I cannot...' Pain crumpled her features, and he hurried to reassure her. 'I cannot lie to you. I do remember you, but only fragments. You comforted me and helped heal me. And I am grateful...' She began to gasp loudly, panic taking over her, until he hurriedly cried, 'I remember I did give you a promise. I am sorry that I forgot it before now and caused you worry. That you were forced to come here and remind me of it...' He took a deep breath, knowing that his words condemned him, but he was bound by duty and honour. If his word meant nothing, he was no better than Mila's father. 'I will honour my promise. I will marry you, Freydis.'

Freydis stared at him for a long moment, and then she began to cry, grabbing hold of his tunic with tight fists and sobbing into his chest. 'Thank you, Egill...thank you.'

Egill held her, his body heavy despite the emptiness inside.

He had wanted a family—to finally claim a path and life of his own. But he would never have imagined this...that he would fail Mila for the sake of his honour.

Egill swallowed the lump in his throat. His future stretched ahead of him like a slaver's chain, and he finally understood why Mila hated her debt.

It had been a long and exhausting day. Mila led the pony and cart into one of the barns of Orla and Hakon's home. Grimr walked ahead of her, carrying a torch to guide the way.

He wasn't a talkative man, had barely said anything to her all afternoon, and even less during their journey back to the hall. He seemed irritated to have been left with her, which she could understand. After all, the man had travelled across an ocean to see his brothers, and had instead spent his first day on dry land keeping her company.

She didn't mind his bad temper. She preferred it. Far

better to deal with her own heartbreak over Egill in silence and solitude. It was easier that way.

Brave Mila. One step at a time.

The memory of Egill's words was like a lash, and she swallowed down her tears for the hundredth time that day. She wasn't brave, she was broken...there was a difference, and she knew it well.

'I am going into the hall,' said Grimr. 'Unhitch the pony and see to it. Then come in for your own meal.' Grimr seemed to think for a moment before gesturing towards the cart with a jerk of his head and adding in a softer tone, 'Unpack it tomorrow, though. We can leave talk of *that* for another day.'

She nodded, bowing her head respectfully as he left.

That.

He meant the one pathetic basket of pottery she had to offer Master Hakon and Mistress Orla. The rest of it still lay within the kiln, mostly shattered. Very few pieces had fired correctly. The bowl she and Egill had made together was ironically one of the few pieces that remained intact after firing.

After untying the pony from the cart, she took it to an empty stall, and was grateful that someone had left a bundle of hay and a trough of water waiting. It was probably Wynflaed or Nora. They were the type to do such a thoughtful thing.

It made tears prick at her eyes, but she tried her best to banish them.

Not yet.

She couldn't allow herself to feel it yet. There was still more to do, endless chores and labour...the life of a lonely bondswoman. She grabbed her bedroll from the cart, ignoring the feather pillows and other fleeces Egill had used, and took her torch from the wall sconce.

A short walk across the stone yard and she was at the doors of the hall, the small door set within the much larger doors left slightly ajar. It glowed with a golden light around its edges, the murmur of voices from within floating out into the cold night. Normally the sight of it would have been welcoming, but Mila dreaded entering the hall—the faces of pity that might await her. She stopped a few feet away and stared at it with growing unease, unable to take another step.

How could she pretend all was well when everything had gone wrong...? Everything.

Even the parts of herself that she'd always presumed would remain safe had crumbled into dust. Love and trust had failed her again, and nothing remained...not even hope for a better future.

Mila sucked in a choked gasp of horror as the door slowly opened. She couldn't run. The light from her torch would give her away. And so she remained still. Caught in a web, she clenched the torch until the wood pricked beneath her fingers.

But thankfully it was a familiar and welcome face that appeared. 'Mila?' whispered Wynflaed, flying around the door quickly and closing it softly behind her, as if afraid someone might see Mila if it remained open for too long. She then ran towards her, arms outstretched. 'What happened?'

Mila could not hold back the flood of tears a moment longer, and she dropped her bedroll to the ground. Using her now free arm to grab her sister around the shoulders and pull her close, she sobbed into the nape of her neck as if she were a child.

'Oh, Mila,' breathed Wynflaed softly, reaching around to cradle her. 'It does not matter. We will find our own way in this world... Who cares about silly pottery? You never loved it anyway. It was just...all that we knew...wasn't it?'

Mila continued to cry, unable to voice the true reason her heart had broken into a thousand shards, like her pitiful pile of pottery.

'It's not just the pottery, is it?' said Wynflaed softly, clutching her tighter.

'No...' whimpered Mila, recovering enough to pull slightly away and swipe angrily at her tear-stained cheeks. 'I have been such a fool...*again*! Such a stupid *fool*!'

'You could never be that.' Her sister's eyes filled with sympathy, and she tilted her head towards the barn. 'Do you have any food left over?'

Mila nodded, sniffing away the last of her tears.

Wynflaed scooped up her bedroll from the ground with one arm. 'Come, let's break some bread and talk about it.' Wynflaed started striding towards the barn, and Mila gave one worried look to the hall doors before following her.

'Won't we be missed?'

Wynflaed didn't stop walking, and Mila had to hurry to keep up with her.

'No, I told Tyr that I wanted some time alone to speak with you. He owes me so many water duties, he'll be grateful to have one taken off his hands.'

Despite her misery, Mila couldn't help but chuckle at that. 'Why does he keep playing against you?'

Wynflaed shrugged. 'Maybe he likes the excitement of it? Life would be boring without risk...don't you agree?'

Mila's heart ached, and she knew her sister meant more by her words than commenting on Tyr's bad luck. But she wasn't sure what to say except, 'Is Egill in the hall...with Freydis?'

They'd reached the barn by then, and Wynflaed took the torch from her and set it in one of the back wall sconces beside the cart. She then threw her bedroll down before fixing Mila with a no-nonsense look that was clear and honest. 'Yes, and I don't like her.'

'Are they going to marry?'

Wynflaed threw some blankets down from the cart onto a nearby hay-bale and gently nudged her to sit. She obeyed, perching on top of the blankets and gathering one around her. Mila shivered, suddenly aware of how clammy her body had become. Her skin was as cold as a dead fish.

Wynflaed sat down in front of her, giving her a deep and careful look, as if she were trying to judge how Mila might react. 'Yes.'

Mila nodded, tears tumbling down her face, as if she could no longer stop crying now that she had allowed herself to start. 'There is some Frankish wine. In a flagon at the front of the cart. Let's drink it.'

Wynflaed frowned. 'We might actually get in trouble for drinking that...'

Mila shook her head. 'No, we won't. If there's only one thing I can rely on about Egill, it's that he's generous... *Idiotic man!* Go on, get it.'

Wynflaed gave her a sympathetic nod and was quick to grab the wine and food. 'So be it,' she said on her return. 'As always, we'll face the consequences together.'

A short time later, they'd spread out a feast of leftovers on a blanket in front of them and had drunk all the wine— with surprising speed. They had now started on what was left of the barrel of mead.

Nora poked her head into the barn. 'There you are!' she said cheerfully, placing her torch in another sconce.

'Come join us!' declared Wynflaed, slapping the blanket beside her. 'We have all manner of delicacies...and mead!'

Nora chuckled and joined them. She was short and curvy with long blonde hair. Because of the feast, it was uncovered and on display, the thick braid draped over her shoulder prettily.

Mila stared at her hair with a rush of sickening envy.

'Why are you frowning at me, Mila? Have I interrupted? I can go back to the hall if you prefer?' asked Nora, glancing at Wynflaed with concern.

Mila winced, not realising how easily her emotions had bled through into her expression.

I need to be more careful!

'No, ignore me! I am not in good spirits. The pottery was a failure.'

Wynflaed swayed slightly as she poured Nora a cup. 'She's refusing to admit her feelings—as always.' Wynflaed—who'd never handled her drink well, slurred as she pointed to Nora. 'I told her that Freydis looks a bit like you.'

'Ah...' said Nora as if understanding it completely. Mila wondered miserably if everyone had suspected she would fall for the handsome warrior on their short trip together.

Did they truly think her such a simple fool?

Except...obviously they were right, Mila thought grimly as she plucked at the blanket beneath her. She had to pretend as if it didn't hurt, and then eventually she might believe it.

'She has Nora's colouring and shape, but she is not as pretty. And she is far more emotional—spoilt almost,' Wynflaed grumbled. 'Not that she has any right to be. Her father is a farmer up in the mountains of their homeland...

You would think she was the daughter of a jarl the way she's been acting!'

Mila shrugged. She should not encourage people to think badly of Freydis. It wasn't her fault. Mila knew all too well how persuasive and tempting Egill could be. 'I think she is very brave…to come all this way, from so very far away, with nothing more than a hope for a better life. The voyage is not easy, and there was no guarantee that Egill would have kept his word.'

'Why should he keep his word? He does not love her. Surely a powerful family such as theirs can ensure both mother and child are well cared for without marriage?' Wynflaed argued, and Mila knew her sister would never have said such a thing if it wasn't for Mila's disappointment.

'He is honourable…and he made her a promise.'

Nora took the cup of mead Wynflaed offered her with a grateful smile before leaning forward to ask gently, 'That's what I don't understand. Why did he not keep his promise from the start? Or go back with Grimr? It's almost as if he's avoiding her…'

Mila shook her head. 'No, he had a bad head injury during the attack against Hakon. He told me himself before she arrived. He barely remembers the days of his recovery, but he did mention a woman tending to his wounds… He just didn't remember…*bedding* her.' The word brought bile up in her throat, and she took a deep gulp of her drink to force it back down.

She could not judge him for his past mistakes, especially when he had not judged her.

Nora's head tilted thoughtfully. 'Is he sure the child is his?'

'Oh! That is a good question!' declared Wynflaed, clapping Nora's shoulder in approval as if she'd made some insightful comment. 'Perhaps the child isn't even his! If that's the case, he wouldn't have to marry her, and he would be free to marry Mila!'

Mila shushed her sharply. 'Don't say such things!'

Wynflaed, who knew her better than anyone, frowned at her sharp reaction. 'But you love each other! It is plain for all to see! He has been courting you ever since he arrived!'

He has made a fool of me!

Humiliation rushed through her, and she recoiled as if she'd been slapped.

'No!' snapped Mila, the anger bursting out of her like a whip. She could not bear to admit another defeat. She had failed so much in such a short time, and she found herself denying the past week and a half as if it were a mere dalliance. 'Such nonsense! We do not love each other. We barely know one another. I had hope for something more. He is our master's brother, after all...but it was not meant to be, and I shall accept it. I am grateful that I was cautious with my heart, or I might have been more upset and disappointed than I am now—'

'*Mila...*'

All three women jumped at Egill's voice.

Chapter Seventeen

Egill winced at Mila's declaration, but he was also glad in a bittersweet way. If she truly did not love him, then his betrayal of her would not hurt as much, and only he would suffer the consequences of his injury.

But he could tell a lot of Mila's denial had been a show of bravery. She hated to appear weak, even around those she trusted. Her eyes were red from crying, and she looked pale in the torchlight. She did suffer—even if it was only with disappointment.

The shock of his arrival hardened into unrepentant resolve, and Mila's chin lifted a little as if daring him to question her words. She was right to deny him. He had no right to want her love. Not when he had agreed to marrying another pregnant woman only a short distance away.

Nora and Wynflaed scrambled to their feet and dipped respectfully at his presence, but Mila remained where she was waiting for him to speak.

Why had he sought her out? What could he possibly say to make this better for her?

'Mila, may I speak with you?' he asked quietly.

'We should go back to the hall...help clear up the feast,' said Nora, grabbing Wynflaed's hand and rushing out with her before even Wynflaed or Mila could make any form of protest. He didn't miss the way Wynflaed stumbled past him as if drunk, or the sharp glare she gave him—which he thoroughly deserved.

Mila stared at him warily as he approached and joined her on the hay-bales and blankets. He purposely sat opposite her a good arm's length away, but she still shuffled a little farther back, as if suspicious of his intentions.

'I insisted we share the supplies. Wynflaed and Nora are not to blame,' she said coldly, and it took him a moment to realise she was talking about the food and drink.

'I do not care about that,' he said dismissively, before adding with a weary sigh, 'That is not why I am here. I am here to apologise. I am so sorry...' He looked into her eyes and put all of his shattered emotions into the word. *'Truly.'*

Mila's expression softened, and she shook her head, wiping a hand across her face as if she were exhausted. 'There is no reason for you to feel bad. You owe me nothing. Thankfully, we were...*cautious*.' She coughed, as if the word had caught in her throat. 'At least now you can start your family with a clear conscience.' She smiled weakly. 'Imagine how much worse things could have been...'

Regret weighed heavy on his shoulders. He only wished he had convinced her sooner to accept him as a suitor. That way, they might even be married now. It would have been terrible, for Freydis, and guilt immediately churned in his stomach. He should not wish such pain on another—especially not the mother of his child. 'I suppose you are right. But I still wish things could have been different.'

'You made your promise to Freydis—before we even met. We...were not meant to be.' She began to twist the fabric of her skirt, avoiding his gaze.

Egill sighed and ran a hand through his hair. 'Loki is laughing at me. I do not remember laying with her. The promise, I only realised about it recently—and even that, I do not remember fully... I swear to you I would not have courted you if I'd known. I do not love her... You must know that.'

'Given time, perhaps it will come back to you?' Mila still refused to look at him—as if she couldn't trust herself to do so. But he would not make any more demands of her, not even to believe him.

Could he one day forget Mila and love Freydis instead?

'I doubt it,' he said.

'Egill?' a woman's voice called out from the doorway, and Egill stiffened, recognising it as Freydis's. She was like a barnacle, never willing to let him go.

'Freydis, I will only be a moment. Go back to the hall,' he prodded gently, not wanting to seem harsh, but also needing this time with Mila.

Unfortunately, Mila did not want to listen to him. She jumped to her feet and began to tidy the baskets and cups. 'Go ahead, Master Egill. I will clear up this mess. Inform Master Hakon that I will tell him all about the pottery in a moment.'

Reluctantly Egill nodded. He had not seen the rest of the pottery leave the kiln, but the weights had done well, so he'd been hopeful. Grimr had been too deep in conversation with Sigrid, so he'd not been able to ask him about it.

'Come, Egill,' said Freydis, her hand slipping around his.

Mila turned away from them, and he allowed himself to be pulled out of the barn. Torn between doing the right thing and following his heart.

A short time later, Egill was sat beside Freydis at the high table, feeling as wretched as a worm. Mila placed a basket in front of them and took three steps back. It was obvious she was drunk, and she swayed a little as she waited for them to examine the pieces. Hakon and Orla passed silent, worried glances between them, but were mercifully quick in their dealing with her.

'So, that is everything?' asked Hakon, looking down at the open basket that had many loom weights and a couple of smaller cups and oil lamps amongst them. There were no large pots, urns or flat-bottomed bottles, and Egill noticed with a heavy heart that even the bowl they had made together did not seem to have survived. It did not look hopeful, and guilt that he'd not been with her when she discovered it gnawed at his insides. He'd promised to help her, and when she'd needed him most, he'd not been there for her.

Mila nodded. 'I am sorry, Master. I tried, but this was all that baked successfully. Your neighbour Snorri is correct. Iceland's clay is too filled with the fire of this land. It will not set as it should. I can produce smaller items to save you buying them in from the merchants... But that is all.'

Orla's green eyes filled with sympathy. 'I am sorry to hear that, Mildritha. I know you hoped to make a living from it.'

Mila shrugged, a cheerful smile on her lips that seemed heavily forced. 'It cannot be helped. I wish to thank you for letting me try it, at least. I will make up for the lost time at the looms.'

Orla waved her hand dismissively. 'Wynflaed has made up for your absence, and you have provided me with some useful loom weights and new cups, which would have cost me silver to buy. I shall take off an extra ten ells from your debt...and I think you and your sister deserve a gift for your hard work. Perhaps you would like to spend the morning at our hot pool tomorrow?'

Mila dipped respectfully, 'Thank you, Mistress. That

is very kind.' She lifted the basket and moved back to the benches at the other side of the room, sinking with obvious relief beside her sister.

Egill understood how difficult admitting her failure would have been for her, even though it wasn't her fault... None of this was her fault.

His stomach churned with nausea for the hundredth time that day. It must have destroyed her to realise that her hopes for a livelihood in Iceland were ruined.

What would she do now?

'May I suggest,' Egill said loudly, drawing everyone's attention, 'that when Mila and Wynflaed's debt is repaid... if they wish it... I return them to Jorvik or perhaps one of the other trading ports? It would be no trouble, as I will be travelling back to Norway anyway...after my child has been born, of course, which should be around the same time as their debts are repaid. Mila is too fine a potter to give up her trade.'

There were a couple of condescending snorts from the warriors, who viewed pottery as one of the lowliest of professions. But Egill glared at them until they were silenced.

However, Freydis seemed the most horrified by his suggestion, as she quickly turned to him and asked, 'You want to return to Norway? Why not stay here in Iceland?'

'But...wouldn't you like to be close to your family? Your friends?'

'I will be happy as long as I am with you,' declared Freydis, wrapping her arm around his tightly. Egill quickly realised he was a horrible man, because he recoiled at the touch.

'I want us to marry here, with your family, as soon as possible,' she said in a rush of excitement, followed by a teasing, 'You have made me wait long enough!'

Had he?

He'd barely known Freydis before the attack. Sitting next to her felt strange and uncomfortable, like a badly fitted tunic that pulled at his neck and wrists.

Sigrid leaned forward. 'Perhaps tomorrow you could take Freydis to look at the golden waterfalls and geyser. I hear they are very beautiful.'

'Would you like to see them? I will take you if you wish it.' Grimr smiled at his wife lovingly, and Egill was so surprised that it took him a moment to realise that much had changed since he'd last seen them together. They'd fought like a cat and dog after meeting one another and being forced into an alliance.

But now they had not only accepted their marriage... but were happy.

'If you want to see something spectacular, we should take you to the Gullfoss waterfalls and the mushroom geyser! Afterwards we can go to Snorri's hall. He has a nice hot pool too!' declared Hakon. 'I can show you all that our land has to offer now that winter's chill has gone.'

Everyone was delighted by the suggestion and started to discuss their plans. But Egill stared down at the table and drank heavily from his cup. He could not bear to face Mila, see the betrayal in her eyes as he made plans to see the places she'd longed to visit.

'Perhaps,' he said thoughtfully, 'Mila and her sister could join us? Mila mentioned to me that she has always wanted to see the golden waterfalls and geyser.'

There was a worried exchange of looks from his brothers and their wives, but it was Freydis who surprised him by saying, 'Yes, they should come. Mila is a friend of yours, is she not? I would like to know her better, and perhaps she could keep me company while we travel... I doubt I can ride a horse or walk if it is far...'

Orla reassured her. 'We will take the large hay-bale cart, and if we stop at Snorri's hall for the night, we can enjoy the waterfalls for a little longer.' She then called towards the two sisters, 'Mila, Wynflaed? Would you like to join us as your reward instead of the pool?'

Mila and Wynflaed both nodded, trying hard to hide their own surprise at the offer. He knew it would be rude for them not to accept it, and when else would they see such wonders? Most thralls and servants spent their entire lives on the same parcel of land of their masters, never venturing farther than the port or market.

Egill hoped he was doing the right thing by offering them this rare opportunity. But then again, was he just making it worse? Was part of him unwilling to let Mila go?

Chapter Eighteen

The next day, the women climbed into the largest hay-bale cart for the journey to the mushroom geyser. A pair of strong oxen pulled the cart, and the men rode horses, leading the way.

Thankfully, Mila didn't have to look at Egill, except for his back, which gave her some comfort at least. She was sure that the previous night he'd heard her deny any feelings for him. She was glad of it, even though he'd seemed hurt by it at the time. She didn't want him to pity her—to offer her a loaf of bread as recompense and send her on her way as Dunstan had done. And that was what this trip felt like…recompense, for having her hopes and dreams burned to ash. At least if he thought there was no love lost between them, perhaps she could hold on to a little of her dignity.

Mila and Wynflaed sat on the front seat, driving the oxen forward with occasional flicks of the reins, whilst the wives sat inside the cart on hay-bales and blankets, eating apples and soft cheese with salted biscuits, and drinking flagons of spring water lightly sweetened with a berry wine Mistress Orla used for flavour.

Mila was glad of their position up front. It meant they were turned away from the women and largely forgotten about. There was only so long she could look at the pretty, luscious and pregnant Freydis without feeling some kind of resentment towards her.

But it also meant they could listen in on the wives' conversations. Even though Mila knew she shouldn't, she was too curious not to. Strangely, she wanted to know everything about Freydis, whilst also wanting to have nothing to do with her.

'Hakon mentioned your family live up on a mountain, Freydis. That must be hard work—to run a farm so isolated from everyone. It must be especially difficult in the winter!' exclaimed Orla conversationally.

Freydis chuckled. 'It is. My father and I kept sheep and goats up there—just us, with no other help. But now that I am to marry, Jarl Grimr has arranged for my father to come live at a cabin nearer the hall.'

Sigrid spoke next, her tone apologetic. 'I hope your father isn't too disappointed by the decision. That life suits Ragnar and his brothers better. It was too much for the pair of you to manage alone.'

'I agree!' declared Freydis, without a glimmer of ill will. 'But I would be lying if I said my father was happy about it. His family have run that farm for many years. He would not question the jarl's decision, of course, but he blames me for it regardless—and always will.'

'I am sorry to hear that,' said Sigrid.

Freydis did not seem concerned by her father's criticism of her, because she explained smoothly a moment later, 'Do not worry. I had already disappointed my father greatly—before the last Haustblót feast actually. Losing the farm made no difference to his feelings towards me. I have always struggled to manage it, and only did it to please him.' She paused for a moment, and then added brightly, 'I am so grateful to you, Sigrid. For convincing Jarl Grimr to allow me to come here. I don't think my father would ever forgive me if I delivered this child before marrying Egill. At least now he can be glad that I did *something* right.'

Mila couldn't help but wonder how things might have been different if Freydis hadn't come... Might they have married, as Egill wished?

Except Grimr would have still brought news of Freydis's pregnancy. So things wouldn't have been much different in the end. Egill would have left to seek the truth of it, and he would never have returned.

Would that have been better or worse?

Here, Mila was being forced to watch him marry another, but at least she understood why.

'Well, I am grateful you came,' said Orla kindly. 'I am nervous about becoming a mother. It will be nice to go through it with a friend.'

'*Friend*? You would consider me as a *friend*?' The question sounded so fragile and hesitant coming out of the usually forthright Freydis, and Mila almost felt sorry for her. If she wasn't going to marry Egill, Mila might have even pitied her.

Orla must have nodded, because Freydis said sweetly, 'I would like that...*very much.*'

A few moments later, Orla asked, 'I take it Grimr is settling in well as jarl, and you as his lady, Sigrid?'

'He is doing very well, and King Harald is pleased with our marriage...finally,' Sigrid replied with a weary sigh.

'I'm sure you will fall pregnant soon,' reassured the young voice of Alvilda, Sigrid's sister, who was little more than a child herself, and could not understand the struggles of women.

Mila knew of many women who made sacrifices and cast spells in a desperate attempt to become pregnant. Others prayed that it would never happen and fell quickly in spite of their wishes. It was a cruel force of nature that many struggled to control. She was grateful every day that nothing had come of her time with Dunstan.

However, Sigrid's response was surprisingly calm and relaxed. 'I fretted about it for a long time. But I am content now. Grimr has given me the confidence and reassurance to know that we will weather any storm together. We are partners, and my struggles are his. A child will come in time, or it will not. We shall leave it up to the Norns of fate to decide.'

'It took a while for me to fall,' said Orla, and there were murmurs of agreement that such things were uncontrollable. 'And honestly,' she added, 'I am glad of it. As you know, Hakon and I married under strange circumstances...'

Mila and Wynflaed exchanged a knowing smile, as they'd been among the few people to witness it. Their flame-haired mistress had marched up to the slaver's block, taken one look at Hakon beaten and bound, and immediately proposed marriage. Not because she was entranced by him—although later she would be—but because she needed a warrior to help protect her lands. Hakon had proven himself quickly, and had become a loving husband and a powerful protector.

Orla continued on thoughtfully, 'It was good to get to know each other first. Like Sigrid, we were strangers on our wedding day. At least you know Egill well already, yes?'

Wynflaed raised a brow deliberately in Mila's direction, but Mila ignored it. It was true that Egill had not once spoken of Freydis the entire time he'd been in Iceland. It was also true that both Hakon and Grimr seemed surprised by Freydis's pregnancy as well as Egill's relationship with her.

Perhaps their mistress was trying to pull on a loose thread?

Unfortunately, Mila knew the truth. Freydis was the woman who had comforted him during his recovery from an injury, and he had sworn a promise to her in thanks. Perhaps he had lain with her before that too? She knew from bitter experience that men could easily forget a woman they had bedded.

Freydis also seemed unconcerned by the comment. 'I only came down from the mountain for the feasts and festivals, but a lot can happen at a feast... How long until we arrive?'

Talk then turned to their journey, and less interesting topics. Mila was relieved. She didn't think she could stand to hear about their romantic relationship. The evidence was clear for all to see that it had been a fruitful one.

The group dismounted from their horses and cart a short distance from the golden waterfalls. Gunnar, as one of Orla's trusted men, was asked to stay behind with the animals, while they all walked the short distance to the edge of the rushing water.

The wide turquoise river carved through the rocky landscape like a mythical serpent pouring down from a giant ice sheet farther away. The rocks on either side of it were carved like giant steps, worn down from the weight of the water. The falling water looking like streams of white hair. A rainbow arched over the land and water like a bridge, glistening in the sunlight.

The rocky land surrounding the waterfalls was covered with emerald-green moss, and small puddles of water gathered from the mist created by the falls—even on sunny days like today.

Mila and Wynflaed took a seat on the ground, a little farther away from the rest of the party who wanted to get nearer to take a closer look. They were content to respectfully admire it from afar. The loud thunder of water was enough of a warning to keep their distance and enjoy the view.

The cold mist kicked up from the rushing water rained down on them constantly, and they draped their cloaks over their heads to stop them from becoming soaked.

'I cannot believe we gave up a morning in a hot pool to sit out in the rain—when it's not even raining,' said Wynflaed with a throaty laugh, and Mila smiled.

'The rainbows are pretty though,' she replied, gesturing towards the streak of colours above the waterfalls. 'I am glad we came. It is a beautiful sight—I have never seen anything like it.'

'True, I suppose it was worthwhile in the end,' Wynflaed grumbled, and then passed her an apple from beneath her cloak.

Mila took it gratefully, and bit into the crisp skin and tart, juicy fruit. 'I am glad to see it... What do you think of Egill's offer to take us back to Jorvik, or any other port?'

Wynflaed frowned, and Mila could sense she wouldn't like the answer. Neither one of them had mentioned it until now, which suggested they were both confused by it. 'I like it here. Jorvik, or at least our life in Jorvik...was miserable in comparison. We were always cold and hungry.'

Mila nodded in agreement. 'But we could have a fresh start. Be potters again... If we worked hard now, and exchanged any of our extra cloth for silver, we could buy better tools. Own a decent workshop and sell better pots. It wouldn't have to be like it was before—'

'With Father stealing from us?' Wynflaed asked dryly, nodding when Mila winced. 'That's what happened to our best pots, I bet. The ones he took to the other markets, the ones that *broke* along the way. I think even Mother suspected him of stealing the coin… I just presumed he spent it on drink… Not another family entirely.'

'We believed everything he told us. There were so many signs…and we still believed his lies.' Mila sighed, but tried her best to focus on the future. 'He won't be a burden to us this time around. We can work for ourselves, and ourselves alone.'

'True,' Wynflaed mumbled, looking less than pleased by the suggestion. 'But… I am a better weaver than I ever was a potter. I could not weave in Jorvik…not unless we had a small holding with some sheep, and even then…without menfolk, people might steal from us.' Wynflaed sighed. 'I hate to admit it. But we are vulnerable alone.'

Mila nodded thoughtfully; she'd suspected as much, but it was still a bitter blow. 'You wish to stay, then.'

Her sister nodded, but there was a crease of concern along her brow. 'I know…how hard it must be with Egill. But hopefully, he will buy land farther away—or go back to Norway. That would be ideal. You may only see him occasionally then.'

'But…what will we do? Once our debt is paid. Do you not have any other ambitions? Perhaps for a smallholding here? Under Master Hakon's protection? Nora could join us. I could tend the sheep, and you two could make cloth.' Mila was desperately clawing for something, anything that would take her away from a life that had no place or purpose for her.

'If that is what you wish. We shall try for that… But… I think Master Hakon would not approve of me leaving his looms to set up our own cloth production on his land.'

Mila had not thought of that. 'Perhaps… I could marry… and you could come and live with us?'

'Who? Bolli?' Wynflaed shrieked, her head snapping up

so fast the cloak momentarily fell off her head, and she had to scramble to recover it. Mila shushed her, looking around them, and noticing Egill wasn't that far away, looking out at the falling water. She hoped he couldn't hear them.

Mila leaned closer and whispered, 'What other choice do I have? I am not a good weaver like you... There is *nothing* for me here.'

'There is a life here for all of us.' Wynflaed gave her a hard look that reminded Mila of their mother telling her off. 'You can stay and weave with us.'

'I am not very good.'

'And I am not very good at milking that stubborn brown cow! But we all have our skills, and Orla won't mind if you prefer to do other chores instead of weaving.'

'I know...' Mila wasn't sure how to explain herself without sounding ungrateful or arrogant. 'I just wanted more... Independence for us...' She took a deep breath and forged onwards. 'I like Mistress Orla, but our lives depend on hers. I want my own life...my own home. Without pottery, my only other option is marriage.'

Wynflaed shook her head, her mouth falling open with shock. 'You would do that?'

'Wouldn't you? For your own home, there are plenty of farmers here that require a wife,' Mila argued, although the thought soured her stomach a little.

Wynflaed shook her head, staring out at the roaring waterfalls ahead of them. 'No. Marriage is another kind of bondage.'

'Not always. Orla and Hakon are happy together. If you marry the right man... Choose wisely with your head first,' Mila said, the realisation kicking her in the gut. 'That's where I went wrong before. I always let my heart lead, first with Dunstan and then with Egill. I need to follow my head in future.'

'Nora and I have vowed never to marry,' Wynflaed replied firmly.

'But—'

Wynflaed cut her off quickly with a resolute expression. 'We won't.' She then looked back towards the waterfall and the rushing water ahead. It gleamed and frothed with the colour of sapphires and milk.

It reminded Mila of Egill's eyes.

Could she ever love anyone else's eyes quite so much?

She doubted it, and it filled her with anguish that she'd so foolishly fallen again.

Another impossible match.

Mila tilted her head onto her sister's shoulder, realising something she'd never understood or spoken of until now. Recognising her own feelings towards Egill had allowed her to see her sister's better.

'You love Nora, don't you?' she asked quietly.

There was a moment of hesitation, and then a soft sigh of relief. 'Yes...'

'Does she love you back?'

This time there was no hesitation. 'Yes.'

Tears of happiness gathered in Mila's eyes. 'Then I am happy for you.'

Wynflaed reached for her hand and gave it a tight squeeze. 'I love you too. How about...we pay off our debt, and then use our extra ells to pay for a small cabin to be built near the hall. We would have Master Hakon's protection then, but we could live more independently most of the year. Only going into the hall for warmth when the winter gets very bad. Nora would like that. I am sure of it.'

Mila sighed. 'I will think on it.'

Wynflaed's voice cracked a little as she asked, 'You are not angry at us for keeping it from you? I don't want you to think we deceived you—'

Mila gathered her close and pressed a kiss against her cheek. 'You didn't keep it from me. I was just blind. As I was with father, Dunstan…and even Egill—to some extent.' He had not deliberately betrayed her, but she should have known that a man so opposite to her in every way could never be hers. 'I don't want to make the same mistake again.'

Wynflaed nodded. 'I understand. But you don't have to marry. You could live with us.'

'I know…' Mila nodded thoughtfully. Part of her wanted to say yes, to enjoy a life beside her friend and sister. 'But that's your life, your happiness with Nora. I want…a life of my own making.'

Wynflaed nodded. 'I understand…just don't go too far away.'

'I won't. I swear it,' replied Mila. There really was only one other option left to her.

Chapter Nineteen

After exploring the countryside and seeing many fountains, geysers, waterfalls and magical pools, they arrived at Snorri's hall and were welcomed inside to eat with the family.

'Why don't the women go and bathe before *nattmal*?' suggested Snorri cheerfully, who seemed delighted by his unexpected visitors. 'My pool is not as close as yours, Orla, but it is certainly bigger!'

Orla laughed at Snorri's competitiveness and replied with a teasing tone, 'If you say so, Snorri. But perhaps it is not as warm as mine *because* it is bigger?'

Snorri was good-naturedly outraged by the suggestion. 'Steam rises from it all through the winter! I even have a sauna built close beside it. I will have one of my thralls run and light the fire! Ingrid, my mother, and Dagny, one of my daughters, will help you.'

Ingrid and Dagny stepped forward and briskly took them into another chamber to gather soaps, combs and linen for the women.

'Wear these,' said Dagny, a tall and strong woman who looked as if she could wrestle with a bear and live to tell the tale. She handed them each loose linen shifts to put on.

Ingrid, a much smaller but equally fierce woman with

long ash-coloured hair wrapped around her head like a coiled snake, explained, 'We wear these down to the pool. Keep your cloaks with you, and we shall see that your clothes are cleaned. Do you each have something to wear for tonight's *nattmal*?'

All of the women nodded except Wynflaed and Mila. 'We do not, but leave ours. You do not need to worry about cleaning them,' said Mila.

Dagny did not seem pleased by this. She examined them closely with a scowl before admitting, 'I would give you some of our clothes, but mine are too long, and Ingrid's would be too short.'

'Perhaps one of your møther's dresses?' Ingrid suggested to Dagny, followed quickly with a chuckled, 'She was in between us in size.'

'Oh, please do not go to any trouble—' Mila could think of nothing worse than wearing the fine clothes of a woman so far above her station. Especially a woman that sadly no longer lived—judging by her lack of presence in the hall.

But Dagny gave a flick of her wrist as if dismissing any further argument. 'You are our guests. You two will also sleep on the floor in my chamber as you have no husbands to share a bedroll with.'

Ingrid nodded. 'Our Bolli speaks well of you, Mildritha. He will be glad that we cared for you and showed you kindness.'

Dagny thrust a bundle of linen, soap and combs into Mila's arms. 'Bolli is very dear to us,' she said firmly, as if to explain their kindness—which was far beyond what should have been granted them. Bolli's women folk were odd, but in a nice way, so Mila took the bundle meekly with a grateful 'Thank you.' She then walked to one of the benches against the wall and removed her boots and clothing before slipping the linen shift over her head.

'I think they like you,' whispered Wynflaed with a mischievous smile. She also had a bundle. 'But I am not complaining! Saves me washing my dress for another week!'

A thrall with a large laundry basket came over and took their clothes. Mila could well imagine they would be scrubbing at them for the next couple of hours, and she hoped they wouldn't dislike them too much for it. She made a point of thanking them as well.

The women left the hall through the main door, their cloaks wrapped tightly around them, their naked feet shoved into their boots for the short trip to the pool. All of their hair was loose, flowing behind them in waves of grey, red, gold and brown, like the seasons of womanhood and nature.

The warriors whooped and cheered as they passed, as if it were some seductive parade meant just for them. To everyone's amusement, Ingrid flashed a little of her leg as she passed, and Snorri gave a disgusted, 'Away with you, Mother!'

A couple of them were handed torches, and their procession walked out into the cold night air. The sun was little more than a milky glow that dipped just beneath the horizon. In the far distance, the grey sea stretched out endlessly, the Saxon Kingdoms of her birth invisible to the naked eye, as if they did not exist at all.

The stone path led them down through a pasture, and then onto more rocky terrain covered with thick moss.

'Be careful, it can be slippery around this part… I keep telling Snorri to put in steps!' said Ingrid as she began to walk down the rocky slope. There was a rope on poles staked into the ground, something for people to hold on to, and everyone took turns following the path, gingerly find their way down the slope to the stone floor.

'My husband, Snorri's father, first dug out this pool,' said Ingrid cheerfully as she reached the flat bottom of the slope and placed her torch in one of the braziers. It flamed quickly, and she then began to light little stone oil lamps and handed them to Dagny to place around the stone pool. 'It may look as if it were scooped out by Odin's hand. But let me tell you! It took many oxen and several back-breaking days to build this. We had to pull out the larger boulders and making a deeper pool. Building up the sides with just the right stone.'

Everyone admired it with murmurs of agreement and admiration, which seemed to please Ingrid.

A large, flat, circular area laid with stone surrounded the water, dropping down to another rocky, moss-covered slope below. A waterfall of gently steaming water came from the rocky far side, appearing to burst out of the rock face. There was also a bench, and a small cabin to the side, which was smoking lightly from the back. Mila presumed that was the sauna.

Mila began to follow the direction of the other women, placing their bundles on the bench and removing their boots and shifts. Orla's hall didn't have a sauna, so Mila and Wynflaed weren't entirely sure what to do. They shivered self-consciously as the other women stripped nude. She couldn't help but notice Freydis's belly was very large and round, the skin taut and covered in stretch marks. She could give birth tomorrow and Mila would not have been surprised.

They then all entered the sauna which was filled with hot air. It was tight inside, the wooden panelling creaking with the heat, but there were two levels of seating. 'I am not good with too much heat,' explained Orla as she sat down on the bottom level, while most of the others jostled to sit as high as possible.

Wynflaed and Mila sat beside their mistress, closest to the door, grateful for the draught that whispered in through the cracks. There was a small charcoal fire in the corner that emitted some light, but Ingrid's lamp placed on the floor by the door gave off enough light to see by. On top of the charcoal were some large, flat rocks, and Ingrid liberally sprinkled water on them with a bunch of birch twigs and woody herbs dipped into a bucket of water. The resulting swell of aromatic steam and smoke had Mila's chest tightening and her eyes streaming.

The women then began to scrub at their bodies with their soap, and she did the same. Sweat already beginning to bead on her skin and then drip off in rivers. The blunt, curved bone knives were passed around. They were used to scrape off the dirt and sweat from their bodies, and then were cleaned by wiping them on linen handcloths.

Mila gave Wynflaed a helpless look as the rest of the occupants appeared content to sit back and remain in the sweltering heat. Ingrid even muttered about it being a chilly day and threw yet more water on the stones. Then she poked the charcoal shards beneath with her twigs until they smoked and glowed.

'Sorry, but this is too much for my Irish blood,' gasped Orla, who had turned the colour of a beet, almost matching her red hair in brightness.

'You are not alone. I feel a little faint! I must be tired. Usually I love a steam bath!' gasped Sigrid, a little embarrassed as she picked her way down from the top seat. 'Stay if you wish, Alvilda,' she said when her little sister rose to follow.

'Maybe for a little longer,' Alvilda replied shyly, tucking up her feet and beaming with pride at the looks of approval from Ingrid and Dagny.

'I will join you in a moment. My legs are aching, and this feels blissful,' said Freydis, who seemed untroubled by the heat despite her condition.

'I gave birth to Snorri in here,' declared Ingrid with a pleasant reminiscing smile. 'It was a terrible winter, and it was the only place I felt warm and safe.'

Mila and Wynflaed had already leapt to their feet to allow Sigrid room to climb down before stumbling out into the deliciously cool air after her. They were followed shortly by Orla, who closed the door behind her. They all exchanged a look of blissful relief as the cold breeze hit their skin, and then giggled with mutual understanding.

'You well?' asked Orla gently, taking hold of Sigrid's arm with concern when she swayed a little.

'Are you?' joked Sigrid, nodding towards Orla's flushed face.

'No!' she replied, and they all began to laugh again. 'Come, let's cool off.'

They each took a bucket of water from the side of the pool and pulled up enough to rinse their bodies. After a few moments of rinsing, they were beginning to shiver again, so they each lowered themselves into the rocky pool with sighs of relief.

The water was hot, but not unbearably so. It felt pleasant after the fire and ice of the steam bath.

They swam around in the water until they each found a reasonably smooth boulder or ledge to perch on. By the time they had settled themselves, the others were out of the sauna.

Joining them shortly after rinsing to talk in the pool,

Freydis seemed blissfully happy, asking if such hot pools were common on Icelandic farms.

'Not all,' admitted Dagny, and then she seemed to fix her gaze on Mila. 'But Bolli lives close to the hot river, so he enjoys the heat from the springs all year round.'

Ingrid nodded with agreement. 'He has two such pools. He had to make another because he kept finding his livestock sitting in his bath! Such a sweet man, my grandson, strong as an ox, but as gentle as a lamb.'

Everyone laughed except Mila, who merely smiled politely. She had the feeling that an invisible Bolli was standing on a slaver's block, and his women folk were definitely trying to sell him to her.

After they returned to the hall, the men went for their bath. They were warned by Ingrid to not stay for too long as their meal was almost ready.

Dutifully they returned just after the women had dressed, and sat down for the evening meal.

'I should never have let you ladies go bathing first! Waiting for you is like waiting for Ragnarök!' said a bad-tempered Snorri as he and the other men marched in from their bath and had to hurry to the antechamber to dress.

'Oh, should I throw your meal to the pigs?' asked Ingrid cheerfully. 'I am sure they would appreciate it better.'

'No need for that!' grumbled Snorri, stomping his boots through the hall while wearing only his linen shift, his hairy legs unfortunately on display for everyone to see. The shifts were a little more revealing on the men than they had been on the women. They had all decided against wearing cloaks too, in a strange show of masculine strength against the elements.

The other men followed, and many of the women

whooped and cheered in the same teasing manner they'd received earlier. The men either laughed or flexed their muscles for greater cheers, and even the warriors that hadn't gone bathing joined in.

It wasn't long until everyone was dressed and sitting down for their evening meal. The firepit blazing in the centre of the room. The high table was filled with Snorri and his family, as well as Orla and Hakon, who were considered honoured guests—as Hakon was a *godi*—an elder of Iceland—and Orla was the only woman to have a vote in the island's assembly.

The rest of them sat on long tables and benches around the narrow fire trough in the centre, with all the guests muddled together. Thankfully, Mila was sat next to Sigrid and Wynflaed. However, Freydis sat opposite her with Egill next to her. Mila comforted herself in the knowledge that at least she didn't have to face Egill directly or break bread with him, so she was grateful for that mercy.

Mila took care to spread a linen cloth over her lap, trying her best to protect the gown she wore. 'I hope I don't drop anything on it,' Mila whispered to Wynflaed, who nodded in agreement, checking the draping of her own cloth.

'I'm going to avoid the mutton soup...less chance of spillage,' she whispered.

'Good plan. I will do the same.'

The dress was the finest she'd ever worn. The shift beneath was a deep ocean blue that must have cost a fortune in labour and dye to make. On top, she wore a bright yellow apron dress, with gold turtle brooches connected by a string of colourful glass beads. The jewellery alone could have paid off her debt, but the apron dress was also trimmed with Byzantine gold silk and embroidery. It was obviously a treasured heirloom.

Wynflaed wore a similarly beautiful gown in shades of green, although her brooches were iron and her beads painted stone. It was clear who Ingrid and Dagny favoured, and Mila squirmed under the implication.

'You look pretty tonight, ladies,' said Snorri as he took a seat at the high table. His gaze lingered on Mila before he looked at the rest of his female guests. 'It seems the Eriksson brothers are constantly surrounded by beauty. Tell me, Mila, how was your pottery in the end?'

Mila flinched, knowing that she would face his amusement and ridicule as he'd been the one to question her initial plan.

Egill spoke before she could even open her mouth. 'There was some success on smaller objects. Oil lamps, loom weights, crucibles...all useful items, I am sure you can agree.'

Snorri frowned and fixed his piercing gaze on Mila. 'Enough to make a living?'

Before Egill could say anything, Mila answered quickly with her head held high. 'No. Not enough for that. A few small items, nothing more.'

'Ah,' said Snorri with a nod of understanding, which was not as smug as she might have imagined it to be. 'At least you tried. That must be a comfort to you...otherwise you might have always wondered at what might have been.'

Mila's mouth dropped open in surprise at Snorri's kindness, and it took her a moment to gather her wits. 'Yes... that is true. Thank you for saying so, Master Snorri.'

Snorri shrugged. 'My Bolli said much the same thing to me when we last spoke of it. It is a shame my son Bolli is not here.' He turned and pointed towards Egill with his horn of ale. 'He could have wished you a hearty congratulations on your upcoming marriage. I am sure he will be pleased to hear of it. You may not have been here long, but you are well-known and admired on the island. I believe there are many who will want to wish you well on your wedding day.'

Egill's jaw flexed, and he stared down at his meal with a sour gaze. 'When the time comes, I am sure we will invite most of Iceland. You and your family are all welcome to attend, of course.'

'When will it be?' asked Snorri. 'Before or after the birth of your child? I would wager you do not have long either way.'

Freydis nodded, the colour high on her cheeks and her eyes eager. She searched Egill's face as he began to eat his meal. 'I would like it to take place as soon as possible...the next Frigga's day, perhaps? To have the goddess's blessing?'

Egill coughed as if struggling to swallow his bread. 'As you wish.'

Freydis frowned at his lack of excitement, but then smiled brightly as she turned back to the high table. 'Next Frigga's day, it is!'

The entire hall lifted its cups and horns of ale. Mila did the same even though her arm felt heavy.

'Skol!' cheered the crowd.

Chapter Twenty

Egill stood outside his brother's hall two days after their return from the feast at Snorri's hall. He stared at the dipping sun with a growing sense of dread. It rose and fell relentlessly without any hope of him changing his fate.

Frigga's day…his *wedding* day…was less than four days away. Tomorrow the festivities would officially begin.

How had that happened?

Just over a week ago, he had been dreaming of a future with Mila. Now they were like strangers, never meeting, barely speaking more than two words to one another.

Freydis wanted him, was desperate to rekindle their connection, but he felt like a lying coward in her presence. To distract himself, he'd helped to prepare for the wedding entertainments in whatever way he could. Working alongside Mila had obviously rubbed off on him, and he could no longer sit idly by while there were chores to be done.

Knowing the feasts would require plenty of fuel, he'd taken the hay-cart to the north-eastern beaches to collect driftwood. Unlike his homeland, Iceland didn't have large forests, and many of their trees were small and bushy. Most of the Icelanders' fires were fed on the huge quantity of driftwood that landed on their beaches, or the peat and turf they dug up. Driftwood was easily replaceable, unlike turf, and so he and Grimr had gone to fetch as much as they could carry in the hay-cart.

Which was a significant amount, judging by the surprised look on Orla's face when they returned late that afternoon. Grimr had gone to spend some time with Sigrid and her sister in the hall, and had suggested they leave the unloading to Hakon's men.

But Egill did not want to go into the hall. He didn't want to see Freydis's hopeful face or Mila's disappointed one. He had failed everyone, including himself, and worse, he continued to do so, even when trying to do the honourable thing.

Perhaps he should call off the wedding?

Throw aside honour and duty to do as he wished, and marry Mila. But could he break his vow to Freydis? Abandon the woman who had stayed by his side in his darkest moment? Could he forgive himself for such a crime... *and could Mila?* She would not want him to hurt another woman, especially not a pregnant one.

So instead of facing his bride, he spent the rest of the afternoon chopping and stacking the driftwood in the nearby log store.

'Greetings, brother!' said Hakon, who came out of the hall and stood beside him, admiring the now much smaller pile of unchopped driftwood. 'You have made good progress.'

'I was hoping to be done by sunset,' grumbled Egill.

Hakon shrugged. 'You chop, and I shall carry them to the store...if there's any room?'

'Some... After I filled it, I started stacking them on top and to the side.'

His brother chuckled with amusement, but with a nod began to pick up the chopped pieces from the ground. When

Hakon straightened up, he said quietly, 'You don't have to do it...marry Freydis. We will support and look after her, whatever you decide. She and the child will want for nothing.'

Egill's chest tightened painfully. 'I made a promise.'

Hakon nodded with understanding. 'But you made that promise when you were badly injured, and you barely even remember making it, according to Grimr. I wasn't there after you were hurt, but Grimr said you were confused for days after.'

Egill frowned. He didn't like his brothers discussing him behind his back. It reminded him of when they protected him as a young boy. He was no longer a child. If anything, Freydis's arrival proved it. 'I made a promise...that much I remember. Would you have me break my word? Dishonour our family name, and become an oath breaker?'

Hakon, with a pile of wood in his arms, raised a single brow and said, 'If it makes you happy? Then yes, I would support you in your decision.' He turned then and walked over to the wood store.

Unsure of what to say or do, Egill rolled a log towards him, and began to swing his axe, cutting into it with heavy chops.

When Hakon returned, Egill's anger still hadn't cooled, and he muttered between clenched teeth, 'Of course *you* would say that! You gave up your jarldom for a woman... but remember *you* had Grimr to pick up the pieces of *that* decision. I do not!'

Egill regretted the words as soon as he'd said them, and stopped what he was doing to turn and apologise.

To his surprise, Hakon seemed untroubled, and Grimr now stood beside him with a deeper scowl than normal on his face. Grimr was quick to speak. 'I feel the same as

Hakon. You should not marry her if it will make you unhappy. I had hoped that being around her again would return your memories. Perhaps make you understand why you offered such a promise in the first place—'

'She is carrying my child.'

'Perhaps,' said Hakon with a shrug. 'I remember she was also friendly with Frode at a lot of the feasts and gatherings.'

Egill frowned. He wasn't sure if he remembered who Frode had flirted with, he wasn't close with the warrior. 'Frode died during Ingvar's attack.'

'Yes,' said Grimr with a thoughtful look. 'He fought off Ingvar's men as they ambushed our boats. If it wasn't for him cutting our ship loose from the dock, we might not have made it out alive... Is that why you feel indebted to her? Could the child be Frode's?'

Egill shook his head, dismissing the suggestion. 'You are saying that because it is *convenient*, but I still made a promise to Freydis.'

Grimr muttered a bad-tempered curse and began to break up some of the smaller pieces of driftwood with his bare hands. 'What good is a promise if it leads to misery for all?'

'Of all people, I would not have imagined *you* to say such a thing,' said Egill, horrified that his loyal brother, who valued honesty and honour above all things, would suggest he now throw away his!

'You do not love her,' Grimr said firmly. 'We all know how a loveless marriage ends. We saw it with our parents, and I would not wish the same for you.'

Hakon nodded. 'Agreed.'

Egill slammed the axe-head into the cutting block and turned to face them. 'Neither of you loved your wives when you married them. Love came after, as it might with Freydis and me.'

'It might have...' Hakon agreed, 'if you were not already in love with—'

'Freydis!' Egill half yelled her name as she stepped out of the hall doors. He was desperate for her not to hear the next damning words of his brother.

She smiled hesitantly, probably surprised by his over-enthusiastic welcome. Sometimes his older brothers were blind idiots when it came to subtlety. They desperately rushed into action, taking the axe and wood with embarrassing speed as if they'd been caught stealing eggs from the henhouse.

'I was just...coming to tell you that *nattmal* would be served soon,' she said, glancing in confusion at the odd behaviour of his brothers.

'Great news! We'll be done with this soon, and then we shall come and join you. Go inside. There's a chill in the air,' Egill said, offering her a bright and reassuring smile. She returned it with a happy expression and left.

Turning to his brothers, he said sharply, 'No more talk of such things, understood? It is *my* life, and I will do what *I* judge is best for *me*.'

They nodded in uncomfortable agreement, and the three of them worked on, finishing their task as quickly as possible.

After *nattmal* everyone settled into groups and either played games or talked amongst themselves.

Egill played a dice game with Freydis in a corner not far from the rest of the women, who were working the looms.

After her absence, Mila was keen to make up the loss of

her time weaving cloth, so she had decided to use the light of the nearby fires to work.

Unfortunately, Wynflaed's and Mila's looms happened to be near where Egill and Freydis were sitting. She was sure Egill probably hadn't noticed their presence. His back was towards them, and he had settled there well before she went to work.

'Are you sure you want to stay in Iceland?' Egill asked Freydis softly, and Mila was certain it was the first time she'd seen him talk privately with Freydis since their trip to see the waterfalls.

As Mila checked the threads with the comb, she prayed Freydis would want to return to Norway and never return.

'I prefer it here,' replied Freydis. Wynflaed gave Mila a sympathetic look as Freydis's voice carried over to them, as sweet as birdsong.

'I am tired of my father. I love him, but recently, I realised a horrible truth—he's been using me my entire life,' said Freydis bitterly. 'I cook and clean for him. I tend to the animals all by myself on that cold, miserable mountain, and he has never once thanked me! Has actually refused every man who has even shown the slightest bit of interest in me, saying that they are not good enough. I know the truth now—he never wanted me to leave—never wanted me to live my own life! When he heard I was pregnant, despite knowing all that I had done for him over the years, he told me he was disappointed in me. *Me!* I took great delight in telling him that you were the father of my child. I knew he could not refuse you or shame me for my choice. You are greater than him in every way! You are the son of the great Jarl Erik Eriksson, brother to Mighty Jarl Grimr and Hakon the Wise. Your family rules the very mountain he lives on. I am finally free! I can finally begin my own life…with our child.'

Egill nodded sympathetically before asking hesitantly, 'But are you sure you want to do the same again here? Farm and tend animals? It won't be much different from living with your father.'

Freydis shook her head with a laugh. 'I would not mind the work if it was for the good of myself and my children, and I know you would be a good husband, not lazy like my father or bad-tempered. I am sick of being lonely on that mountain! I want to be surrounded by people and joy!' She grinned as she looked around them at Hakon and Orla's hall. 'Perhaps your brother could help us find a parcel of land to farm. I was speaking with Orla, and she said she recently inherited a lot of land but had to give some of it to Snorri and other landowners to ensure their loyalty. Perhaps we could buy some from them? Or come to an arrangement? I think this would be the perfect place to settle, especially when you can have hot baths in the middle of winter! At home I would have been exhausted just carrying and heating the water for a simple barrel bath. But here the rivers and springs are already hot!' She laughed. 'Please say we can have a farm with its own hot pool, like Snorri and your brother have.'

'I will try my best,' answered Egill, and Freydis threw her arms around him with a squeal of excitement that made Mila's stomach clench with jealousy. She was appeased only slightly when she saw the awkward way Egill unpeeled himself from her. He never seemed comfortable around his ex-lover, and that gave her some comfort—even though she knew it was spiteful of her.

'Let's go speak with Hakon and Orla,' he said, rising up and turning to help Freydis to her feet. As if some invisible thread connected them, Egill's eyes found Mila's, and for a moment she forgot how to breathe. Could only stare with longing at the man she had once hoped to call her own.

'Yes...let's do that,' said Freydis loudly, and Egill broke the connection with Mila first. He busied himself with taking Freydis's arm and walking with her towards where Hakon and Orla sat.

'Did you hear that?' Wynflaed hissed, dragging Mila's gaze back to her. 'She's *lying*!'

'What?' asked Mila, more shaken by the caring manner in which Egill had spoken and guided his betrothed away than anything else.

'She said that her father was disappointed with her *until* she told him that Egill was the father of her child.' Wynflaed grinned, spreading her hands in front of her as if she were offering Mila some great prize. Nora moved closer and stood beside them, blocking them from the view of others. It was a technique they had used often to hide their gossiping.

'So?'

With an exasperated sigh, Wynflaed explained, 'Do you remember her speaking to Sigrid on the journey to the waterfalls? She said, *"My father has been disappointed in me since before Haustblót."* That's the Norse festival celebrating the end of summer and the beginning of autumn!'

Mila rolled her eyes. 'So?'

'Sigrid's marriage to Hakon was meant to take place the week *after Haustblót*! So Freydis had disappointed her father with her pregnancy *before* the attack! But Egill was meant to have slept with her when he was recovering from his injuries. It doesn't make sense, unless...' Wynflaed leaned in close to whisper, 'Freydis was already pregnant before she slept with Egill...or...she *never* slept with Egill at all! You said he was wounded and couldn't remember that time well. Perhaps Freydis made it all up?'

'Oh, you are clever!' whispered Nora excitedly. 'I bet she did!'

Wynflaed nodded, accepting the complement as if it were her due. 'So... Freydis disappointed her father by becoming pregnant by some...other Viking,' she said with a dismissive wave before poking Mila in the chest with her finger. 'And afterwards, she took advantage of Egill and claimed the child was his! He has no reason to marry her!'

Mila swallowed the information slowly, as if it were a shard of broken pottery. 'Except...he made a promise. He does remember *that*!'

'But she's lying!' hissed Wynflaed indignantly.

Nora nodded. 'She's right. You should still tell him.'

Mila sighed. 'It won't make him change his mind. You don't understand... To him, a promise is a promise. He has to keep his word.'

'When have men *ever* kept their word?' said Wynflaed with obvious disgust before adding, 'Anyway, it doesn't matter. *For once* you can use it to your advantage!'

'Egill is different. He would not break an oath, and what good would it do anyone to tell him this? It could ruin their future together.'

Wynflaed threw up her hands in defeat, and Nora said quietly, 'But...even if it *doesn't* change his mind, he should know the truth from the start. Otherwise he could blame and resent her *and* the child later on.'

Wynflaed gave the parting blow. 'Wouldn't *you* want to know the truth? Even if it hurt?'

Mila sighed. 'Fine, I will talk to him.'

Wynflaed let out a deep sigh of relief before she grumbled, 'Finally, good sense has prevailed!'

Chapter Twenty-One

Three days before his wedding and the hall was filled almost to bursting with wedding guests. Many had resorted to sleeping in the hay barns or had set up tents in a nearby pasture.

'Why are there so many people?' asked Egill in disbelief, when he noticed more unfamiliar faces arrive. 'They barely know me, and many of them have never even met Freydis!'

Orla chuckled and gave his arm a consoling squeeze. 'They do love an excuse for a celebration. Snorri must have put the word out far and wide, telling them that it will be a big celebration. I suppose I owe them a feast, considering I married Hakon so quickly and without much ceremony.'

'Still…it's a lot of people to manage…' moaned Egill, his stomach twisting and his chest tightening with an aching pain that seemed to grow worse with every day that passed.

'All will be well,' Orla reassured him.

But Egill's apprehension remained. He couldn't sleep at night, just lay beside Freydis wondering how his fate had changed so completely on the turn of the dice. He searched his mind and the fog of his memory trying to find the reason for his promise, to remember the moment he had apparently lain with her.

Only blackness stared back at him.

He couldn't stomach the thought of lying with her—thankfully, Freydis hadn't initiated anything between them either. But when he tried to remember that first time, he couldn't. The memories were as intangible as smoke, with no thought or meaning.

The touch of her hand, the kindness of her voice, his weeping as he struggled to concentrate. She had been kind to him in his weakest moment, and he had clung to her to save himself from drowning in the darkness. But when he looked at Freydis now, he couldn't fathom how he had slept with her, and certainly not why he had made such a ridiculous promise... Only that he had.

Of all things to forget, why couldn't he have forgotten that?

Thankfully his brothers had not questioned him since their ambush yesterday, when he'd been chopping driftwood, and they'd urged him to go back on his word. But doubts still tormented him, and Mila's dark brown eyes watched him wherever he went, reminding him constantly of what he would lose.

When he did sleep, he dreamt of Mila, and it sickened him that he would betray the woman he had vowed to marry—the mother of his child—for another. He'd not remembered his oath before. He could be forgiven for that. But now he remembered, and he should not yearn for Mila. If he could have cut out his heart to stop it beating for her, he would.

He was brought back to the present by Orla's pondering, 'Feeding them will not be a struggle. Especially as many of them brought gifts of food and drink. But I do wonder about how we are going to entertain them... I would prefer to leave the big feast until after you are married.'

Egill wasn't sure if he could sit around for another three

days, eating and drinking and slowly waiting for the day of his wedding to come. He wanted the uncertainty and doubts to end. Once he was married, his fate with Freydis would be set, and he could accept his new life fully. Until then, the waiting would be unbearable...

'How about some games?' asked Orla thoughtfully. 'I think our neighbours might enjoy that, especially if we give out some prizes?'

'That sounds a good idea,' he replied, quickly adding, 'I will take part and help set up anything you need.' He needed to keep himself busy.

'Thank you, Egill!' Orla said cheerfully. 'I will go and find Hakon, ask him what sort of games and challenges we should organise. Let me know if you think of anything too...'

Egill nodded and went back to staring at the horde of wedding guests walking around his brother's home, like flies on a corpse cheerfully buzzing around, oblivious to his misery. They waved happy greetings and wished him good fortune with his marriage.

They were looking at him, but not truly seeing him. The only person who truly saw him was Mila. Whose sad eyes matched his own.

He was both surprised and relieved when Mila came out of the barn and approached him. Usually she would have avoided him at all costs, but today she strode with purpose as if she'd been looking for him—or at least waiting for him to be alone, which was rare these days.

'Egill...' she said, and then seemed to lose all confidence, because her face became flushed and her expression turned hesitant.

'Are you well?' he asked, concerned. She had not sought

him out once since the night of Freydis's arrival. 'Is there something wrong?'

'I am fine,' she said, and then she took a deep breath as if to brace herself before jumping into deep water. Releasing it in a rush, she said, 'I need to tell you something...well... not really tell. It's more of a thought, really...it might not be true...and really it is not my place to tell it...you might think I am being deliberately unkind...which isn't true...' She sighed as her words failed her.

He looked around him at the passing people. 'Should we speak more privately?'

She nodded, and then she lifted her hands. He realised she was carrying four empty buckets. 'Will you help me fetch water from the stream?'

It was the perfect excuse for them to be alone together. 'Yes, of course.' He took two of her buckets, and they began to walk. Their long strides ate up the ground and took them away from curious ears.

'What is it?' he asked when they arrived a few steps away from the stream.

Mila sat on a nearby boulder, placed her buckets at her feet, and then looked up at him with soulful eyes. 'Are you sure the child is yours?'

Egill stared back at her, unsure of how best to answer. He was damned either way, so he answered honestly. 'She says it is. But I do not remember bedding her. I swear it. Otherwise I would not have...courted you as I did.'

She nodded. 'But...do you think she is telling *you* the truth?'

His earlier doubts and what Hakon had said about Frode niggled at the back of his head. 'Why do you doubt her?'

Mila squirmed under his gaze and then said briskly, 'It is something she said to Sigrid... It contradicted something she said to you last night. Perhaps, I misheard, or misunderstood...' She looked up at him then, her jaw lifting with sincerity. 'I do not say this out of jealousy, or with any ill will towards Freydis...'

'Go on,' he said firmly, folding his arms in front of his chest, anything to stop himself from going to her. He desperately wanted to touch her, to comfort her, but also himself—knowing that holding her close would soothe him.

Mila's eyes dropped to her feet. 'She told Sigrid she had disappointed her father before the Haustblót feast... That was before Ingvar's attack and your injury. If you hadn't bedded her before the attack, then why was her father already disappointed in her?' Mila's gaze rose to meet his, and she sighed wistfully. 'It doesn't matter, though, does it? My telling you this...you still made a promise.'

He nodded, the pain so raw and thick in his throat that he couldn't bring himself to speak.

Tears gathered in her eyes, but she blinked them away, brushing off invisible dirt from her skirts and getting to her feet with her buckets in hand. 'Let's fetch the water, then, and not speak of it again.'

Finally he found the courage to speak, and his voice sounded husky and desperate. 'I wish I had not made it... the promise...but... I did, and I must stand by it.'

Her back was stiff, her shoulders low, as she answered softly, 'I understand, and I am sorry... I should not have spoken of it—I do not wish to cause trouble. I just...thought you should know.'

As they walked back with buckets full of water, they were met by an impatient-looking Freydis, who put a protective hand over her belly at the sight of Mila. It was a sharp reminder of his future obligations. He only wished he were happier about it.

Freydis scowled at Mila. 'That is not work for a jarl's brother. You should have asked another thrall to help you.'

'I offered to help,' said Egill firmly, hating how rude Freydis had become towards Mila recently. She glared at her often and spoke sharply to her when she served the meals. Had Freydis heard his brothers talking about him being in love with another woman, and she'd then assumed they'd been speaking about Mila? He hoped not, but it would explain her recent change in attitude towards her.

Egill flinched at the turn of his thoughts.

Did he love Mila?

Surely it was too soon for that? Yes, he had cared for her, courted and wanted her. But...*love*?

Freydis called to a passing servant, who happened to be Wynflaed, 'You! Come help Master Egill with the water.'

Egill stiffened with anger and snapped, 'I said I would do it!'

Freydis flinched as if he'd struck her, and then her bottom lip began to tremble.

'Freydis, I am going to take this inside, and then I will help you with whatever you need,' he said softly, hoping to ease her distress after his harsh tone.

Tears filled Freydis's eyes, and her golden head gave a sharp nod as she turned and hurried back inside the hall.

Wynflaed approached. 'Are you sure you don't want me to take them?'

He shook his head. 'No, I said I would do it, and I will.'

Afterwards he went in search of Freydis, who sat on the guest bed in the antechamber, wiping tears from her face with a small linen cloth. Immediately he felt like the worst of men and went to sit beside her. He hated to see women cry, even more so when he was to blame.

'Freydis, I am sorry for being sharp with you, but you have to understand...' He sighed, unsure of how to explain himself.

'You like her.' Freydis sniffed. 'Have you lain with her? Could she be carrying your child too?'

'No, and...my memory is fine now. I would not forget.'

Freydis's shoulders remained stiff despite his reassurance. 'Do you love her?'

'No,' he said quickly, not wanting to upset Freydis with matters that neither of them could control. 'We must look to the future.'

'Yes.' She nodded, gripping his hands and clutching them tightly. 'I am sorry. I was jealous... I know I have no right to condemn you—'

'Of course you do,' Egill said solemnly. 'Even if I do not remember...our time together. I can understand your anger and hurt that I would have forgotten it...'

Freydis shook her head and stood up, wiping at her face and forcing a bright smile. 'Not at all. Come, let's find out about the games Orla is planning. It looks like it's going to be lots of fun!'

Chapter Twenty-Two

'I can't decide! There are so many contests to choose from!' declared Nora with a shake of her head as she poured steaming stew into bowls, and then placed them on trays for Wynflaed and Mila to serve.

Mistress Orla had just finished announcing the contests before the evening meal, and the entire hall was buzzing like a beehive with excitement. Mostly because of the prizes. There were bolts of Orla's cloth, and bags of silver and fat piglets brought over by Grimr. Hakon had a finely made axe that he'd smelted himself. All prizes that were coveted by everyone in the hall, both high and low.

Wynflaed laughed, rearranging the bowls on her tray so that she could take more. 'Well, you don't have long to decide. It all starts tomorrow after *dagmal*.' She lifted the tray of bowls easily with one hand and walked over to the tables to begin handing them out.

Tyr was busy filling jugs of mead from a nearby barrel, and he shrugged. 'What is there to decide? You can only do the craft contest, and that's one of the last ones.'

Mila didn't like his assumption that women could only take part in the craft contest. But it was true that most of the contests were designed for the men. However, she was particularly sore about the craft one—especially considering her recent pottery failure. It didn't leave her with many options. 'I think I could do well in the barrel run... You don't need to be strong for that, just have a good sense of balance.'

Nora nodded enthusiastically, 'And the foot race. I could do that...and Wynflaed would be good at *hnefatafl*—that only needs wit and cunning. She's got plenty of that. You don't actually have to be a warrior for some of the contests.'

'You think a serving-woman could beat a jarl or a seasoned warrior at *hnefatafl*?' balked a man a few feet away from them. He was one of the farmers from the north, and he hadn't looked sober since he'd arrived yesterday.

Nora's confidence disappeared under the weight of his harsh tone, and several curious eyes turned towards them. Mila gently took the last bowl from her and placed it on the tray, turning back towards them and blocking Nora from view. 'My sister is good at games. If the mistress allows it, I don't see why we can't take part.'

'Why would they allow their thralls to join in?' snorted the man as she walked past. 'Your sort are only good for one thing.' The smack on her bottom was hard, and she winced with pain and stumbled a few feet with the force of the blow. The bowls wobbled and a little of the stew slopped onto the tray, but thankfully none fell.

'Not so good at balancing after all!' declared the man with a nasty cackle, and many of the surrounding men laughed with him. Mila vowed to serve them last, and as she concentrated on readjusting her tray back onto her shoulder, she noticed the sudden silence that descended over the hall.

Mila turned back to the man, wondering what had caused the change in mood, and was surprised to see that the man was now pinned to the table. His neck and shoulders pressed down by Egill, who must have sprinted from his seat at the high table to arrive here so quickly.

The man mumbled something garbled from the table, his jaw so firmly pressed into the wood he could barely speak.

Egill spoke for him. 'You are a guest at my celebration. But even guests are not allowed to strike a woman of this hall. Apologise, or I will take the hand that caused such offense!'

The pressure must have eased a little, because the man was able to raise his jaw up slightly. 'I am sorry. I thought she was a thrall!'

'It doesn't matter what she is! I still demand an apology!' roared Egill, thrusting the man so hard against the table he began choking from the pressure.

If Mila were completely honest, she didn't mind the man's discomfort. After all, he had assaulted her, and although a slap on the rump or a pinch of the hip was common at feasts, she'd always hated them. Thankfully she didn't suffer from them normally as Mistress Orla frowned on such behaviour, but at big feasts, it happened more often. Mainly because the servants were too busy to run complaining to their mistress over every minor insult.

But Egill seemed furious, his face was flushed, his jaw tightly clenched and his eyes filled with hatred. Mila quickly became aware of how dangerous the situation had become, as men around them carefully moved their hands to the hilts of their weapons.

'He's apologised. You should let him go, brother,' said Hakon slowly, his voice commanding, but also calm and reasonable.

Grimr stood up a few feet away and said gently, 'I am sure he will promise never to do it again.' He spoke as if he were trying to soothe his brother's temper. Which was strange in itself. Egill was usually the negotiator, the voice of reason—not Grimr.

Egill slowly lifted his hands, and the man jerked away to wipe some spittle from his chin, looking shocked and humiliated. Not far from how Mila had felt moments before. It was a satisfaction she tried her best not show. She merely nodded meekly when the man gave a swift promise not to bother her or any of the other servants again.

To ease the tension, she placed a bowl of stew down in front of him and carried on swiftly down the table, handing them out.

Every single person made a great show of thanking her politely.

Egill strode back to his position beside Freydis and took a seat. She stared at him with open dismay. He ignored her, opening and closing his fists repeatedly on the table as if to ease the rage that had consumed him moments before.

Mila flinched at the cold and condemning look Freydis sent her way, but she could understand the woman's anger. It must be humiliating to have your betrothed protecting another woman's honour—especially one he was known to have courted.

Sighing, Mila went back to her work, trying her best not to think about how Egill's behaviour might reflect badly on her.

Would they think she was his?

And how would that make poor Freydis feel? When she was due to marry him in only a couple of days? Unlike Wynflaed, she felt no real malice towards Freydis. She'd been in a similar position herself. She couldn't condemn her for forcing Egill to make good on his promise...even if it made Mila miserable.

It all felt so *wrong*!

Mila set down the last of her bowls, not realising who she was serving until a kindly voice asked, 'Are you hurt, Mila?' Bolli was staring up at her with an expectant and compassionate gaze.

'I'm fine. Thank you, Bolli.'

Bolli nodded. 'Sit next to us if you wish...when your work is done. There is plenty of room.' He elbowed his sister, who nodded in agreement, shifting slightly away to demonstrate there was indeed space.

'Oh, yes...and I have been meaning to speak with Orla for a long time. Come take my seat whenever you are ready.'

'And mine, for your sister,' said his grandmother cheerfully. 'I'm sure we'll done eating by the time you've finished serving this lot!' She waved about the packed hall, and the many tables that still needed serving.

'Yes, I will be a while. Thank you for the kind offer,' Mila said with a chuckle. She had been about to politely refuse, but after the incident with Egill, she didn't wish to burn her bridges...especially one that might lead to security for herself and Wynflaed in the future. 'I will come as soon as I can.'

Bolli seemed delighted by the prospect. 'I am going to compete in the wrestling... Will you cheer for me?'

Mila nodded. 'If you wish.'

Snorri gave a loud cheer of delight, drawing all eyes to them. 'Bolli will be a hard man to beat, especially with pretty Mila championing him!'

Mila cleared her throat, trying her best not to seem foolish, despite the blush heating her cheeks. 'In return... I hope you will cheer for me in the barrel run?'

'Of course!' Bolli shouted with a raise of his cup, and his entire family loudly agreed. Mila had to admit that Bolli's family were incredibly likeable, and even Snorri had his moments of charm.

Should I consider him? For when my debt is paid?

There were certainly worse paths, like the horrible beast who had slapped her. She went back to work feeling an odd mixture of gloom and hope. She did not want to marry Bolli, but she was also a practical woman, and she doubted there were many more options open to her.

A kind, honourable man with a farm of his own was not a match she should dismiss easily. But as she walked away, she caught the sour look of Egill staring at her, as well as his sad-looking betrothed at his side, helplessly trying to gain his attention. Embarrassment, shame and finally anger washed through Mila in waves.

How dare he judge me for this? He is about to marry someone else! I must let my mind guide me...not my foolish heart.

Chapter Twenty-Three

Wynflaed bit her lip and stared at the stone board in front of her. Mila held her breath for the hundredth time since the match between Wynflaed and Grimr had begun, but eventually Wynflaed moved her stone king forward.

Grimr leaned closer, scrutinising the board, as it was now his turn to move, and then with agonising slowness he moved his pawn, advancing slowly on Wynflaed's king. The crowd around them muttered in approval or dismay, depending on the wagers they'd placed.

Mila's own nerves were stretched thin, and she placed a hand on Wynflaed's shoulder, silently offering her support. Her sister reached up patted her hand, and then gently placed her king piece down in surrender. 'Jarl Grimr, thank you for an exciting game and for letting me face my defeat with dignity.'

The crowd cheered with approval, pleased that their man had won—as many had bet on Jarl Grimr winning the contest. However, Wynflaed and Grimr had battled many opponents to finally face each other, and Mila was proud of her sister despite her losing the final match.

Jarl Grimr had proven himself a formidable adversary, his skill and tactics unquestionable. His wife placed a kiss on his cheek. 'Well done, my love! I am delighted with the bolts of cloth you have won for us!' she said, and her little sister Alvilda squealed and clapped in agreement.

Grimr smiled and gave Wynflaed an approving nod. 'You were an excellent player, Wynflaed. You have a talent for the game... Keep the board and pieces. I want you to practice—for the next time we play.'

Wynflaed's eyes bulged. The board and pieces were intricately carved treasures. She had never owned anything of such value, but Mila knew she would never sell them—despite the amount of silver she could get for them.

'Thank you, Jarl Grimr... That is very kind of you.'

As Wynflaed got up and carefully put the pieces back inside the box beneath the board's square top. Nora and Mila took it in turns to give her hugs of congratulations.

'It's your turn next,' Wynflaed said, nodding towards Mila.

Mila groaned and rolled her eyes. 'I am already regretting my decision!'

Nora laughed. 'You can't be any worse than me!' Nora had unfortunately come last in the morning foot race.

'You would have come second if Sten hadn't pushed you over!' snarled Wynflaed, and she glared at the man from across the room.

'Stop it!' hissed Nora. 'You will get us in trouble! And what would we have done with a piglet anyway?'

'True...' Wynflaed's ill humour fled her expression, and she nudged Mila in the ribs. 'But a silver chalice...*that* we could sell. Pay off all our debts in one go!'

Mila nodded enthusiastically, but she didn't feel as excited by the prospect as she should.

What will I do when I am free? Join my sister or marry?

She wasn't even sure if she was ready to make such a

decision. But for Wynflaed and Nora's sake, she would try her best.

'Well, don't be disappointed if I fall off straight away!' she laughed. 'Come, let's go.'

All the hall and its guests had to walk or ride out to the nearby river for the next three contests, as they needed plenty of space and water.

The river was one of the cold ones flowing down from the mountains, but it was deep and slow enough for the barrel balance. Everyone moved out with baskets of food, blankets, and the crafts many were still working on to enjoy the afternoon's entertainment.

Mistress Orla, Sigrid, Alvilda and Freydis sat down on a blanket beside them, while Bolli and his family sat a few feet away. Deliberately, Bolli greeted her with a smile, and his family all watched with obvious glee at her polite response. Mila felt as if she were a hare surrounded by hungry foxes.

Unfortunately, she had to wait a long time for her challenge as it was the last one of the day. She sat with Wynflaed and Nora and watched the men prepare for the axe-throwing and archery contests. The targets were placed on the opposite riverbank, straw figures with red hearts painted on their chests.

It was reasonably wide in this stretch of the river, and some of the men lost their axes in the water. They had to wait until everyone had thrown before they could wade into the water and retrieve their weapons. It was a double humiliation that most men took well, either with a laugh or a loud curse at the wind.

Hakon was the only man who hit the target in the centre of its red heart, but a few men managed to hit the straw body, including both of his brothers.

'What is the point of giving out prizes if you win them all back!' declared Snorri with a bad-tempered huff as Hakon was handed a fat piglet. He raised it proudly to his adoring crowd, petting it afterwards as if it were a kitten.

Sigrid raised a regal brow at Snorri. 'Then you Icelanders should try harder. Nothing comes to us easily. Odin taught us that. He gave an eye for wisdom! All you need to do is win a simple game.'

'Hmm,' growled Snorri, who never liked to be challenged, but he seemed to grudgingly accept her point, because he said decisively, 'I will take part in the next toga honk!'

There was some good-natured teasing by his family and friends as he strode towards the next challenge.

'I have to see this!' declared Sigrid, getting up with many of the others to go and watch. All were curious as to how Snorri would do against much younger men.

Bolli stayed behind, as did Freydis, Nora and Mila, which she didn't realise until too late because she'd been busy trying to untangle some threads from Nora's latest effort to win the craft challenge—a disastrous attempt at nalbinding a pair of colourful socks.

'Remind me again, what is toga honk?' Nora asked, frowning at Snorri, who was now lying on his back with his feet up in the air, waiting for his opponent. Several other men were doing the same.

Bolli chuckled but took his time explaining, 'Two people lie on their backs, their feet pressed against each other. They both hold the end of a rope placed between them. It has a central mark. Whoever can pull the mark over to their side is the winner.'

Freydis smiled at him. 'Is your father any good?'

Bolli shrugged but nodded. 'He is…but I am better.'

Freydis laughed but said with an admiring look, 'I can imagine you are...don't you agree, Mila?' she asked pointedly, and Mila felt as if Freydis were pushing her towards Bolli with invisible hands.

She nodded in agreement. 'Why not join the competition? If you win, Snorri can't complain the Eriksson brothers win everything.'

Bolli shook his head. 'I would prefer to save myself for the wrestling tomorrow. Besides, this is one of the few games the brothers are not competing in... I suspect that is why he entered. My father is a cunning man.' Bolli grinned at his own judgement of his father.

There was a cheer as Snorri beat his opponent and shouted for the next. Freydis and Mila laughed as Bolli gave them a secretive wink. 'See...he only enters fights he knows he can win!'

'My Egill will be competing in the wrestling tomorrow. Are you sure you want to face him? Or should you follow your father's example?' teased Freydis.

Mila was surprised that Egill would take part in the wrestling. It suited men built like Grimr and Bolli far more. But then, Grimr had played the strategy *hnefatafl* game, so perhaps she was wrong to make presumptions about their strengths.

Bolli merely shrugged. 'I imagined he would enter. Especially after my father announced I would be taking part.'

He glanced at Mila, and she looked away. Did he believe Egill had only decided to enter to prove something to Mila? She had to admit she had wondered the same, and rather than being flattered, she felt sick at the prospect. She did not want to be fought over, especially by a man who was already betrothed to another.

'I hear you are neighbours to Orla, Bolli. Do you have a

large farm?' Freydis asked casually, her amusement dipping after the look Bolli had given Mila about Egill.

'It is a good size. I own the land around the hot river, plus some meadows and barley fields to the east. A hundred sheep, twenty cattle. My farm is a good size, and of course, combined with the power and influence of my father, we do well here.'

Freydis exclaimed loudly, 'That is most impressive, Bolli! Do you not agree, Mila?'

Mila nodded with a weak smile. She felt as if she were being sold to again.

'And the hot river! What is that like?' asked Freydis, seeming to have a genuine interest this time.

Bolli explained in detail about the landscape around his home, the hot pools and springs, the danger as well as the benefits of his land. Mila was convinced that Freydis had started the conversation to encourage her to considering him as a potential match. But as they talked and laughed, exchanging stories of both their homelands and the striking differences and similarities between them, Mila began to feel more like an outsider in their conversation. Not that she minded. She concentrated on untangling Nora's threads as she listened to them speak.

Freydis knew a lot about farming and livestock. She even gave Bolli tips on growing vegetables in rocky soil and harsh winters. They laughed about the strange temperament of sheep and the stubborn cows that enjoyed his hot pool, knocking over every fence he'd built until he surrendered it to them and built his own bath.

Mila was beginning to realise that Freydis would make a far better wife to Bolli than she ever could. She knew nothing about farming. She'd grown up digging clay out of riverbanks and selling the simple efforts of her labours in market stalls. Even now, she could barely weave enough cloth to pay her debts.

'And your sister mentioned you had children. Are they with you?' asked Freydis cheerfully, glancing around them with interest.

Bolli laughed, looking a little embarrassed as he confessed, 'Yes, but my sister tends to indulge them whenever we get together as a family, and I barely see them.'

'I would love to meet them,' said Freydis, and then pointedly looking at Mila as she asked, 'Have you met them before?'

Mila had been so distracted by her own thoughts that it took her a moment to understand the question, and the answer only filled her with more doubts and embarrassment. 'I...ah...a long time ago, I think...'

Bolli's smile turned brittle, but he shrugged. 'You did... before my wife died...'

Freydis's expression fell, and she reached over to touch his arm, drawing his attention. 'I am sorry. That must have been very difficult for you.'

Bolli smiled, patting her hand gently. 'Thank you, but it is best to always focus on the future, and not linger too much on the sadness of the past. Especially when you have children... Ah, there they are!' he said with a grin, pointing to Dagny, who was walking towards them with three children in tow.

Mila remembered them then, three russet-haired children with blue eyes and sweet smiles. Her stomach churned as they ran over. The oldest boy hadn't seen more than ten winters. The youngest, a girl, had seen only around five or six. They were quicker than Dagny, and they tumbled into their father's welcoming arms with excited squeals.

'Let me introduce you to my children, ladies,' said Bolli

proudly. 'My eldest son, Bolli the younger—we call him Bol—then Tormund, and finally Sigrid.'

'Sigrid? Jarl Grimr has a beautiful wife called Sigrid, and you, sweet girl, are just as pretty,' declared Freydis.

Little Sigrid giggled with delight and then said shyly, 'Hello, Mildritha!'

The adults stared in confusion at the child's obvious mistake, and Bolli the younger quickly explained—with the authority of an eldest child. 'Papa said you were kind and beautiful. He wants you to become our—'

'That's enough, Bol!' Bolli interrupted his son quickly, a flush running up is neck. He said sheepishly, 'You are mistaken. This lady...' he pointed at Mila '...is Mildritha, and this lady, who is also very beautiful and kind, is called Freydis. She is betrothed to marry the jarl's brother, Egill.'

The children, especially little Sigrid, did not seem impressed by the revelation. Nausea rolled in her stomach, and she cringed under their innocent gaze.

Of course they were disappointed. How could she be a mother to them? She could barely look after herself. They deserved someone who wanted to be their mother, not some cold-hearted woman who only wanted to have feather pillows in her bed!

Freydis's voice interrupted her thoughts for a second time as she spoke to the children. 'It looks like your grandfather is about to battle in the final contest of toga honk. Shall we go and cheer him on?'

'Yes please!' declared the children, and they all walked over to watch Snorri's final match, leaving Mila alone with Bolli...on purpose, probably, judging by the encouraging smile Freydis and Dagny gave her. Nora had been dragged away too, but she gave Mila a guilty look, obviously sorry for not staying behind.

When they were out of hearing, Mila couldn't keep silent a moment longer. She turned to Bolli, feeling more resolved when she saw the hope in his eyes.

'I have considered your offer, and... I am sorry, but I cannot accept it.'

Bolli's face fell. 'My children are good. They just... misunderstood...'

'No...and please do not worry about that. If anything, your children are too good for me. I cannot accept them—because they deserve better. Someone with a heart that is open and loving. My heart...it is broken... I cannot offer them what they need, and it would be selfish of me to believe otherwise...' She struggled to find the words to explain. 'I do not think I will be happy with you...and because of that, I know I can never make you or your children happy either.'

'Mildritha, please reconsider. I know you have been... *disappointed* by Egill, but there is a lot that I can offer you.'

'I know you can, and I don't want to seem ungrateful.' She tilted her chin up. 'But I have made my decision.'

Bolli shook his head as if denying her words. 'I once felt as you do now. Heartbroken, but it was my children that gave me strength to continue. Their love that gave me hope for a better future when I thought all was lost. I will not give up on you, Mildritha, and you...you should not give up on yourself either. There is *always* a chance to find happiness again, but you must let it in—and give love a second chance.'

Mila's eyes filled with tears, and she fought to find the words. How could she tell this sweet man that she'd already given love a second chance? That it had already failed her more than once?

A cleared throat drew their attention to Freydis only a

few feet away, her eyes wide and her mouth slightly parted in awe. 'Sorry to interrupt, but your children...they want you to come and watch the match.'

'I'm coming,' said Bolli, and after a gentle smile towards Mila, he hurried away.

Freydis stared at her for a moment in confusion before she shook her head and said coldly, 'You are a fool.' Without another word, she walked away.

Yes. I am a fool, thought Mila hopelessly, but she couldn't mislead Bolli and his family by accepting him. That would be cruel.

Chapter Twenty-Four

Hakon was still cuddling his fat prize as Egill lined up with his family to watch the barrel run.

Grimr raised a golden brow at the piglet. 'Remind you of anyone?'

Hakon jiggled the squeaking bundle of wriggling pink flesh. 'Of course! It looks just like him!'

'Who?' asked Orla, confused.

'Baby Egill!' Hakon and Grimr both declared at the same time, and Egill rolled his eyes at their ridiculous sense of humour.

Orla and Sigrid laughed, and Egill gave them both a horrified look. 'I was a delight!'

'You cried all the time,' grumbled Grimr. 'You had to be held every waking moment.'

Orla's brow wrinkled with suspicion. 'Or did your brothers insist on holding you, Egill? Hakon, do put that animal down! Only Loki knows why you are cradling it like a babe. We might need to eat it come winter!'

Hakon clutched the piglet tighter to his chest, looking appalled. 'No! This will be my prize sow! You will see. She will birth a hundred piglets every year!'

'I hope for *her* sake she doesn't!' grumbled Orla.

Hakon grinned. 'You don't want a hundred babes from me?'

Orla shook her head in horror. 'One or two, yes, but don't wish a hundred on me!'

'Or me, Grimr! I am happy with the current one...' said Sigrid, and her hand strayed to her belly with a shy smile.

Everyone stared at her in confusion for a moment, until a grinning Grimr pulled her close and declared proudly, 'It is still early, but we think Sigrid might be with child.'

Immediately everyone burst out into jubilant congratulations, and Sigrid was covered in hugs and kisses. Laughing, she tried her best to hush them. 'Please shush! Do not tell Alvilda yet. I do not want her disappointed if nothing comes of it. I just thought it might be best to mention it now. In case you have any advice for the tiredness and sickness, Orla? I want to delay telling Alvilda until I am certain.'

Orla nodded. 'Do not worry. We won't say anything. But you might want to eat little and often. I found that helped with my sickness. The tiredness... Try to take naps whenever you can. I am sure we can distract Alvilda whenever you need to lie down.'

Sigrid sighed with relief. 'Thank you— Oh, where is Freydis? I should have told her as well.'

Egill hadn't been thinking about Freydis for a long time. In fact, most of the day he had tried to avoid her, and it seemed to have worked, as she was nowhere to be seen. He glanced around at the thick crowd along the riverbank. 'She's with Bolli and his family,' he said after a moment, pointing her out.

Freydis also noticed him, and with a wave she hurried through the crowd to reach them—much to Egill's dismay. Unable to help himself, Egill searched for Mila amongst the surrounding group of Bolli and his family. But he couldn't see her anywhere, not even with Wynflaed or Nora.

'This sounds like a fun game! I have never heard of barrel running before!' declared Freydis as she joined them.

Hakon nodded. 'It is a little odd. Tyr invented it one midsummer festival, and it's become a bit of a tradition.'

'So...people stand on the sides of a barrel...in a river?' asked Freydis, gesturing to the men up to their waists in the water who were currently keeping a barrel steady in the water.

'Yes, and then each challenger gets on top and tries to make it to the other side of the river.'

'How?' laughed Freydis. 'Do they have an oar?'

'Watch,' said Egill, strangely losing patience with her questions as he became increasingly frustrated by his inability to find Mila's face in the crowd.

Where had she gone?

A man clambered onto the barrel using a plank from the riverbank. Once he was firmly standing on its side, the plank was pulled away, and the men either side of the barrel released it. The man tried to roll the barrel with his feet, but fell into the water less than a heartbeat later.

'Not many manage it,' said Hakon with a deep, rumbling laugh.

The contest continued much the same with hoots, cheers and laughter from the crowd as each man stepped onto the barrel and promptly fell off it again, straight into the chilly water below. The losers were made to hold the barrel for the next person.

'Tyr looks to have gone the furthest,' said Grimr. 'No wonder he invented the game!'

Hakon laughed. 'True, but he only managed halfway.'

'Surely there are no more people?' Egill sighed, frowning up at the sky. The sun hadn't set, but it was beginning to paint the sky in splashes of reds and pinks.

Grimr wrapped his arms around his wife. 'The tents

are up, and the bonfires are lit. I am looking forward to our night outside—in the wilds of nature.' Grimr wiggled his eyebrows suggestively and then pressed a kiss into his wife's neck.

Sigrid giggled and swatted at his arm before giving a loud yawn. 'I think I will be ready for bed straight after dinner. I am exhausted!'

Egill laughed at the look of dismay on his brother's face, but when he turned back to see the next competitor, his heart leapt into his throat, because it was Mila that stepped out onto the barrel.

She was only wearing her shift. But she'd looped it through her legs and tied it to her belt to create a billowy pair of trousers. It left half of her legs on display, and many of the men were giving loads cheers of approval at the sight. Enjoying the arrival of those shapely limbs rather than cheering for Mila's brave attempt at the contest.

'What is she doing!' snarled Egill, and Freydis looked up at him with a glare.

'She is free to do whatever she wishes.'

'But she will hurt herself! And for what? A miserable chalice!'

Grimr scowled at him in disapproval. 'It is a fine prize, made of pure silver. It could easily pay off her debt and that of her sister.'

Egill glared at his brother, but he knew he spoke the truth.

'You are not her master,' muttered Freydis bad-temperedly. 'Let her do as she wishes.'

It was a stark reminder that he was embarrassing himself.

He was behaving like an idiot!

He clenched his jaw tightly to stop himself from saying anything more.

Mila wobbled a little as she climbed on top, then dropped to the planks of the barrel on all fours. The crowd roared with laughter that she'd stumbled before the men had even let go. But after a moment, she reached out with her arms and stood up again, balancing on her bare feet on the wood.

It was an interesting technique that not all men had used. Some had kept their boots on for better grip. Others had kept low, while others had done as she was doing. None of them seemed to have done particularly well regardless. To his surprise, it was Tyr the current champion who was holding Mila's barrel, and he was taking great care to keep it steady while she readjusted her feet.

Good. Otherwise Egill would have been the first to reprimand him.

It was then that Egill recognised the other man holding the barrel, and it made jealousy roar in his veins, because it was *Bolli*. He'd not even competed in the barrel contest previously, but he'd still stripped off his tunic and strode into the water to offer Mila his help. The lack of a tunic seemed particularly unnecessary...

Mila gave a little nod, her face sharp with concentration as the men stepped away from the barrel and she began to step lightly back and forth in a dancing motion. The crowd began to roar with encouragement, but rather than race to the other side, she allowed the barrel to float her gently downstream. She only took light steps to readjust her balance. It was a clever technique.

Mila was used to working with nature, and she allowed the river to carry her with little effort. When she reached the halfway point, she danced a little faster, the barrel swaying dangerously from the movement, but somehow, she managed to stay upright.

She was farther across than Tyr, but she still didn't give

up. Perhaps she hadn't even realised she'd won? She was certainly concentrating hard.

Slow and steady, she managed to roll the barrel towards the opposite bank as the people behind her clapped and cheered. Her face never once broke in its grim determination. The barrel began to stick in the mud, rocking dangerously back and forth.

She took a deep breath and then leapt with all her might, falling on the opposite bank with very little grace but a roar of cheers behind her. Her triumph was clear for all to see.

Tyr and Bolli raised their fists in the air with a screaming cheer of pride and then Bolli dove into the water to swim to her. When he reached her, Bolli lifted her high up to set her on his shoulder, carrying her back across the water like a queen.

Jealousy and pride stormed within him. But it was her smile that stole Egill's breath. She looked radiantly happy, and he wanted nothing more than to go to her. To congratulate and kiss her thoroughly.

But he couldn't.

Bolli put her down on the riverbank after carrying her across the river, and all around her, everyone was cheering and clapping her on the back for her astounding achievement. She couldn't quite believe her luck either.

Wynflaed and Nora started to help her back into her apron dress. Giggling, Wynflaed gasped, 'How were you able to do that? It looked impossible!'

Nora helped pin on her bone brooch. 'You were magnificent! To complete the run on your first try! Incredible!'

Mila laughed. 'I doubt I will ever manage to do it again! Honestly, I don't even know *how* I did it. I was just determined to try my best.'

Tyr laughed as he rubbed himself down with a blanket. 'Well, that was certainly your best! You are not even wet! I am going to have to find a new game next year—as you are too good at this and will always beat me!'

Bolli moved to stand in front of her and smiled proudly down at her. She was still shocked he'd been so gracious about her earlier refusal of him. It was as if he hadn't even heard her, which should have been infuriating—but his words had been so heartfelt. He'd also remained as kind and as generous as before. Even swimming across the river to carry her back. Mila only hoped she could count on Bolli to hold no ill will against her in the future if she continued to refuse him.

In his usually sweet manner, he said, 'Come, friend, let me carry you to your prize.'

'You have already carried me once! And honestly, there's no need. It was just a balancing game!'

'*Just a balancing game?*' Tyr cried, aghast at the suggestion his challenge was easy. 'No one has even come close to crossing! You are a legend! Your name will be written in the sagas! Mildritha—the lady who can walk on water!'

Another cheer rang out, and a round shield was laid flat on the ground. 'Sit! You can be carried like a victorious queen!' said Bolli, and Tyr nodded in agreement.

Mila laughed but did as they asked and sat on the shield, gripping the edges tightly and squealing with fear and delight as she was raised high. The shield balanced between Tyr and Bolli's shoulders as they strode forward towards Master Hakon and Mistress Orla. Bolli's children and Sigrid's sister Alvilda ran ahead of them with excitement while the rest of the people walked behind.

Orla smiled warmly at Mila as she approached. All the Eriksson brothers stood in a fan around her like golden giants. With beautiful Sigrid beside Grimr and pretty Freydis beside Egill.

Mila was curious about Egill's expression. He was staring at her with an intensity she found almost suffocating.

How could he look at her with such longing when his betrothed stood by his side?

Swirling anger and jealousy almost overpowered her, and she forced herself to look down at her sister, walking with Nora.

They would be her future. Not Egill.

'A glorious procession for a worthy champion!' declared Orla as Mila's shield was carefully lowered and she was able to hop down to the ground.

'Thank you, Mistress!'

Orla took the silver chalice from her cloak and raised it high. The crowd answered with a deafening cheer.

Mila stepped forward, but she didn't take the chalice. Instead she asked, 'Mistress, may I use that chalice as payment?'

'To pay off your debt and your sister's?' asked Orla. 'It is worth more than what you both owe, but I can arrange for the difference to be paid in coin or cloth.'

Mila shook her head, surprised at her mistress's kindness. 'Can it pay off Nora and Wynflaed's debt? And, also, with your permission, I would like a cabin built on your land, near the main hall, so that when my sister and Nora are free, they can live there together but remain under your protection and continue to work your looms for payment. Would that be possible? I can work longer on the looms if you need more payment.'

Wynflaed gasped and stared at her. She looked as if she was about to say something, but then Nora took her hand and shook her head subtly. Wisely Wynflaed remained silent.

She would answer their questions later.

Orla handed the chalice to her husband and then covered her heart with her fist. 'Then I swear to take this chalice in payment for Nora and Wynflaed's freedom and construction of their cabin. Now, let's speak no more of debts. Tonight, let us enjoy the full moon and bonfires. Tomorrow we shall have the final contests, followed by a wedding feast!'

The crowd roared its approval. With a clap of Orla's hands, the drums began to beat a dancing rhythm, and the bonfires were lit.

Wynflaed grabbed her arm and pulled her through the crowd until they stood not far from one of the smoking bonfires. 'What about you! I love you, and offering to do that is very kind. But why? Why not pay off your debt first? And, why the cabin... Unless...' Her eyes widened, and she snapped, 'You *are* going to live with us, aren't you?'

Nora, who had been following them, said quietly, 'Well... we should probably go help with the food... The meat is roasting, but they'll need help with the cabbage and onions, bread and... I will go on ahead, tell them you're coming...'

With another glance at the furious Wynflaed, Nora gave a grimace and headed off to the kitchen tent.

Mila tried her best to ease her sister's concerns. 'It won't take me too long to pay off my own debt. Especially now that you are free and can help me. Besides, it was what you wanted, wasn't it? A home for you and Nora.'

Wynflaed was not reassured, judging by the continued scowl on her face. 'Yes! But that was *our* dream, not yours! That's what you said! What will *you* do? And please do not say you will marry Bolli! He's a good man, but—'

Mila interrupted. 'I'm not going to marry Bolli.'

Wynflaed's brow smoothed. 'Good! So you *will* live with us.'

'I do not know.'

'What do you mean, you do not know?'

Mila sighed. 'The cabin—that's your dream. But... I don't know what mine is yet. I think... I'd like to go to Norway. Perhaps Sigrid and Grimr will take me with them when they return?'

'What?' Wynflaed looked truly horrified now. 'Why would you go there?'

To leave Iceland and never see Egill or his bride ever again.

'Perhaps they will have clay that I can work with...or a position in their hall. Jarl Grimr seems a good man, and Sigrid a kind mistress.'

Mila flinched as hurt briefly crossed her sister's face, followed swiftly by concern. 'I understand that you're not happy here currently...but is Norway truly the answer?'

'I want to see more of the world...see what else it can offer me.' It was decision that had not come easily to her, and the reason for that stood in front of her.

Tears filled Wynflaed's eyes. 'What will I do without you?'

Mila grabbed her shoulders and hugged her fiercely. 'You will be happy. I insist upon it!'

Wynflaed nodded and then hugged her back before stepping away, and forcing herself to take deep breaths to stop from crying. 'It will be like losing an arm. But if it will make you happy...' Mila nodded at her questioning look. 'Come, let's help out with the food. Before Tyr curses both of our names.'

Freydis looked gloomily at Egill's cup as it was refilled by one of the servants. 'You shouldn't drink too much. It's our wedding day tomorrow.'

'Yes... I know,' he said bitterly.

There was laughter and dancing around the fire, but it might as well have been a funeral pyre to Egill. He noticed Snorri and Bolli were some of the most boisterous revellers. He even caught Bolli smiling more than once in his direction.

Of course he would be happy! Mila had agreed to be his bride!

That much was clear after the refusal of her prize. She had no need of her silver chalice, and Bolli had been the one to carry her across the river. Perhaps he would pay off her debt too, even though she'd refused Egill several times. It was obvious she'd agreed to marry Bolli and become the mother of his brood. It explained why she had arranged for her sister and friend to be well cared for in the future, and had not mentioned herself at all.

He placed his cup beside him on the bench and stood up. 'I am going to the latrine,' he explained, and Freydis gave him a fragile smile of acknowledgement.

She would never question him, or laugh, or fight with him as Mila had.

Odin's teeth! Would he ever be happy with Freydis?

No.

The answer was simple, but it might as well have been fifty lashes across his back.

As he stumbled away, he walked through the revellers. Many wore animal skins, flower wreaths or antlers on their heads. It would be a debauched night, and he felt as if all the spirits of this wild land were taunting him as they danced past.

Then, to torment him further, Mila's dark hair twirled by. He grabbed hold of her arm and tugged her out of the dance. She gasped, falling hard against his chest, her face flushed and her breathing heavy.

He stormed away from the fires and chaos of the dancers, pulling her with him behind one of the nearby tents. There wasn't much light to see her face by, but someone had lit a brazier in the nearby tent, and the moon was full so there was just enough to see her shocked expression.

'You can't marry him!' he growled, hating how desperate he sounded—like a wounded bear.

'What?' she gasped, her eyes wide in the dim light.

'Bolli, curse him!' He shouted spitefully, 'Bolli, and *both* of his hot pools, and his hundred sheep, and his brood of children! You can't marry him! He's not right for you! And he will *never* make you happy!'

Her eyes narrowed, and then she ripped her arm from his grasp. 'My life is not your concern!'

'You do not *love* him!' he growled.

Mila's anger seemed to boil over, because she smacked him on the arm. 'And you do not love Freydis! But you will still marry her, will you not?'

'I...' He ran a hand through his hair hopelessly. 'Please don't...don't ruin your life, as I have done.'

Mila stared at him for a long moment, and then snarled through gritted teeth, 'You have no right to say what I can and cannot do! You gave up that right when you said *yes* to marrying Freydis!'

She spun away from him then, storming back into the whirlpool of dancers and disappearing moments later. He did not see her again for the rest of the night.

Chapter Twenty-Five

There were many sore heads the following day. At dawn, the camp had been dismantled, and everyone returned to Hakon and Orla's hall for *dagmal*. Even after a hearty meal of porridge to start the day, many still winced against the spring sunlight, and there were more than a few people who decided against competing in the contests that day.

Egill was not one of them. He welcomed the physical pain that fighting would bring, anything to distract him from his heartache. Freydis kept fussing over him, which only made him feel worse. Thankfully she was currently away with the other women preparing for the ceremony...

Odin's teeth, the ceremony!

The day he'd been dreading had finally arrived, and it might as well be the day of his execution.

He might have been happier if it were.

Last night he'd dreamt of running away with Mila. That instead of walking away from him, she grabbed his hand, and they had disappeared like mist into the darkness. When he woke up beside the smoking ash of the campfire, he'd felt as if his heart had been pulled from his chest.

What sort of man would dream of another woman on the eve of his wedding?

Not an honourable one. His mother and father would have been ashamed of him.

A man went flying into the people beside him. There was laughter and cheers as he helped to lift the fallen warrior and then pushed him back into the fighting circle. No one was done until they surrendered, lost consciousness or died. Hopefully none would die, as it was a celebration, and death would cast a bad omen an already miserable match.

Grimr and Hakon came to stand on either side of him. 'Are you sure you want to compete?' asked Hakon, and Egill had to acknowledge that Freydis wasn't the only one who'd been fussing over him all morning.

'What else should I do? Drink? I doubt my bride will appreciate me being drunk at our wedding.' She'd definitely not been pleased with his behaviour last night, leaving him by the fire to seek her tent early.

'But the wrestling *and* the sword contests...are you sure about this?' said Grimr with a frown.

Egill snorted. 'Ah, look, my miserable brother has made an appearance. I was worried your newfound happiness had changed your personality for good!'

Grimr's scowl deepened. 'I will bet against you in both finals. If the gods are kind, they will ensure you have some sense beaten into that thick head of yours.'

'So you believe I will make the finals, at least,' he replied dryly with a slight tilt of his head. 'That is comforting.'

'You would embarrass our family name if you didn't make it that far,' Hakon replied absently, crossing his arms to watch the current contest drawing to a close. To Egill's surprise, Hakon's comment only made Grimr's scowl deepen.

'Our *family name* is not as great or as honourable as either of you believes. We should all look to being true to ourselves first. I urge you to do the same, Egill,' said Grimr cryptically before walking over to Gunnar, who was already taking bets on the next challenge.

An unconscious man with a bloody nose was dragged from the circle, while the victor waited for his next opponent.

Egill stepped forward, his wooden sword and shield raised.

Mila was busy all morning with preparations for the feast later. She was grateful of the distraction. Occasionally she watched a few moments of the contests whenever she was passing by, or she would listen to people discussing who had lost or won the most recent matches.

Which was how she knew Egill was competing in both the sword and wrestling competitions. No one else was doing the same.

When Tyr came into the hall, he gave all the bondswomen an update on what had been happening. 'We have a finalist for the wrestling. But they've had to delay his final match against Egill. At least until Egill has fought Karl for the sword match.'

'So it's drawing to a close, then?' asked Nora.

Tyr nodded. 'But Mistress Orla says we should all come out and watch the final matches. There's not much more to do in the kitchens until after the wedding. We can all have a cup of ale too.'

Mila's stomach heaved at the thought of Egill's wedding.

How would she manage to witness it without crying?

Wynflaed wiped her hands on her apron and then took Mila's hand gently in hers. 'Come on, then. Let's be done with this.'

Mila nodded, unable to speak, and grateful that Wynflaed and Nora were with her. Tyr handed them each a cup of ale, and they walked out to find a seat.

Nora and Wynflaed gave her sideway glances as they shuffled over to one of the haystacks and climbed to the top for a better view of the fights.

She immediately noticed Egill in the fighting circle. His chest was bare and glistening with sweat from back-to-back matches.

He must be exhausted...

But Mila tried not to feel too much sympathy towards him. She was still furious with him after his outburst last night.

How dare he make demands of her when he was going to marry another?

Yes, she'd not told him the truth, but a callous part of her wanted to torment him.

Let him think she was doing the same! Perhaps his jealousy would make him change his mind...

Mila sighed.

She shouldn't wish such a thing!

It would leave a mother and child abandoned. Freydis had said her father would shun her. Perhaps the rest of her settlement would too? If it was anything like Jorvik, they would.

Mila knew that from her own experience growing up with an absent father. She'd thought at the time it was because her parents had not been officially married. Now she realised it had been much worse than that. Perhaps other people had known the truth about her father, or at least suspected? She would never know.

She took a deep gulp of her ale, and Wynflaed gave her a sympathetic look before pouring some of hers in Mila's cup. 'You'll need it more than me,' she said.

Karl, one of Grimr's fiercest warriors, stepped forward into the circle to fight Egill. It was an even match of sword skill, and the two men danced around one another for a few moments before Egill attacked hard. The thud of wooden sword on shield made Mila's hands clutch her skirts, and she flinched a few times when she saw Karl's sword swing dangerously close to Egill's head. But Egill managed to duck and then roll away in time to lift his shield and thrust forward with a lunge.

The fighting was intense and went on for a long time. Both men were breathing heavily and struggling to raise their shields as the strain of the last dozen matches began to finally take their toll on them. But eventually Egill managed to wear the warrior down, raining blow after blow on his shield until Karl made a mistake with his footing and dropped down to one knee. It was enough for Egill to kick aside his shield and claim the match by pressing the wooden sword to Karl's neck.

The crowd roared in approval, jumping up from their seats and yelling Egill's name. But Egill was a compassionate winner, and he clapped Karl on the shoulder and helped raise him to his feet.

Mila could tell Egill was exhausted by the way he struggled to lift his sword when he was named the official winner of the match. He barely even acknowledged the silver chalice he'd won before he was being urged to disarm for the final wrestling match.

'Who's he matched with for the wrestling?' asked Mila, curious and also a little nervous that he might get seriously hurt.

'Your champion,' said Tyr, shrugging as if it were obvious, and Mila swallowed hard as she watched a barechested and far better rested Bolli step into the circle.

Bolli turned, searching through the crowd. When his eyes fixed on her, he grinned and waved at her. Mila gave a weak smile and raised her hand awkwardly in return. After his help and support during her own contest, it would seem churlish not to return the favour. But the glare and anger that passed over Egill's face made her stomach clench. To make matters worse, Freydis had finished dressing in her wedding gown and bridal crown and had come out to watch the final match.

Looking as lovely as the fertility goddess her name was derived from, Freydis stepped into the circle with a beaming smile upon her face. 'Good luck to you both! I must insist on marrying someone at the end of this match. But be careful! I would rather not start my wedding with a funeral!' laughed Freydis.

Egill did not seem amused by her teasing, and he stepped into the centre without replying. Bolli followed him after a brief and shy bow towards Freydis.

They began to circle one another, each of them looking for an opening. Egill slammed forward first, and she could have sworn she heard the meat of their muscles slap together like a crack of thunder. The crowd hissed and cheered depending on who they championed, and Mila could do nothing more than clench her hands tightly in her lap. Sick with worry for *both* men, although for different reasons.

Loud grunts and curses filled the air as the two men grappled, their skin reddening under the strain.

There was a moment when Mila thought Bolli was defeated. His back was bowed in an unnatural arch that made her wince. Egill was slimmer than Bolli, but his muscles were so tightly corded and his skill impressive. As he twisted, she thought she could see every thread and fibre of strength along his back ripple with tension. He pressed harder, Bolli's face turning almost purple in the death grip Egill had around his neck.

'Odin's teeth!' Tyr muttered in horror. 'He's going to kill him!'

Mila couldn't bear it.

He was going to kill Bolli, and it was all her fault!

She'd baited his jealousy last night and made him believe she had chosen Bolli.

She closed her eyes and clasped her hands in front of her chest, begging whatever god ruled the heavens to save both men from a terrible fate. Bolli from dying, and Egill from regretting his vengeance for the rest of his life—as she knew he would.

The crowd inhaled sharply and then burst into a loud cheer.

Had he killed Bolli?

In Norse society, death at a feast was merely inconvenient. But Mila knew she would never forgive herself or Egill if he'd killed Bolli. She was afraid to open her eyes and look.

'Bolli! Bolli! Bolli!'

The crowd's excited chanting forced her to open her eyes, and that's when she realised it was Egill who had lost the fight.

'It's like he gave up! All the strength just left him—at the very last moment! *Curses!* I placed a silver coin on him winning both!' grumbled a bad-tempered Tyr beside her. She stared in shock at Egill, who lay flat on his back, staring up at the sky in obvious defeat.

Mila's hands were shaking as she lowered them back to her lap. Nora picked up her discarded empty cup of ale and poured some of her own into it. 'Here...' she urged, placing it carefully in Mila's hands.

But she was still staring at Egill, wondering what had caused him to change his mind. Freydis rushed to his side a moment later, and Mila wasn't sure if it was relief or pride that washed through her at that moment.

Egill had done the right thing...because he always did the right thing.

Chapter Twenty-Six

'Egill!' cried Freydis as she hurried to his side, concern and worry written all over her pale face. 'Are you hurt?'

'Come on, brother,' said Grimr, lifting him up off the ground and half carrying him past Hakon, who gave him a consoling pat on the shoulder as he passed. His brother would have followed him into the hall with Grimr and Freydis, but as the host, he had to give out the prize to Bolli.

Bolli, the man who had won not only the wrestling match, but Mila as well.

Perhaps he even had her heart now, as well as her hand in marriage?

He had seen the way she'd prayed for Bolli. Terrified that Egill would give in to the darkness of his jealousy and kill the one man who had yet to disappoint her?

Egill had no right to do such a thing. If Mila could not be with him, he wanted her to have a chance of happiness, because *that* was true love. His mother had explained it to him once long ago, and it had always stuck with him.

'Love is fighting for another person's happiness before considering your own.'

He sank down onto a bench, Freydis rushing to sit beside him.

'Did you bang your head?' gasped Freydis, her fingers

moving over his skull, and he shook his head to get rid of her touch.

I am defeated.

Egill leaned back against the wall, staring straight ahead, and out of the corner of his eye he could see a worried look pass between Freydis and Grimr. But he didn't care. He felt as if his insides had been scooped out with a hot spoon, and all that remained was an empty burnt shell.

He could still feel the meat of Bolli's neck beneath his arm, the strain of the skin, and the heat of the pressure he'd inflicted. Blood lust had raged within him. He'd wanted to kill him, to snap his neck. Then he'd seen Mila, and he'd realised what he was doing and why.

Shame had poured down on him like hot coals, and he'd instinctively let go. Allowing the poor man to breathe once more. Not moving or fighting back when Bolli tried to flip him. He hadn't the heart to do so, not after what he'd tried to do.

Grimr made a huffing sound before saying, 'I will get you some water.' He walked across the hall to the kitchen, leaving him alone with his betrothed.

Freydis fussed over him, checking his eyes to see if there was any blood or confusion in them. Despite his lack of feeling towards her, he had to admit that Freydis was a kind and compassionate woman. She reminded him of his mother with her golden hair, and part of him wished he could fall into her arms for a second time and weep like a child. It still shocked him that he would have slept with her, despite her prettiness. The similarity was disturbing.

'I am sorry. I do not deserve either of you,' he said, the words raw in his throat. 'I have tried to be a good and decent man...but I constantly fail...'

Her eyes met his, and they began to glisten with unshed

tears. 'No, you haven't failed anyone, Egill. I... I have failed you. Can you ever love me?' There was still hope in her eyes, and he looked down at his feet, ashamed of himself.

'I will care for you and the child...always. But I cannot love you, Freydis. I wish I could...'

Grimr came to stand beside them, offering Egill a cup of water, which he took gladly. As he drank, Grimr looked down at Freydis and asked solemnly, 'Is this *truly* what you want?'

Freydis swallowed, her face so young and vulnerable as she stared up at Grimr. 'What choice do I have?'

Grimr sighed. 'Tell me what you want, and I will do all that I can to help.'

Her bottom lip trembled. 'I want a husband, and a home of my own.'

Egill shook his head and rose to his feet. 'I made you a promise, and I will keep it! I am honour-bound to do so. Come, Freydis.'

Grimr grabbed his arm as he tried to walk past and hissed, 'Do not do this for honour! Or for *anyone* but yourself! If you think our father would be ashamed of you, you are wrong! He is the shameful one in our family, not you!'

Egill frowned. 'What are you talking about?'

Hakon walked up to them at that moment and stared at Grimr in confusion. 'What has happened?'

Grimr looked between his two brothers and then, with a defeated roll of his head, said, 'I have kept it a secret for too long. But our father...he was not a good man.'

Egill nodded slowly confused. 'I know he was never faithful to Mother, but—'

'No!' snapped Grimr. He was silent for a moment before confessing quietly, 'I never wished to tell you this. But Sigrid believes you should both know the truth—especially since Egill is about to make a terrible mistake. I only hope you can forgive me for passing this burden on to you...'

Hakon and Egill exchanged a worried glance, and then Egill placed a hand on his shoulder. 'Grimr, your burden is ours. Speak. Keep nothing from us.'

Grimr's head lowered as if a great shame rested on his shoulders. 'Our poor mother. I didn't realise how ill she was...or I would never have done it.'

'What?' asked Hakon, disturbed by the obvious guilt and heartache that Grimr had carried for many years.

Grimr looked at both of them in turn, as if checking that they would be able to bear the wound he was about to inflict upon them. 'Our sister...'

'Was born dead,' Egill said, remembering with a shudder the wail of grief his mother had given at the news.

Grimr shook his head, his face pale. 'No, she lived... for a while. I followed Father while the women were looking after Mother.'

Egill felt a sudden swell of bile rise in his throat. The way that Grimr spoke was beginning to worry him. 'What happened?'

Grimr looked him in the eye, the truth of his words piercing his heart like a lance. 'Father killed her... He said she wouldn't have survived anyway, that she was malformed. But he had no right!' Grimr's head and voice rose with anger. 'And I kept his cursed secret! Allowed Mother to take her last breath believing she had failed our sister.'

Grimr's anger roared through all of them. Hakon's fist clenched, and Egill had to swallow a shout of outrage. They each took a moment to digest the confession, and then Egill realised how difficult this must have been for Grimr. Not only to tell them, but to have kept their father's terrible secret for so many years. So Egill squeezed his brother's shoulder gently and said, 'No, he had no right to do that. But you were just a child, Grimr. There was nothing you could do.'

Grimr took a deep breath and nodded. 'Sigrid says the same.'

'She is right,' said Hakon, placing an arm around his younger brother's shoulders.

They embraced each other in grief and silent agreement.

Afterwards, Grimr stared at him, his eyes intense with conviction. 'Please Egill, do not believe you have to live up to our family name or our father's *honour*... He had none. He murdered his own child.' Grimr looked down at Freydis, who was clutching her hands tightly in front of her, her face pale, and the bridal crown slightly askew on her head. 'You are one of my people, Freydis. All people have value. Even if your father disowns you, I will not.'

Tears fell down Freydis's cheeks, and she wiped them away angrily. 'What will you do when he shuns me openly? Cast him out?'

Grimr nodded. 'If he fails to do as I ask, he is not welcome in my hall.'

Freydis shook her head helplessly. 'I don't want that.'

'It's time for the wedding!' shouted revellers pouring into the hall, sweeping around them in a matter of moments, and playfully tugging at them to come outside again.

Egill and Freydis were swept up in the chaos.

As they passed through the open doors, he noticed Mila standing in the doorway, her expression worried and uncertain.

Had she been waiting outside this entire time?

Hundreds of thoughts ran through his mind. Grimr's revelation about his father, the growing sense of unease that Freydis wasn't telling him the whole truth, but most of all the pull of Mila calling to him. As if their souls were bound together by the threads of fate.

She reached forward through the crowd and grabbed his arm urgently. 'I am not going to marry him! I just want you to know that!' she said, and then let go of him, releasing him back into the tide that thrust him out into the light.

He flinched as if he were battling a storm in his mind. Beside him walked Freydis, but she was not looking at him. She was staring down at her swollen belly and the protective hand covering it.

My child.

Egill was suffocating under the weight of responsibility and haunted by dark eyes filled with longing.

He glanced back but couldn't see Mila.

If she wasn't going to marry Bolli, then what was she going to do? Live with her sister? Leave?

Dread pooled in his stomach, and he tasted metal in his mouth.

She was going to leave!

He would never see her again, and she would disappear into the shadows, just as she had in his dream...but without him by her side.

His arm burned where she had touched him. Denial and pain roaring through him like a merciless army. He needed Mila... He couldn't live without her.

But they had already arrived at the pretty archway made of willow and heather. It was to serve as the altar for the handfasting ceremony. The local *gothi*, who performed marriages, awaited them, rope in one hand, ceremonial twigs in the other.

A whip and a chain.

What was he doing?

Egill spun around, searching the crowd desperately for Mila's face, half-afraid she had already turned into mist.

When he spotted her, his body slumped with relief. She stood on a hay-bale not far from where she had spoken to him. Her sister was beside her, holding her hand tightly. It was then that he noticed the tears pouring down her face, and guilt threatened to choke the life from him.

Oily liquid splashed against his face, and he realised the *gothi* was anointing them with the ceremonial oils.

It was finally happening... His happiness was dying.

Freydis was watching him with a pained expression. His fists clenched and unclenched as he struggled to breathe.

The *gothi* offered him the rope, loudly reciting the official words that he would need to repeat while he wrapped the rope around their hands. Binding himself to a woman he barely knew, while the one he loved watched in tears.

Freydis stared back at him, and then said in a quiet voice, 'Forgive me.'

Chapter Twenty-Seven

'I...cannot...' he croaked, his voice raw as if he'd been strangled. He stared at the rope offered to him by the *gothi*, ignoring them when they thrust it impatiently towards him a second time.

Instead, his gaze swept back to Freydis and the tears in her eyes. She nodded, a weak smile on her lips, and he was not sure if she had heard him, or if he had even voiced his own denial. His mind was shattered, not this time by injury, but because of his own doing. The promise finally broken.

Egill opened his mouth to speak again, but was silenced when Freydis did the most unexpected thing. She pushed the rope away from him, and then took his hand, turning to face the crowd.

In a loud voice she bravely declared, 'Egill made me a promise. He was injured and barely remembers it. But I will tell it to you now.' She took a deep breath, and then, with the confidence of a queen, she said, 'I told him that I was with child, and that the father of my baby...had died in Ingvar's attack. Frode was a good man...' Her voice broke a little, but she pushed forward with courage. 'Frode had sworn that he would convince my father to accept him. But he was once a thrall—until Hakon freed him, and my father would not accept a man such as him to marry me.' She squeezed Egill's hand before continuing, 'Egill pitied me, and he swore that he would find a suitable husband for me. If he could not, he would marry me himself, because no one had ever owned his heart.' Tears gathered in Freydis's eyes as she turned to face him. 'But that is no longer true...is it, Egill?'

He shook his head, dumbfounded by her confession that rang so true in the dark corners of his mind. He was also plagued with guilty for not being able to help her as he'd promised.

Freydis nodded. 'So I will release you from your promise.' She dropped his hand and wiped at her face self-consciously. The next words were said behind her hands, quiet and sniffled like an ashamed child's cry. 'Please... forgive me. I should not have lied to you.'

Her fragile, frightened voice rang in his head like a bell. Unlocking the memory within, and in a rush, he remembered her weeping by his side. Their hands entwined in mutual fear, his promise heartfelt. His reaching for her and embracing her as a friend, patting her back lightly as she wept. *'You will not be alone, Freydis... When I am well, I will help you, I swear it.'*

Memory and emotion blinded him, and he rushed forward, sweeping her into a hug. Patting her back once again, he whispered, 'I forgive you.' Her small body sagged against him with relief. Then her golden head bobbed in acknowledgement, and she pulled away, wiping at her tears.

'You should still get married today,' she said, and then gestured with her chin towards Mila. 'Before you miss your chance.'

Freydis walked towards the hall, the crowd parting to allow her to pass. She held her head high, but her eyes avoided everyone, fearful of condemnation.

'I will marry you, Freydis!' shouted a man from the crowd, loud and confident.

The crowd gasped in surprise, and everyone turned towards the voice. It was Bolli, and he was pushing through the crowd like a bull, sending several men flying in different directions.

Freydis stilled and then spun towards him, obviously shocked by the offer. 'Bolli?'

Bolli finally reached her, and he took a deep breath before nodding solemnly. 'Your child would be welcomed as one of my own...that is...if you agree to be a mother to mine?' He gestured to his children, who had followed in his wake, gathered around him and eagerly smiling up at her.

Bolli took another step forward and reached for her hand. 'I would love and cherish you, Freydis. I have had my eye on you ever since you arrived. Now that you are no longer betrothed, I would gladly offer you my hand.'

Freydis frowned. 'But...you have been courting Mila this entire time!' she snapped angrily, and there were a few chuckles from the surrounding crowd.

Egill heard one of the bondswomen to the side of him mutter, 'This is as good as Egill's play!'

'Better!' replied her friend.

Bolli shrugged, holding his hands up to the crowd in surrender. 'What can I say? I am as cunning as my father.'

'That is certainly true!' shouted Snorri from the back of the crowd.

'Yes, there was a time I would have accepted Mila. But then you arrived...' He shook his head with a boyish grin. 'I showed interest in her because I wanted to make both of you reconsider your betrothal...by making him jealous...' He rubbed his neck with a wince. 'I think it worked.'

Most women would have been horrified by such a confession, but Freydis had always been an odd woman, and she flushed with pleasure and pride. 'Well...that *is* clever... I suppose.'

'Will you marry me, then?'

Freydis considered him for a moment. 'You said you have *two* hot pools, yes?'

He nodded eagerly. 'I do.'

'Then...' She paused dramatically before grinning. *'Yes,* I will marry you! Although... I am sorry to say I have no dowry to speak of—'

'I will pay it,' interrupted Egill, and Freydis gave him an appreciative smile before turning back to Bolli.

'Then... Bolli, I expect to receive your silver chalice as my bride price—because if I am unhappy with you, I will divorce you and take my silver with me.'

Bolli grinned at her warning and pulled her into his arms. 'I will never give you a reason to leave me, beautiful Freydis.' And he swooped down, kissing her soundly on the mouth—to the entire crowd's roar of approval.

Egill walked past the happy couple towards Mila, barely noticing the thumps of approval his brothers gave him as he passed. His eyes focused solely on Mila—drowning in the sea of longing he felt for her. 'Mila, I have been a fool...'

She gazed up at him, her face flushed and still wet with tears.

'Can you forgive me?' he asked, already dropping to his knees to beg for her to accept him, knowing that he should have done this much sooner.

'Not...' she sobbed, struggling to get the words out. 'Not unless...you marry me first.'

Relief and joy burst from his chest, and he kissed her sweet hands. 'Yes—I swear it.'

She laughed. 'No more promises, I beg you! Just...stay with me, wherever I go, whatever I do...stay with me.'

He nodded. He understood now. Love was sacrifice and vows, but it was also action. 'I love you,' he said, finally breaking the last chain that had kept them apart. 'I will tell you it every day, not just with words—for who can trust a serpent's tongue? But I will tell you with action by remaining always by your side, and with my touch, and my kiss.'

He pressed another kiss against the leaping pulse in her wrist.

'I love you,' she replied, cupping his face in her palms and running her thumb across his lips in a tender caress.

Slowly he rose to his feet, cupping her face in his hands, and kissed her deeply and passionately. 'Let's get married now,' he whispered against her lips, pulling slightly away to see her better.

'Agreed,' she replied, her smile radiant and without a trace of worry or doubt.

Orla and Sigrid rushed over to them. 'While Bolli and Freydis get married, lets prepare you for yours,' said Orla, reaching for Mila's elbow as if to steer her away.

Mila shook her head. 'There is no need. I can marry him as I am.'

Egill nodded. 'Agreed. I will marry her as she is, gladly.'

They stared into each other's eyes, blissfully happy. But Sigrid took one look at Mila's old and dirty ochre skirt and snapped, 'Absolutely not! Come along!'

Wynflaed and Nora laughed, and they hurried after Mila as Sigrid dragged her into the hall. Orla appeased Egill's outrage with a sharp, 'Patience, Egill!' before following close behind.

Mila was escorted into Orla's chamber by the four women.

'My cobalt gown will look nice with your hair,' said Orla thoughtfully as she rushed past them and started rifling through her chest.

Sigrid nodded in agreement. 'I have some lovely silver turtle brooches and blue beads that will go beautifully with it.' She hurried to her travelling chest, just as Orla retrieved the gown, and held it up for Sigrid's approval.

'Perfect!' declared Sigrid, ducking back to pull out her small jewellery chest and bring it over to them. Mila looked helplessly at Wynflaed, who shrugged and smiled, mischievously delighted by it all.

'Please...do not trouble yourselves!' implored Mila. 'There really is no need!'

'Nonsense!' said Orla, tapping her foot impatiently, until Mila began to peel off her apron dress obediently.

Wynflaed took the old dress from her and put it aside. While Orla draped the gown over her head. Nora was then instructed by Sigrid to go and gather combs.

The flurry of activity was dizzying, and breathlessly Mila gasped as the gown fell into place. Her hands brushed down the soft wool, unable to stop herself from admiring it. 'The gift of letting me borrow this is too kind, Mistress. What if I mark it?'

Orla took her by the shoulders and fixed her with a firm look. 'This is not my gift, Mildritha. You are merely doing as any member of my family can. Understand?'

Mila gasped again. Strangely, she had not considered what marrying Egill would mean.

Had these two women now become her sisters?

She glanced at Sigrid, who seemed in agreement with Orla, because she cheerfully matched Orla's smile.

Mila shook her head, embarrassed. 'I am your bondswoman. Until I have repaid my debt—'

She had been about to explain that she was not worthy enough to be called family. But Orla interrupted her. 'How can you be bound to me when you are marrying Egill? Your debt is repaid. Consider that your wedding gift—if you must. I have already branded your tablet with your freedom. I did so when I marked Nora and Wynflaed's earlier.'

Mila stared at her in shock. 'But that was before...'

Orla nodded, busying herself with tying the gown and putting the brooches Sigrid handed to her in place. 'I was hoping Egill would see sense, and even if he didn't, I thought he had caused you enough tears and trouble for my family to owe you far more than fifty ells—or whatever it is.'

'Forty-eight,' Mila answered, and Orla's hands stilled after attaching the final brooch.

'Well...' she said, taking a step back and catching her eye with a sincere look. 'The debt is repaid.'

Tears pricked in her eyes.

'No tears!' declared Orla sharply, grabbing a stool and patting it. 'Sit. We need to brush out that beautiful hair of yours.'

Nora had returned with combs, and the four women gathered around her to brush out her hair from its cap and braid.

When they were done, Sigrid reached for her jewellery chest again and removed a silver bridal crown. 'It's not the most beautiful piece of jewellery...but my grandmother, mother and I have worn it at our weddings. Each of us have become powerful women in our own right since. Would you like to wear it for your wedding, Mildritha?'

Mila's eyes filled with more tears, and she nodded. 'I would be honoured...and call me Mila. That is what my family call me.'

Sigrid smiled and gently began to place the bridal crown on her head.

'What is keeping you? Egill wants you to hurry!' shouted Grimr from the other side of the door, and Sigrid rolled her eyes.

'That's the second time he's done that—interrupted me putting on this bridal crown!' she grumbled with a chuckle before smiling brightly and taking a step back. 'You look beautiful, Mila.'

Wynflaed walked out with her to meet Egill. Mila held tightly to her elbow for courage, nervous of the crowd and their watchful eyes.

Would they condemn her for stealing Egill from Freydis?

To Mila's surprise, Freydis stepped forward from the crowd and gave her a bunch of flowers. 'I hope you can also forgive me?' she asked shyly, and the tightness in Mila's chest loosened.

'I never blamed you,' Mila replied.

Freydis gave her a tearful smile before leaning against her new husband Bolli, who pulled her close.

'Good luck!' said Bolli, and as she walked forward, more people wished her good fortune, including Tyr and his wife, her friends, and Egill's brothers.

When her eyes locked with Egill's, all her remaining nerves flew away like butterflies in the wind. She joined him in front of the *gothi*, but Egill refused the rope when it was offered.

Instead, he gathered her hands in his and said, 'Our love is the only thing that binds us, and it will never fall or fail.'

Mila's heart filled to bursting, and when their last promises were done, she didn't wait for the *gothi* to proclaim them married. She leapt into Egill's arms and kissed him hard and passionately for the whole world to see.

Chapter Twenty-Eight

The crowds would sing and dance well into the next morning. But Egill wanted to enjoy some time away with his new bride. It was their first night as a married couple, and he wanted to show her exactly how he would love her for the rest of their lives together.

Eventually he managed to drag Mila away from dancing with Wynflaed and Nora long enough to speak with her.

'Where would you like to spend the night?' he asked. 'Here in the hall, out in a tent, or...' He paused, suddenly uncertain.

Mila frowned. 'If you are going to suggest the cabin... I have mixed feelings about it. The memories we made there are both good and bad—'

Egill nodded in agreement. 'I know. I was going to suggest somewhere else. But I was unsure how you would feel about it.'

'Where?'

Egill smiled. 'Grimr's ship. He landed it on the coast not far from here. He did not want to dock it in the port where he could not keep an eye on it. We could ride out to it—it would not take long—and then...enjoy some time alone.'

Mila grinned. 'That sounds a fine idea.' She laughed at the revellers sailing past them in a chaotic dance. 'I doubt anyone will miss us, but let me tell Wynflaed—and you should tell your brothers. I will meet you outside in a moment.'

After a quick kiss, they left in opposite directions to say their goodbyes. The merry crowd engulfed them as they parted ways.

When Mila arrived outside the hall a short time later, she wondered if Egill was still inside, but a flickering light caught her attention. She noticed it was Egill riding on a horse towards her, two large sacks draped either side of its rump. He held a torch in one hand.

'I gathered some blankets and supplies,' he said, and she grinned as with one arm he helped her to sit in front of him. 'Can you hold the torch?'

'Sure,' she replied, taking it from him as he urged the horse forward.

Thankfully the night was clear, and the path to the coast was easy to navigate. Mila doubted anyone would miss them—Wynflaed and Nora had barely blinked at her leaving, had even pushed her away, claiming she should *'go and finally get on with it'*.

Mila stifled a laugh at the memory. At least there was another bride and groom present at the feast to take the crowd's teasing when they couldn't find them later. She was glad Egill had thought to make this a more private moment for them.

Mila had never liked being the centre of attention, as it reminded her too much of the sneers of the townsfolk in Jorvik, even when it was a happy occasion like today. She was glad to have Bolli and Freydis to take some of the intrusive attention away from her.

She sighed, enjoying the cool air on her face and Egill's

warm chest beneath her back as they rode the short journey to the beach.

The ship gleamed in the moonlight like a giant shell dropped at the very top of the beach, closest to the sand dunes—out of reach of the tide. It was propped up with driftwood and rocks to ensure it was stable, and a ladder was set against its side.

They unsaddled from the horse and tied it to the ship with a net of hay and some water they'd brought with them.

Egill gestured for her to climb first, holding the ladder steady at the base. She smiled when she reached the top. The expensive sail was packed away. The ship protected from the elements with oiled canvas and a fresh coating of tar depending on the area.

Below its towering mast was a small built-up hold with its own timber roof and smoke hole.

'This is very fine!' she laughed, and Egill shrugged as he joined her.

'I believe Sigrid didn't enjoy travelling in the hold last year, so Grimr made some improvements.'

'I can imagine!' Mila laughed, and clambered down into the cabin. The door was a thick fur-and leather curtain, and inside there was a bed big enough for two, as well as a small cot—no doubt built for Alvilda.

The bed was stripped, with only the feather-and-straw mattresses remaining, but Egill had brought blankets and even a luxurious sheepskin with him. Using the torch, they had brought, he quickly lit a few pieces of driftwood in a small brazier, then propped the smaller mattress against the door. 'It will help keep out the draught,' he explained. 'And then we can use the cot base as a bench.'

Mila smiled. 'Perfect!' She opened her own sack and took out one of her pottery bowls.

'Is that...?' Wonder filled his voice as she allowed the light to show the press of their thumbs in the bottom of the bowl. The pattern of their skin was highlighted with two red drops of glaze that had accidentally merged together in a Roman-style heart during firing.

She nodded. 'It is the one we made together... It is the only one that did not break. I thought it a cruel trick of fate. But now... I wonder if it was a symbol of what was to come. That despite everything, we managed to survive.'

He gently cupped the bowl around her hands, their fingers brushing against one another—in the same way they had touched when they'd first made it. 'We have been through a fire together and are stronger for it, I think.'

She leaned across and pressed her mouth to his in silent agreement.

He placed the bowl on the bench safely, and then reached for Mila. The soft firelight glowed on her skin like a kiss of gold and amber on her cheeks.

'I am truly sorry for the pain I caused you...both of us...' he said, cupping her face and searching her eyes intently. He needed to reassure himself that he had not ruined things between them with his own stupidity and pride.

'You were trying to do the right thing.'

'I should have questioned Freydis much sooner. I had doubts, but I was afraid it was my own selfish desires holding sway.'

'You are not selfish, Egill.' She sighed. 'And I should have told you my true feelings.'

'You were afraid of being hurt again.'

Mila pressed her face against his beating heart and sighed with resignation. 'I was a coward.'

His arms wrapped around her tightly, and he kissed the top of her head. 'A true marriage is when two people build a life together. What shall we build, Mila? Pottery? A farm? I will do whatever you wish. Simply tell me what you want.'

Mila looked up at him and confessed, 'I have no idea. Pottery will be almost impossible to make here. But... I do not want to farm either, or work looms. I want to find something that I am good at...but I am not sure if there is anything...and I want to see other lands, even though I know I will miss my sister terribly...' She laughed dryly. 'I am not certain of anything. Except one thing. I want to eat a meal with you every day in the bowl that we made together.'

Egill grinned. 'That sounds a perfect life.'

Mila frowned. 'Is there anything you want?'

Egill thought for a moment before answering. 'Perhaps we can become merchant traders together? Travel between my brothers and all the places in between.'

'I thought you wanted to settle down?' she teased, delighted by the suggestion that they could explore the world *and* return to see her sister whenever they wished.

Egill shrugged. 'Settling is for people without a home. I have one.' He kissed her nose for emphasis. 'I have you.'

She reached up and undid the cord of his tunic. 'And I have you.'

Egill did not seem to need any further encouragement; with a grin he shrugged out of his tunics and threw them on the bench. Mila laughed and then began to carefully undo the ties and brooches of her own borrowed gown and jewellery.

Egill grew impatient at her care and began to help her. 'I will have to earn a lot of silver. As I suspect I will be ripping fine clothes off you many times in the future.'

She chuckled. 'Then should I continue to wear my two plain gowns and bone brooches? To save you spoiling fine cloth?'

Egill gave an indignant huff. 'And have the other merchants laugh at us? No, you shall wear the finest gowns, trimmed in silk and fur. You will wear only gold brooches and will be perfumed with the spices from sun-drenched lands.' As he spoke, Mila began to kiss and stroke his chest, making her way down to his waist, where she tugged at the ties of the wide-legged trousers, loosening them. She was confident now that she no longer had to hide her desire from him.

When she glanced up, his blue eyes were filled with fiery lust. With a smile, she slipped the last remaining fabric from her shoulders and let the dress and shift pool on the floor. Normally she would not have dared treat a fine dress so poorly, but now she knew that dreams and hopes *could* come true.

Groaning, he scooped her up and laid her on the soft bed, only pausing to remove the last of his clothes. When he returned to the bed, he lifted one of her legs, kissing and licking his way up from her ankle to her knee. He rested her leg on his shoulder as he dipped between her parted thighs and began to nip and kiss the pillow of her inner thigh.

She groaned, arching her spine with pleasure as he teased her flesh and made her core melt like warm honey. She ached for him, and without realising what she was doing, she raised her hips towards him eagerly.

Egill rose up, a powerful and magnificent warrior, spreading her legs on either side of his hips, positioning her just how he wanted. 'This time,' he groaned, his muscles tense and his voice husky, 'I am going to take you so fully that you will be screaming my name more than once tonight. I will have you in every way that I imagined, and it will be slow and soft, fast and deep. We will know each other in every way.'

Mila moaned at his words. She wanted nothing more than to be taken, and yet his words were a torturous promise that caused her heart to beat wildly in her chest. Biting her bottom lip, she nodded eagerly. 'Show me.'

He began to touch himself in long, firm strokes. Up and down, teasing her with the sight of his desire and the anticipation of pleasure that only he could bring her. She reached between them, joining her hands with his, her fingers moulding around his hard member and squeezing it lightly with every stroke at the head and base with a tight grip.

He groaned beneath her touch and pushed her back down on the bed, easing down between her thighs, their hips coming together to fit in perfect and natural harmony. His manhood pushed into her and filled her with heat. Pinning her hips with his hands, he guided each movement into her body, her arms snaking around his neck like ivy.

'I love you, Mila,' he moaned. Sweat beaded on his skin as he drove into her with slow, steady strokes of his hips.

'I love you!' she gasped, her body beginning to rock against him as his controlled thrusts teased her with the blissful pleasure to come. A tightening desperation built within her until she was panting and moaning his name, clawing at his back and buttocks like a wild woman. She rubbed her sex against him each time they came together.

But she whimpered with disappointment when he pulled out of her, gasping, and seemed to take a moment to control his breath.

'What's wrong?'

Egill grinned and then brushed a kiss against her lips. 'Do not worry, sweetling. I am not done with you yet. Turn over, my darling.'

Confused, but trusting him completely, she did as he

asked. He reached around her waist and pulled her up so that she was kneeling in front of him. The full heat of his body against her back was as hot as a kiln. He placed her hands against the wall and then kissed her neck and back as his fingers began to rub in soft circular motions on the bud of pleasure that seemed to throb with increasing waves at his touch.

He pressed her forward and lifted her hips, his thick staff slipping between her thighs and entering her with delicious ease. Egill groaned against her neck, and she pushed her bottom against him, eager for him to fill her completely.

'Please, Egill,' she moaned, desperate now for the release she knew only he could provide.

She gasped as he began to thrust into her with fast, quick strokes, holding her in place tightly as he rode her from behind. Her hands splayed against the wooden walls of the cabin as she surrendered to his powerful claiming of her body, moaning with pleasure and relief as finally the orgasm ripped through her in wave after blissful wave.

Never had she felt so possessed, and so free.

All her fears for the future had dissolved into smoke and disappeared into the starry night above.

Epilogue

Iceland, Five Years Later

A mighty dragon ship sailed into the harbour. It was market day and the height of summer, when the midnight sun would shine almost endlessly. Many people were trading at the market stalls that day, and the arrival of such a magnificent ship caused a ripple of worry to run through the crowd.

Was it war? King Harald seeking to claim their lands for his own?

Two of the elders happened to be in town that day, and they were called for immediately to negotiate with the new arrivals. But when the plank hit the jetty, the couple who strode down were not the king and queen of Norway, although they looked the part—wrapped in luxurious fox furs and silk-trimmed robes, expensive jewellery and the smell of exotic perfume lingering in the air around them.

The crowd sighed with relief as they recognised the couple.

'It is Egill and Mila!' declared Hakon cheerfully. He'd been one of the elders called forward and was glad to see his brother and sister-in-law after such a long separation.

'Hakon! Bolli! Greetings!' shouted Egill, striding forward to clasp his brother's arm and slap his back with affection.

Mila joined him, smiling warmly. 'Greetings, friends. How have you been? Are my sister and Nora well?'

Hakon grinned. 'Very well indeed! I have two boys now—Grimr the younger, whom you have met, and baby Egill, who was born only recently.'

Egill grinned at his brother's choice of baby name, and Mila gave her husband's arm a squeeze. However, Hakon was not finished, and he added cryptically, 'Wynflaed and Nora also have some good news to share with you!'

Mila glanced towards Bolli, who was also nodding with agreement. 'How are Freydis and the children?' she asked.

Bolli had been delightfully happy with Freydis the last time she'd seen him, and continued to be—as his next statement proved. 'She has given me another beautiful girl. The boys are annoyed that they are outnumbered now.'

Mila laughed, and Bolli gave her a shrewd and teasing look. 'You look different, Mila. Marriage and the life of a merchant agrees with you, I think.'

Mila tilted her head thoughtfully. 'Perhaps... I am the same, but I am definitely happier. Who would have imagined a life aboard a ship would suit me so well...but it does.'

Egill pulled her close and proudly declared, 'She is a menace in the eastern markets! Mila bends those men to her will and accepts only the finest quality at the lowest price. If it were not for my wife, I would be a poor merchant indeed!'

Mila shrugged, accepting the compliment lightly. They both knew it wasn't false praise. However, they worked in partnership, and she was quick to explain her husband's role. 'Egill knows what to buy, where and when to sell it... I only ensure we make a handsome profit when we do.'

'Well, we missed you last year. But by the looks of your

new ship, I would say your trip to Constantinople went well.'

A sly look twinkled in Egill's eye. 'Very well indeed. We also have a new addition to our crew, and some guests we picked up along the way!'

Mila smiled and then waved towards the ship. A warrior ducked out of view and then returned carrying a large basket, followed by Grimr and Sigrid, as well as their son Harald and Alvilda. When he handed the basket to Egill, Hakon and Bolli peered inside, exclaiming softly at the babe sleeping within.

'My son. His name is Floki, and he was born while we wintered at Novgorod,' said Egill proudly.

Everyone admired Floki and then greeted Grimr, Sigrid and their family.

Hakon shook his head in disbelief at Alvilda and Harald. 'You have both grown so much! The last time I saw you, Harald, you were only just walking, and Alvilda! You are a woman full grown!'

Alvilda blushed, and Sigrid groaned. 'I know! We have delayed her marrying for as long as we can, but King Harald insists we match her with someone soon.'

Grimr shrugged bad-temperedly. 'Let him wait! Alvilda can stay with us until she is an old crone if she wishes it!'

'I do not wish it!' snapped Alvilda with a horrified look, and everybody laughed.

'Come, let us go to my hall,' said Hakon. 'We must have a feast to celebrate your arrival. It has been too long since all of us were together. Orla has plenty of wool to trade with you. Our land and ventures are prosperous, and we have much to be thankful for.'

It wasn't long until they arrived at Hakon and Orla's hall,

piled together on the large hay-cart that Hakon had used to bring the wool to market.

As they approached, the entire settlement came out to greet them, the crowd murmuring with curiosity at the large group of travellers with him.

Mila noticed there were a couple more buildings than there had been before, and it was beginning to look more like a prosperous village.

'That's Wynflaed and Nora's cabin beside the barn. It wasn't fully built when you came here last,' said Hakon, and Mila leaned over the cart to see it better. It had its own herb and vegetable patch, as well as plenty of room for two. If anything, it was a very generous size.

'Although in the depths of winter, we all come into the hall,' continued Hakon, 'I suspect I may need to extend it next year. Which will mean...' He looked pointedly at Egill. 'I will need to import some good oak and pine from Norway.'

'We can help with that,' said Egill.

'Where are Nora and Wynflaed?' asked Mila, eager to see her sister. She'd noticed there was no smoke coming from Wynflaed's cabin, so they must either be working at the looms or in the fields. The last time she had seen them, Mila had offered to let them sail with her, but they had refused as they were happy to remain working for Hakon and Orla.

'They are inside the hall,' explained Hakon. 'Some days it's easier that way.'

Mila gave him a curious look, but Hakon simply responded with a secretive smile and continued to drive the cart up to the barn.

They all clambered out of the hay-cart, Egill taking care as he handed down Floki's basket. Mila glanced inside, but he was still sleeping. She suspected he would wake as soon as they were still. She might need to wear him in a sling for a while to get him used to life on land again.

Orla came out of the open hall doors and gave a squeal of excitement when she saw them. 'All of you?' She clapped her hands with delight. 'How wonderful!'

Others began to come out of the hall, curious, and Mila gave her own shriek of excitement when she saw her sister. They ran towards each other, wrapping one another in a tight and tearful embrace.

'How have you been?' they both asked at the same time and then laughed, answering together again, 'Good!'

'Did Hakon tell you?' asked Wynflaed, glancing towards Hakon, who shook his head with a smile.

'Tell me what?' asked Mila.

Wynflaed turned and called out for Nora. She walked through the crowd slowly, a young baby in her arms, no older than Mila's Floki.

Confused, Mila looked towards her sister, whose face was filled with joyous love.

'Eadith...she's our daughter,' said Wynflaed. 'Her mother died, but we promised to raise her as our own. Oh, Mila, I have everything I could have dreamed of...and more than I thought possible.'

Mila gasped and then hugged Wynflaed tightly. 'Eadith? Mother's name... Oh, look at her! Mother would be so proud. She's beautiful!'

Egill stepped forward, taking Floki's basket and holding it up to Eadith and Nora. 'Floki, meet your cousin Eadith.'

Mila laughed, wiping away joyful tears. 'They're both fast asleep!'

'Best way to be,' said Orla. 'Let us take them somewhere quiet while we talk. I want to hear all about your travels.'

Mila followed Orla into the hall, and they put the babies down in the same rocking cot, while baby Egill slept in the other. Nora, who had followed close behind, said, 'I will keep watch over them. Go and talk. If they need feeding, I will come and get you.'

As they left, Mila asked, 'Do you feed both babes?'

Orla nodded. 'It seemed for the best.' Her face became sad for a moment. 'The mother was in such poor condition when she arrived. She died giving birth. I am only glad we were able to comfort her in her last days.'

'She was a thrall, like us?' Mila asked quietly.

Orla nodded. 'Although I am glad to say less come every year, and the freeing of thralls has become common practice. Even the elders are beginning to see the wisdom of it.'

Mila sighed, and said a silent prayer for the soul of her niece's mother. It was a timely reminder of how her own fate could have been very different. 'I never thanked you for buying us... Life could have been very different without you. Thank you.'

Orla shook her head. 'Do not thank me.'

They entered the hall. Already it was bustling with activity as people gathered to begin preparations for the feast. Mila smiled as she took her seat at the high table and sipped from a chalice of Frankish wine. The same wine she had haggled hard to win at a decent price, it tasted of sharp blackberries and rich oak.

She enjoyed her little luxuries, but each morning they still shared porridge from the simple bowl they'd made together.

Egill was already sitting on the bench beside her. The children had a table of their own, with Alvilda grudgingly taking charge of the unruly boys, who were a mix of red and golden heads.

'Ah, it is good to see you all. It has been too long,' said Hakon.

Grimr nodded. 'I wish we could visit every year, but it is impossible. There is always so much to be done.'

'Perhaps we can help?' said Mila thoughtfully. 'On our trading voyages, we can take you back and forth. At least then, we will meet every couple of years. Occasionally we will travel to Constantinople, but otherwise we can ensure we see each other whenever we can.'

Egill looped an arm around her shoulders. 'A perfect suggestion.'

'To prosperity, feasts and safe travels!' declared Hakon, raising his chalice, and everyone raised theirs as well. 'But most of all to *family*.'

'Skol!' They shouted in unison.

Another cheer rose around them. Egill tapped his cup against Mila's, drawing her gaze to his. 'Family...' he repeated, and she smiled.

'Family.' She tapped her chalice against his.

They were family and partners, bound together by both word and action. Their hearts and souls united in all matters.

* * * * *

If you loved this story,
check out Lucy Morris's previous captivating
historical romances
'Her Bought Viking Husband'
in Convenient Vows with a Viking
How the Wallflower Wins a Duke

And why not pick up the
A Season to Wed miniseries,
featuring Lucy Morris's charming romance?

Only an Heiress Will Do *by Virginia Heath*
The Viscount's Forbidden Flirtation *by Sarah Rodi*
Their Second Chance Season *by Ella Matthews*
The Lord's Maddening Miss *by Lucy Morris*

Get up to 4 Free Books!

We'll send you 2 free books from each series you try PLUS a free Mystery Gift.

FREE Value Over **$25**

Both the **Harlequin® Historical** and **Harlequin® Romance** series feature compelling novels filled with emotion and simmering romance.

YES! Please send me 2 FREE novels from the Harlequin Historical or Harlequin Romance series and my FREE Mystery Gift (gift is worth about $10 retail). After receiving them, if I don't wish to receive any more books, I can return the shipping statement marked "cancel." If I don't cancel, I will receive 5 brand-new Harlequin Historical books every month and be billed just $6.39 each in the U.S. or $7.19 each in Canada, or 4 brand-new Harlequin Romance Larger-Print books every month and be billed just $7.19 each in the U.S. or $7.99 each in Canada, a savings of 20% off the cover price. It's quite a bargain! Shipping and handling is just 50¢ per book in the U.S. and $1.25 per book in Canada.* I understand that accepting the 2 free books and gift places me under no obligation to buy anything. I can always return a shipment and cancel at any time by calling the number below. The free books and gift are mine to keep no matter what I decide.

Choose one:
- ☐ **Harlequin Historical** (246/349 BPA G36Y)
- ☐ **Harlequin Romance Larger-Print** (119/319 BPA G36Y)
- ☐ **Or Try Both!** (246/349 & 119/319 BPA G36Z)

Name (please print)

Address   Apt. #

City   State/Province   Zip/Postal Code

Email: Please check this box ☐ if you would like to receive newsletters and promotional emails from Harlequin Enterprises ULC and its affiliates. You can unsubscribe anytime.

Mail to the Harlequin Reader Service:
IN U.S.A.: P.O. Box 1341, Buffalo, NY 14240-8531
IN CANADA: P.O. Box 603, Fort Erie, Ontario L2A 5X3

Want to explore our other series or interested in ebooks? Visit www.ReaderService.com or call 1-800-873-8635.

---

*Terms and prices subject to change without notice. Prices do not include sales taxes, which will be charged (if applicable) based on your state or country of residence. Canadian residents will be charged applicable taxes. Offer not valid in Quebec. This offer is limited to one order per household. Books received may not be as shown. Not valid for current subscribers to the Harlequin Historical or Harlequin Romance series. All orders subject to approval. Credit or debit balances in a customer's account(s) may be offset by any other outstanding balance owed by or to the customer. Please allow 4 to 6 weeks for delivery. Offer available while quantities last.

Your Privacy—Your information is being collected by Harlequin Enterprises ULC, operating as Harlequin Reader Service. For a complete summary of the information we collect, how we use this information and to whom it is disclosed, please visit our privacy notice located at https://corporate.harlequin.com/privacy-notice. Notice to California Residents – Under California law, you have specific rights to control and access your data. For more information on these rights and how to exercise them, visit https://corporate.harlequin.com/california-privacy. For additional information for residents of other U.S. states that provide their residents with certain rights with respect to personal data, visit https://corporate.harlequin.com/other-state-residents-privacy-rights/.

HHHRLP25